Murder
on High
A Much Winchmoor Mystery

Paula Williams

Read ***Murder Served Cold, Rough and Deadly,*** *and* ***Burying Bad News,*** *the first, second, and third in the series.*

www.darkstroke.com

Discover us online:
www.darkstroke.com

Find us on instagram:
www.instagram.com/darkstrokebooks

Include **#darkstroke** in a photo of yourself
holding this book on Instagram and
something nice will happen.

To my gorgeous,
talented and absolutely
amazing grandchildren,
Ellie, George and Robert.

This comes with my fondest love
and the promise that you will
never appear in my books
(unless, of course you want to!).

Your parents, on the other hand,
might not get off so lightly!

Acknowledgements

First, my grateful thanks, as always, to Steph and Laurence Patterson at darkstroke books, without whom none of this would have happened. Thank you so much for taking a chance on Much Winchmoor four books ago, and for your continued support, encouragement - and brilliant covers. Thanks, too, to my fellow darkstroke authors from all across the globe. It's been a joy getting to know you all 'virtually' and being part of such a great, supportive and talented community. (Thank you, too, for giving me many hours of reading pleasure!)

The fictional village of Much Winchmoor bears an uncanny resemblance to the small Somerset village in which I live. And once again, my grateful thanks go to my friends and neighbours for the good-natured way they accept the liberties I take with their village. But whilst the location might be (almost) accurate, the characters in Much Winchmoor are very much products of my over-active imagination and my slightly skewed way of looking at things and bear no resemblance whatsoever to any persons living or dead.

My grateful thanks go to Pete Ticknell and Mark Lansdown, whose detailed descriptions of the climb to the top of the church tower spared me the horror of having to climb those steep, winding steps. Thanks are also due to Mark for his ongoing advice on all things agricultural. Any mistakes in this area are due entirely to my failure to remember what I'm told! (Especially if it was over a glass of wine or two).

I cannot claim the credit for the title of this book. That goes to Jane Odriozola and Robert Crouch, following an appeal for help on my Facebook author page (**www.facebook.com/ paula.williams.author**) when I was stuck for a title. Both Jane and Robert came up with the same one and, as a thank you to them, Jane's beautiful black cat, Max and Robert's delightful little dog, Harvey both appear in Murder on High.

My list of thank yous gets longer with each book. But I reserve the biggest vote of thanks to you, my lovely readers, without whom there would be no point in writing my books. And for those of you who are kind enough to leave a review, my thanks are boundless. Reviews really do help an author and each and everyone is very much appreciated.

It gives me a huge thrill to hear from my readers and I can be contacted via my website at **www.paulawilliamswriter.com**

About the Author

Paula Williams is living her dream. She's written all her life – her earliest efforts involved blackmailing her unfortunate younger brothers into appearing in her various plays and pageants. But it's only in recent years, when she turned her attention to writing short stories and serials for women's magazines that she discovered, to her surprise, that people with better judgement than her brothers actually liked what she wrote and were prepared to pay her for it and she has sold over 100 short stories and serials both in the UK and overseas.

Now, she writes every day in a lovely, book-lined study in her home in Somerset, where she lives with her husband and a handsome but not always obedient rescue dog, a Dalmatian called Duke. She still writes for magazines but now writes novels as well. She's currently writing the Much Winchmoor series of murder mysteries, set in a village not unlike the one she lives in - although as far as she knows, none of her friends and neighbours have murderous tendencies.

A member of both the Romantic Novelists' Association and the Crime Writers' Association, her novels often feature a murder or two, and are always spiked with humour and sprinkled with a touch of romance.

She also writes a monthly column, Ideas Store, for the writers' magazine, Writers' Forum. And she blogs about her books, other people's books and, sometimes, Dalmatians on her website at **paulawilliamswriter.com**. She can also be found on her author page at **facebook.com/paula.williams.author** and on **Twitter @paulawilliams44**

She gives talks at writing festivals and to organised groups and has appeared several times of local radio. In fact, she'll talk about writing to anyone who'll stand still long enough to listen.

But, as with all dreams, she worries that one day she's going to wake up and find she still has to bully her brothers into reading 'the play what she wrote'.

Murder
on High
A Much Winchmoor Mystery

Chapter One

The top of the tower of the church of St Bartholomew in the small Somerset village of Much Winchmoor was the perfect spot from which to get a bird's eye view of the area spread out like a relief map below. From one side of the square tower you could see the curve of the Mendip Hills as they stretched away into the distance. If you crossed to the opposite side, you'd look across low lying, willow-fringed pastureland towards Glastonbury Tor.

According to the poster on the church noticeboard, it was also the perfect spot from which to launch thirty-five teddy bears in two weeks' time. The proud owners (or, as was more likely, their parents) had each paid £3 to watch their precious bears abseil down the tower to raise funds for the restoration of the children's play area.

According to the poster, it promised to be a fun day out for all the family with refreshments and bric-a-brac stalls in the church grounds and the nearby village hall.

Realisation came in a flash, because it was also, without doubt, the perfect spot to commit a murder. After all, who was it who said that abseiling was only the second fastest way down a church tower?

***

"What this place needs," Cordelia Hilperton-Jones announced in her best Downton Abbey drawl, "is a jolly good murder or two."

Why is it, do you think, that people who haven't been here for two minutes always think they know exactly what 'this place' needs? I'll tell you what this place needs. A half decent broadband signal, a half decent bus service, and somewhere half decent for the little ones to play would be a start.

What it didn't need was 'a jolly good murder or two.'

Although if it did, I knew exactly where I'd like that murder to take place. Right here. Right now. In Chez Cheryl, which according to the sign on the front gate was 'Much Winchmoor's Finest Hairdressing Establishment'.

This was in fact nothing but the truth as it was also Much Winchmoor's only hairdressing establishment and it was established, more the pity, in our front room and in the not quite finished extension on the back of the house. It was going to be Mum's new beauty parlour, until Dad's company had put him on short time and the money had run out.

Chez Cheryl was also where I was being forced to work, very much against my will, on account of there being a sudden rush of customers all eager to look their best for Fred Wetherall's funeral.

Now if there's one thing that excites the ladies of Much Winchmoor (known collectively - by me at least - as the Grumble and Gossip Group) and sends them rushing off for a shampoo and set, (*none of that fancy blow drying nonsense for them, thank you very much, Cheryl!*) it's a good funeral.

St Bartholomew's would be packed as they turn out in all their primped and permed finery, to give 'dear old Fred a good send-off'.'

Because, you see, 'dear old Fred' was one of the few unattached elderly males in a village full of unattached elderly females and there had always been fierce competition for his attention - in spite of his unfortunate habit of spitting whenever he spoke on account of his ill-fitting dentures. He only put them in when socialising and so had never quite got the hang of keeping them firmly in his mouth.

No-one had dared make him laugh since the time in the Winchmoor Arms when Abe Compton told him that joke about the parrot and the windmill. Fred gave a huge gust of laughter and his top set flew out and ended up in Millie Compton's lap, just as she was about to tuck in to her 'pensioners special' fish pie.

Nor was dear old Fred murdered. He was ninety-three and had slipped away quietly during *Match of the Day* when Manchester United lost 2-1 to Arsenal because of a dodgy penalty decision which, as a lifelong Arsenal supporter, probably pleased him no end. So there are worse ways to go, when you think about it.

And who was I looking to murder that bright but chilly November morning? My grandmother, that was who. Not my dad's mother. She, sadly, had died five years earlier when I was at college. I still miss her, and even now, I can't walk past the house where she used to live without a pang of sadness.

No, the grandparent who was causing me grief that day was my mother's mother, Gran Kingham, who insisted on being called Grandma, which was why I never did. This was in retaliation for the way she insisted on calling me Kathryn, even though my name is Katie (although I prefer to be called Kat).

But Gran K felt that Katie was not posh enough for her only grandchild.

It was her fault I was here in the salon, up to my elbows in shampoo, conditioner and gossip, when I should have been upstairs with my laptop, doing work that I actually got paid for.

Gran K lived twenty miles away in Taunton but had turned up in a taxi four days earlier, bringing with her a teetering pile of Louis Vuitton suitcases and a yowling, growling black cat in a basket.

She had a plaster cast on her right arm. She had, she announced, tripped and fallen over Max, the yowling, growling black cat, and had broken her wrist. She and Max would be staying with us until it healed.

During the short time she'd been with us she'd managed to offend almost everyone she came across. Even our cat Cedric, the laziest creature in the universe, had taken one look at yowling, growling Max and had bestirred himself enough to move into Mrs Chinnery's bungalow across the road. He sat in her front room window and glared every time one of us walked past.

But that morning Gran K had upset Sandra, Mum's assistant. Sandra had worked for Mum for as long as I can remember, apart from when she had a better-late-than-never mid-life crisis and took off to Torquay with a chiropodist called Clint. She'd returned a few months later, minus the bunion that had plagued her all her life, but sadly for Sandra also minus Clint, who had, it transpired, found other toes to tickle.

But once she'd tasted the bright lights of Torquay Sandra never really settled back in Much Winchmoor. And who could blame her? I certainly didn't.

So when Gran K made some pointed comment about how sad it was when women went about looking like mutton dressed as lamb and how they shouldn't wear leggings when they didn't have the legs for it, Sandra turned scarlet, tore off her Chez Cheryl tabard, flung it to the ground, and stormed out, just minutes before the funeral rush started.

So there I was, stuck in the salon, when I should have been upstairs in the tiny store cupboard that was now my bedroom since Gran had commandeered my room. Instead of massaging shampoo into a seemingly endless succession of pink scalps, I should have been up there finishing off an account of Much Winchmoor Parish Council's latest battle to get the village litter bin replaced, after it was vandalised on Bonfire Night. It was due in the editor's inbox that afternoon, but so far I'd only got as far as the heading '*Bin-fire night in Much Winchmoor*'.

However, Gran K wasn't the only person on my hit list that morning. The other was our new local 'celebrity' Cordelia Hilperton-Jones. She wasn't a real celebrity, of course, but once-removed. Her mother was the famous Shakespearean actress and national treasure Dame Hermione Hilperton.

"Katie?" Mum called across at me, her expression harassed. "If you could shampoo Olive, please. I've almost finished Millie and will be ready for her in a few moments. And you can get Mrs Browne a cup of tea. She's been waiting so patiently."

Morag Browne (that's Browne spelt with an 'e', as she was at pains to point out) was the newest member of the Grumble and Gossip Group. She'd only moved to the village six months ago, having relocated from Scotland to be nearer her daughter who lived on the other side of Dintscombe.

She was a short dumpy woman, with steel grey dead straight hair and a permanent expression on her face that would curdle milk. Because while she might have lagged behind in the group's gossiping stakes owing to being a newcomer to the village, she more than made up for when it came to grumbling and was certainly up there near the top of the leader board.

And that morning was no exception. Although she'd arrived for her 10.30 appointment fifteen minutes early (and it was still only 10.25) she hadn't been waiting patiently at all, but had been tutting, huffing and giving me the hard stare every time I glanced across at her.

However, I didn't point this out to Mum because the never ending to do list she'd given me had been accompanied by one of her 'looks'.

She had a whole arsenal of 'looks' ranging from 'You're surely not going out dressed like that!', to 'I don't think that's very funny', and were more effective than any words. Her current 'look' said 'Don't stand around gossiping when there's work to be done'.

She gave Cordelia a strained smile. "I'm really sorry, Mrs Hilperton-Jones, but as you can see, I'm a bit rushed this morning. I could fit you in this afternoon though."

"Good heavens, no," Cordelia barked as she pushed a careless hand through her chin length mousey brown hair. "I haven't come in for a haircut or one of your peculiar sounding beauty treatments, Cheryl. No offence intended, but not my thing at all I'm afraid. I'm strictly a soap and water gal, you know."

Cordelia was a tall, big boned woman, with a long horsey face and a square jaw. That morning she was sporting the sort of tweedy jacket and yellow polo neck jumper that looked as if they should go with a pair of jodhpurs and riding boots. Instead, she'd teamed it with a dark green corduroy skirt that favoured comfort over style.

She was obviously going for the 'country woman, landed gentry' look. She only needed a headscarf and a pair of binoculars slung around her neck and she'd have looked like she was channelling the Queen on a day at the races.

At that moment, Gran Kingham put her head around the door and announced she was going out for an hour. Her thin lips twitched with disapproval as her cold green eyes flickered over Cordelia. Gran K fancied herself a bit of a fashion aficionado and was always ready with unasked for and usually unwelcome advice.

I jumped in quickly before she could do so. "Cordelia's come to see me, Mum."

Cordelia nodded. "Certainly did. I was just walking past - taking the Princess for her morning walkabout, you know - when I saw you through the window. Didn't realise you worked here. Thought you worked for the Chronicle, which was why I wanted to see you. Have I got the wrong Katie?"

I assured her that I was, indeed, the right Katie, although I preferred to be called Kat. There was no point explaining that in this part of rural Somerset decent jobs were harder to come by than honest politicians, and that I was a dog walker, barmaid and (unpaid) hair salon gopher in addition to 'community correspondent' for the local newspaper, The Dintscombe Chronicle.

"I'm just helping Mum out this morning. Staffing problems," I added as I sent a murderous look at Gran K who, as always, chose to ignore me. She'd given up offering me fashion advice a long time ago and was one of the reasons my short, spiky hair goes through all the colours of the rainbow- and some colours no self-respecting rainbow would even consider - depending on my mood. That morning, I was in a purple and orange mood.

"I've got some terribly exciting news," Cordelia said. "And I can spare you half an hour this afternoon."

I would have loved to have said that unfortunately I couldn't spare *her* half an hour. But I'm freelance and get paid by the line. So I can't afford to be choosy. A story's a story.

"What's it about?" I asked.

There was a high pitched yelp as she reached into a shoulder bag that was big enough to hold a small horse. It didn't hold a horse however but a dog. Smaller than our cat, it had pointy ears, a sharp nose and huge worried eyes.

"Hold the princess while I find the flier," she said as she thrust the tiny creature at me. "It's in here somewhere. Now, Persephone. Behave yourself," she added as the dog gave a low warning growl and bared a set of tiny, razor-sharp teeth that could probably shred anything that came within snapping distance. Including my fingers.

Finally, after more rummaging from Cordelia, and a lot more growling from Princess Persephone, Cordelia produced a piece of paper which she handed to me. I, very thankfully, handed the grumpy little dog back. Mind you, I'd probably be grumpy if I'd been shoved in a handbag.

"Well?" Cordelia said before I'd had chance to read it.

It said:

'A MURDER IS ANNOUNCED.
The award winning Dintscombe Players are about to embark on their latest exciting venture. A series of interactive murder mystery evenings, written and directed by Cordelia Hilperton-Jones. Venues to be announced. Be prepared to join in the fun.'

"My latest idea," she explained. "And though I say it myself, a damn fine one. You've heard of the Dintscombe Players, no doubt. You may also have heard that the company is currently homeless, thanks to the greed of unscrupulous landlords who put the rent up so steeply in the Dintscombe Community Hall that the community can no longer afford to use it. Your lovely editor did an excellent piece on it a couple of months ago. I'm sure you remember it. Mitch is such a sweetie."

Now she was wrong there on two counts. For one, Mitch Muckleford was not the editor of the Dintscombe Chronicle but the owner. The editor was a smooth-talking Irishman called Liam who believed there wasn't a woman on the planet immune to his slow smile and a sexy Irish accent that could make your toes curl. And two, Mitch was most definitely not a sweetie. At least, not to me, although to the daughter of a national treasure with an accent like cut glass? Maybe.

"So I came up with this great idea of the Players becoming a touring company. Like actors used to be, years ago," Cordelia said, addressing the entire room as she did so. "And then, I thought, these murder mystery evenings are all the thing now. And where better to start than my own village? One should interact with the local community whenever possible, I've always believed."

Interact with the community? Since she moved to the village three months earlier, Cordelia Hilperton-Jones hadn't just interacted with the community, she'd launched a complete takeover. In that short time, she'd got herself elected as President of the WI, Chairperson of the Floral Arts Society, and was currently engaged in a bitter power struggle on the Village Hall Committee with Elsie Flintlock.

"Especially given Much Winchmoor's reputation as the murder capital of the Southwest," Cordelia said with relish. "It would go down a storm. And is just what this place needs. A jolly good murder or two."

Which is, of course, where you came in.

Chapter Two

I stared at her. "There's nothing jolly or good about murder," I said as I tried to block out the picture that flashed into my mind from a couple of years earlier when my boyfriend, Will and I had discovered a body. The memory was still as fresh and horrible as if it had been last week.

Murder is not funny. It's cruel and messy and takes your nice joined up world, smashes it into a thousand pieces and nothing is ever quite the same again. Even now I can't bear to watch *Midsomer Murders* or *Miss Marple*. As for reading crime fiction, which I used to love, no way.

Cordelia looked puzzled. "But this isn't real, Katie. It's only entertainment."

"And where do you think this so-called entertainment is going to take place?" A voice from the other side of the salon called out. "Because, in case you've forgotten, I'm the bookings secretary for the village hall and I can tell you now, it's booked solid right through to next Easter."

Cordelia's lips tightened as she swung round. "In its present condition the village hall is hardly a suitable venue for my players, Mrs Flintlock. Which was precisely why I advocated some much needed changes. Which some people, for reasons of their own, choose to block at every turn."

Elsie Flintlock glared at her from under the drier, a scarlet flush travelling up her thin, pointy face. "And what's wrong with the village hall?" Her voice rose sharply. "It's good enough for everyone else in the village."

"It might well be suitable for the children's playgroup or the Scottish country dancing group, but my players need a proper stage on which to perform and the one in the hall has a shed on it. A shed, I ask you! I couldn't believe my eyes when I saw it."

She laughed, then turned to the other ladies in various stages of the shampoo and set process. "For heaven's sake," she appealed to them. "Who in the right minds would put up a shed in the middle of a stage? It's utterly ridiculous."

An abrupt silence fell across the room, broken only by the gentle hum of the driers and a collective intake of breath from the ladies. Morag Browne (with an e) paused, her teacup in mid-air, her eyes bright as she sensed a coming storm.

Olive Shrewton, who was at the basin in front of me, head back, ready for her shampoo suddenly sat bolt upright, her face as red as Elsie's.

"That would have been my late husband," she said with quiet dignity. "Reverend Fairweather had the idea that the hall would be the perfect place for Mrs Denby, the parish secretary, to work in, rather than the kitchen table in the vicarage. Only Mrs Denby said it was too cold and draughty. So my Geoffrey, God rest his soul, came up with the idea of putting a shed on the stage. After all, it wasn't as if the stage had been used as a proper stage. Not for years. It was out of the way of the little ones and he made it nice and cosy and warm for Mrs Denby. It was the last thing he ever did because he took ill and died soon after." She wrestled her hands free from the waterproof cape I'd wrapped around her and dabbed at her eyes. "That shed is a monument to him. He made a beautiful job of it. It's not any old rubbish from B&Q, you know. My Geoffrey was a craftsman."

"And after all that, Mrs Denby never used it," Elsie finished as Olive's voice trailed away. "Said it made her feel cluster-phobic. But it makes a very handy storage room. So, that's your answer." She sent Cordelia another glare. "You can blame the vicar, if you must blame anyone."

Cordelia shrugged. "Well, it's all irrelevant. Even without the shed on the stage, the hall is still not suitable. I've got a much better venue planned for my murder mystery evenings. The Winchmoor Arms."

She looked around the room like she was expecting a round of applause. Instead, she got a load of blank stares and a snort of derision from Elsie.

"I'm not sure Norina will go for that," I said. Norina, the landlady was a Welsh whirlwind with very definite views. Things were done her way or no way. She'd already ousted the skittles team from the pub and was in the process of converting their skittle alley into a dining room despite a chorus of protest from the locals.

"She's all for it," Cordelia said, airily. "I've just been running the idea past her. Thinks it will be a perfect way to celebrate the opening of her new dining room. She's very excited about the whole thing and is planning the evening's menu already."

Norina's enthusiasm had obviously been running away with her. It was nowhere near finished. I'd worked in the pub the previous evening and her lovely new dining room still looked like the closing down sale in a builders' yard.

"When are you planning this?" I asked.

"We're in rehearsal now. So we're aiming for the end of the month." She gathered up her bag and gave the princess a pat. "Now if you'll excuse me, I'm in a bit of a rush this morning. But I'm free at 4.30 this afternoon. Come round then and I'll let you have pictures as well."

"But I'm not sure -" I began, but she cut me off mid-sentence with a wave of her hand. She scrabbled around in her bag, took out a small pad of post-it notes, wrote on one and handed it to me.

"My number. Let me know if you can't make it. But like I said, your boss suggested I got in touch with you. I had lunch with him the other day and he said it would make a great story, given the murder capital angle. He was also very keen on my other exciting news, which I am having to keep under wraps for now."

"You had lunch with Liam? But I thought he was in Ireland seeing his folks."

"Not him. Mitch. He's a long-time fan of my mother, apparently and I kind of hinted she might be here for opening night. Not that she would, of course," she added. "Village pubs are not her thing. But he doesn't know that."

"And does Norina also think that Dame Hermione might

make an appearance?" I asked.

She smiled. "Well, I didn't exactly say that. Just that my mother is always very supportive." Her smile faded and there was a lingering sadness in her brown eyes for a brief second. She straightened her shoulders. "She always sends me lovely messages at the start of a new production," she added. "Or, more likely, her PA does."

"That woman!" Elsie hissed as Cordelia swept out. "Not lived in the place five minutes and she's trying to take over everything. First the Floral Art, then the WI. But she'll not get her hands on the hall committee. Not while there's breath in my body."

"Yes, but Elsie," Olive pointed out. "I don't want to defend her, not after what she said about my Geoffrey but, to be fair, no one else wanted the WI job. Our institute was in danger of closing down if she hadn't stepped in."

"That's not the point," Elsie sniffed. "She's got too much time on her hands, that's her problem. Why doesn't she get a proper job like everyone else? And as for the way she chases after the vicar..."

"The poor vicar has been so lonely since his wife went…" Millie Compton called out, joining in the conversation from the other side of the room.

And then it was game on. A roomful of gossips doing what they did best.

"I didn't know the vicar had been married," Morag Browne piped up. "He looks a confirmed bachelor if ever I saw one."

She had a point. The Reverend Lionel Fairweather was a skinny beanpole of a man with the sort of slicked down hairstyle that was last fashionable in the 1940s. He was probably born looking middle-aged. He always wore a multi-coloured fair-isle pullover under his jacket, whatever the season. Elsie was convinced that he had one for every day of the year (except, of course, Sundays) as she swore she'd never seen him wear the same one twice. She also reckoned he was in his early forties but really, he could have been any age.

"Looks can deceive," Millie called across to Morag. "It was so romantic. He went off on holiday to Dorset a few years ago and came back and announced he was about to get married."

"Didn't last though," Olive said.

"His wife ran off the with the organist. Bet he keeps his pipes finely tuned for her," Elsie said with a wicked cackle that earned her a black look from my mother.

"But before then, there was all that trouble with Mrs Fairweather's brother, remember?" Olive said. "Went to prison, didn't he? Still there now for all I know. And well he deserved to."

"What did he do?" Morag asked eagerly. She loved nothing better than the chance to wonder what the world was coming to and to moan on about the shocking way young people behaved these days.

"He only robbed the vicar of the money from the church fete," Olive said. "That was wicked. "

Morag sniffed. "Probably needed the money for his drugs, I shouldn't wonder," she said.

Millie cleared her throat. "Well, I thought he was a very pleasant young man. Had a lovely smile. And he gave me a very nice picture he'd drawn of our farmhouse. I had it framed."

"You're too trusting, Millie. That's your problem," Elsie said.

"Ever since the vicar moved here, we've been trying to marry him off, Morag," Olive explained. "Then it was like Millie said, he came back from holiday and said he was getting married. A whirlwind holiday romance."

"It was never going to work though, was it?" Elsie, who had no time for romance, put in. "He was years older than her for a start," she went on with a quick nod to Morag, "And, as you rightly said, a confirmed bachelor. I said back then the two of them were totally incombustible. And I was proved right."

"I think maybe you mean incompatible," Mum said quietly but Elsie ignored her.

"After Mrs Fairweather left I reckon Mrs Denby thought she was well in there. But her nose has been well and truly put out of joint since Cecelia Hillbilly-Bones, Her Ladyship, as I call her, arrived."

"It's Cordelia," Millie said. "Cordelia Hilperton-Jones."

"Whatever," Elsie said with a dismissive wave. "She's been tossing her bonnet at the vicar ever since she arrived."

"Cordelia and the vicar?" I couldn't help myself, but a more unlikely couple it would be impossible to imagine. She was several inches taller than him for a start. "Surely not."

"I'm not usually wrong about these things. He'd best be careful though. Her first husband died very suddenly, from what I hear. An 'unexplained death', was what they said."

"Oh Elsie, you've been watching too much *Midsomer Murders* again," I said as I wrapped a towel around Olive's head and led her across to the chair next to where Mum was putting the finishing touches to Millie. At least the gossiping had taken the bleakness from Olive's eyes after Cordelia's tactless remark.

Millie sighed. "Well, I for one hope so. They're both lonely souls who deserve a bit of happiness in their lives. Oh, I do like a bit of romance," she said with a faraway look in her eyes.

Millie was married to Abe Compton, the local cider maker who spent most of his leisure time sampling his own products, and the rest of his time sleeping off the effects. So the closest to romance Millie came was within the pages of her beloved Mills and Boon novels.

"Talking of romance," she went on and turned towards me so abruptly she nearly had Mum's styling comb up her nose. "How are the wedding plans coming along, dear? Oh Morag, it's so lovely. Katie and Will have known each other since they were babies and now they're getting married."

That got everyone's attention. More the pity. Half a dozen pairs of eyes, including my mother's, swivelled in my direction. I didn't answer but led Morag across to the basin and helped her into a gown.

When it became obvious that I wasn't going to answer, Mum spoke. "We're still working on it, aren't we, Katie?"

Never have I been more pleased to feel my phone, in the back pocket of my jeans, vibrate with an incoming message. Mum tutted, but it was the one thing I'd held out on. I'd help in the salon for the morning, but I was waiting on a couple of calls so would have to leave my phone turned on.

"It's the vicar," I said. "Is it ok if I head off when I've shampooed Mrs Browne? Only it says he wants to see me right away."

"Oooh, wedding plans?" Millie cooed.

"No," I said more sharply than I meant to which made me feel bad as Millie's face fell. My voice softened. "It's work. For the paper."

Millie's eyes lit up. "Oh Katie, love. You do live such an exciting life, rushing from one news story to the next, don't you? Our Katie's a journalist, you know, Morag. She had a top job in one of the Bristol radio stations but chose to come back here. The Chronicle's certainly a lot better since she started working for them. You must be so proud of her, Cheryl."

Mum just smiled and nodded.

Millie was only partly right. Back in the day, in another life that is now a distant memory, I did indeed have a proper job, not an assortment of rubbish ones like I have now. But it wasn't exactly the top job Millie imagined it to be. I'd been a research assistant in a local radio station, which was a posh way of saying general dogsbody but I loved it. I lived in an 'almost city centre' flat and life was exciting, no two days the same.

Then my ratface boyfriend of the time ran off not only with the contents of our joint bank account but with my best friend and, the final insult, my signed photo of David Tennant as Doctor Who. On the same day the radio station made me redundant and a few months later, unable to find another job, my finances became so desperate that I was forced to give up my 'almost city centre' flat and come back to Much Winchmoor to live with my mum and dad.

And I've been stuck here ever since.

Now, once I'd finished my fifth shampoo of the morning, I was hurrying off to interview the vicar (who could, according to the text message from Mrs Denby, his secretary, spare me five minutes) about a mass teddy bear abseil off the church tower that was planned for next week.

17

And when I'd done that, I was going to write up my account of last night's Parish Council meeting and their ongoing battle to get their vandalised litter bin replaced. And then, of course, interview Cordelia Hilperton-Jones about her murder mystery evenings.

Welcome to my *exciting* life. Not.

Chapter Three

As I set off for the vicarage the early morning brightness had faded and been replaced by a sullen grey grunginess that was more typical of this time of the year. 'Too bright too early', my Gran Latcham would have said and she had usually been right when it came to the weather.

It wasn't actually raining, but the cloud was so low that the air felt damp and cloying. As I went through the churchyard, there was a constant patter as drips from the overhanging yew trees splatted on to the paved path.

I walked through the churchyard every day with Prescott, Elsie's annoying little dog, who would always make a dive for the compost heap in the far corner. Thankfully this time I was dogless (I'd managed to squeeze that particular chore in before starting work in the salon), so it made a nice change to be able to take the main path around the church instead of having to go the long way round to avoid the compost heap. As I did so, a shiver chased down my back that had nothing to do with the weather or the drip from the yew trees that had just landed on my head. It made me wish, for the first time ever, that I had Prescott with me. I stopped and turned around, my heart thumping. But there was nothing, or nobody, there.

And yet, if I didn't know better, I'd say someone was watching me. But the place was completely empty, apart from the incumbents of the ancient, lichen spattered graves, their headstones leaning at drunken angles, their lettering worn away by time and the weather. They were certainly not interested in me. But it sure felt like somebody was. I took a second look. Still nothing, apart from a couple of pigeons prancing about like a pair of hyped-up tap-dancers along the apex of the church roof.

"Get a grip, Kat," I told myself sternly as I quickened my

step. "You've allowed all that murder mystery nonsense to get to you."

As I walked up the dark, twisty drive that led to the vicarage, that slightly freaked out sensation in the pit of my stomach was not helped when one of the overgrown rhododendron bushes snatched at my arm as I passed and I almost made a fool of myself by shrieking. I breathed a sigh of relief when I turned the final corner that led to the front of the house.

St Bartholomew's Vicarage was built when Queen Victoria was still young enough to chase Prince Albert around the royal bedchamber. I'd always found the place with its ivy-cloaked walls and high pointy eaves quite creepy. I was still a bit rattled after my moment of weirdness in the churchyard (I preferred to forget about being freaked out by a rhododendron bush) as I rapped on the imposing front door with its heavy iron knocker. As the sound echoed inside the house, I half expected the door to be opened by Lurch from the Addams Family. But of course, it wasn't Lurch. It was Mrs Denby, the vicar's secretary and general dogsbody who more or less ran the place and did all the important stuff while he played chess with the headmaster of the local private school and composed dreary sermons that nobody really understood.

She was one of those quietly efficient people who just got on with things, preferring to stay firmly in the background. She was a soft, round person with plump, rosy cheeks and the sweetest smile. She was smiling now as she opened the door.

"Katie," she breathed, in her soft West Country accent. "How kind of you to come."

"But you asked me to," I pointed out. "Your text said the vicar could spare me five minutes."

Her smile faded. "Oh dear, is that how it came out? I'm afraid you misunderstood me, my lovely. I meant to ask you to come and see me. Not the reverend. I never was any good with this texting. He isn't here. He's off visiting old Percy Tunstall who's had a fall and broken his hip." She gave a sigh. "That man is a saint," she said as she dabbed the corner of her eye with her little finger...

"Percy Tunstall? A saint?" I was surprised because the last I'd heard he was on police bail for receiving stolen farm machinery, and that his fall had been the direct result of too many pints of Abe Compton's notorious Headbender cider.

Mrs Denby gave me a stern look. "I meant the reverend, of course. That man has the patience of a saint, even for an old reprobate like Percy Tunstall. From there he was going across to see his friend at the school. I'm afraid he probably won't be back until this evening."

I was quite relieved, to be honest. Once Mr Fairweather got going, he was a very difficult man to get away from and I always found I ended up agreeing to do something worthy and useful (and unpaid) that I would prefer not to do.

"That's ok," I said briskly. "I can email him a couple of questions. It was only about a piece I'm doing for the Chronicle about the teddy bear abseil. Unless, of course, you can help me. All I need is a comment about what a fun event it will be and how the money's going to a good cause, that sort of thing."

"I'm sorry, my dear. I'm afraid I couldn't bring myself to say that because, to be honest, I'm not really sure about the whole thing. And I've told the reverend so. The churchyard is a sacred place and shouldn't be used for such…frivolities." She flushed, her apple cheeks now the colour of an over ripe tomato. "Look, I'm not trying to make your life difficult. It's just, well, it just doesn't feel right to me. I've got my principles, you see."

I thought how easily I'd caved in over the story of the murder mystery evenings and kind of envied Mrs Denby her principles.

"That's all right," I said. "Don't worry about it."

"Thank you, dear. Now, to the reason I wanted to see you. I understand you have a dog walking business."

"I do. It's called *Paws for Walks.*" I 'paused' for a moment to see if she would appreciate the name, which I thought was quite clever. But if she did, she was making a good job of hiding it. "I didn't realise you had a dog, Mrs Denby."

"I don't. It's the vicar's dog."

21

"Oh right. You mean Archie. He was his wife's dog, wasn't he?" I'd been spending way too much time in Elsie Flintlock's company, but the words were out before I could stop them.

"His ex-wife," she said gently. "With the reverend being called away suddenly and not being back until late the poor little chap isn't going to get a walk today. And if he misses his walk, he whines and drives everyone mad. Would you be prepared to walk him? The reverend will pay you the going rate, of course. Cash."

"Well, I'm a bit busy this afternoon," I began but Mrs Denby cut in.

"I did mention that this could well be a regular thing, didn't I, dear?" she went on. "Reverend Fairweather was talking about it only the other day. Why don't you take Archie now and see how you get on with him? I'll go and get him."

And before I could say anything she bustled off. I shrugged. It would only take an hour. And it was, as Mrs Denby had said, for cash. With the chance of making it a regular thing.

But it was as well I'd walked the other dogs earlier. Although Archie was a quiet dog with a permanently depressed expression, he and Prescott were sworn enemies and exchanged foul-mouthed canine curses at the mere sight of each other.

I blamed Prescott, of course. He had a talent for making enemies. It was about the only talent he did have. Unless you counted burying himself in compost heaps or getting lost down rabbit holes talents.

The strange thing was, he got along quite well with the other dogs I walked. There was Rosie, the laid-back Labrador who didn't have the energy to fall out with anyone. They got on ok, usually by ignoring each other. Then there was Finbar, the Irish Wolfhound. He was the size of a small horse, with bristly grey fur and soulful amber eyes. For some weird reason, Prescott adored him. And, even more weird, the feeling was mutual.

I'd promised Mrs Denby to give Archie at least an hour's walk ('any less and he whines the place down,' she'd warned) so I decided to take him up on Pendle Knoll, the hill that stands above Will's farm. I loved it up there, even on a grungy grey day like this one.

The view from the top was spectacular and well worth the climb. It looked down across the flat, willow fringed fields towards Glastonbury Tor in the distance. I didn't often take the other three up there as Prescott usually managed to disappear down one of the hundreds of rabbit holes that peppered the hedges.

"You'll like it up there," I told Archie as we set off down the drive. "I'll let you off, and you can have a good chase around."

But he ignored me and continued to plod along, head and tail down. Until, that was, we went into the churchyard when he stopped dead and gave a low growl. Did he, too, feel there was something there, watching us? Like I had earlier? Or, as was more likely, was he merely on high alert looking for his arch enemy?

"Come on, boy," I said. "Prescott's safely at home, snoozing in his favourite armchair. You're quite safe."

I pulled on his lead and hurried him on through the churchyard, along the High Street and up School Hill, before the long, steep climb to the top of Pendle Knoll.

We'd just reached it when the earlier drizzle suddenly changed to cold driving rain that was being blown straight into my face. I pulled the hood up on my waterproof, remembering my earlier promise to Archie to let him off when we reached the top.

I unclipped his lead but he made no attempt to move from my side. Prescott would have been across the field like a rat out of a trap by this time, but poor sad little Archie just stood there, in the rain, looking as wet and miserable as I was.

"Come on then, let's head back, shall we?" I said, taking pity on him. "I know Mrs Denby said you'd whine the place down if you had less than your hour's walk. But I don't somehow think you'll be doing that today."

***

23

I'd been out a little over forty-five minutes when Archie and I made our way up the vicarage drive, dodging the dripping rhododendron leaves as well as we could.

But before we reached the house I stopped at the sound of voices. One was Mrs Denby's soft burr, the other voice, a woman's, was higher, shriller. Before I could get close enough to see who it was there was the slam of a car door.

"And you can tell Lionel," I heard the woman shout. I couldn't make out her exact words only that she sounded very, very angry, "...not getting away with this...never forgive him... make him pay..."

The engine whined and there was the hiss of tyres on gravel as the car took off.

The vicarage drive was very narrow and bendy, so I pulled Archie close to me and jumped deep into the rhododendrons as a small yellow car rocketed past, scattering gravel as it did so. We'd have been flattened if we'd still been in the drive.

The driver, a pale faced woman with light brown hair, didn't even see us.

"Who on earth was that?" I asked Mrs Denby as soon as I'd extricated myself and one very wet Archie from the dripping bushes. "She was driving like a mad thing. She'd have mown us both down if I hadn't heard her coming and jumped out of the way. As it was, I don't think she even saw us."

But I forgot my anger as I got closer to Mrs Denby. She was leaning against the front door of the vicarage, looking as if she was about to faint.

"Katie?" Her voice was barely above a whisper. "I wasn't expecting you yet. You're back early."

"Just as well I am," I said. "Are you all right? You look very pale."

"Did you hear what she said?" Mrs Denby stammered. "She - she actually threatened to kill the reverend. Did you hear her?" She put her hand to her heart. "Oh, my life and heart, I really believe she'd have done so if he'd been here."

Chapter Four

Poor Mrs Denby's apple cheeks had now turned the colour of cold porridge. She clung to the doorframe as if it was the only thing keeping her upright.

"Would you like to sit down?" I asked.

She shook her head. "I'll be fine, thank you, lovely. It's just - just a shock, the way she turned like that. It came on so sudden. Nice as ninepence until I told her that the reverend wasn't at home. Then she went mad. Quite mad. S-said ... terrible things... And her eyes..."

Her voice trailed away as she dragged her fingers through her usually immaculate hair.

"What sort of things?" I asked but she shook her head.

"Who is she?" I went on. "Does she live in the village? I didn't recognise her."

"No. She lives –" She paused, a tiny frown on her forehead as she raked through her memory. "She lives way over the other side of Little Mearefield, I believe. The poor soul has mental health problems. Has done so for some time. Thinks everyone is out to steal from her. Paranoia, I believe the reverend called it. But today was the first time she'd ever shown any tendency to violence. And to direct it at the reverend, of all people. When he's done so much to help her. She's a very disturbed young woman, I'm afraid. Didn't you hear her? She threatened to kill him."

"I just caught the odd word or two. But she certainly sounded pretty wound up about something."

"And you say she didn't see you or the dog?"

"No. Luckily I heard her car coming and managed to jump into the rhododendrons. Which was just as well. She'd have hit us otherwise."

Mrs Denby gave a long sigh. "I'm just so thankful the

reverend wasn't here. Goodness knows what she'd have done. And him in such a state after last night, and all. He hates confrontation, you know. I could see this morning he was terribly upset."

"Why was that?"

"Why, the row, of course. I'm surprised you couldn't hear it all over the village. I was working late, trying to make a start on the old folks' Christmas party which always takes such a lot of organising. They didn't know I was still here, of course. She was in such a rage, I wouldn't have believed it. Talk about 'hell hath no fury like a woman scorned'."

"Do you mean the woman who's just left? She was here last night as well?"

"Oh no. It wasn't her. It was -" She stopped. "What am I doing, standing here gossiping? The reverend would be horrified if he could hear me. Please forget what I said. It was nothing. Now I'm sorry, my lovely, I'm going to have to go and sit down for a bit. Thank you for walking Archie. I'll - I'll settle up with you presently, if that's ok. I still feel all of a doodah, to be honest. And you'd best head off home and get out of those wet clothes. You look soaked through."

I was indeed, right through to my underwear. My boots were full of the water that had run down my legs so that I squelched as I walked and my so-called waterproof jacket had long since given up the unequal task of keeping the rain out and was now clinging to my back.

"We were right up on the top of Pendle Knoll when the rain came. There's no shelter up there. And jumping into those wet rhododendrons hasn't helped matters either. Archie's as wet as me, I'm afraid. Do you want me to towel him off before I go?"

"No, that's ok. I'll do it."

"Do you want me to walk him tomorrow?"

"I'll talk it through with the reverend and let you know." She held out her hand for the dog's lead, but he had his head buried in one of the bushes that flanked the front door and all that could be seen was his furiously wagging tail.

"What have you got there, boy?" I asked as I bent down towards him. He stepped back and allowed me to pick up whatever it was that had got him so excited, which just went to show what a nice dog he was. If that had been Prescott, he'd have swallowed it rather than give up his prize.

It was a keyring. Or, at least, part of one. It was a little plastic frame that, as often as not, contained a school photograph and was usually fixed to the keyring by a metal loop which, in this case, was twisted and broken. So there was no ring or keys, no smirking schoolchild either. Instead the frame contained an exquisite miniature drawing of a house by the sea. Such was the level of detail that I was pretty sure I recognised the place at Stargate Bay, a small hamlet on the South Dorset coast that Will and I both loved.

I showed it to Mrs Denby. "Is this yours?" I asked her.

She shrugged. "I've never seen it before. Just a bit of rubbish that people have left lying around. Give it to me and I'll pop it in the bin."

She held out her hand for it but I stepped back. "Oh no. You can't do that."

"It's only a bit of tat," she said, her hand still outstretched. "You don't want to hold on to it either. You don't know where it's been, do you?"

That's my trouble, you see. If someone tells me I don't want to (or can't) do something, it usually makes me want to do the complete opposite. And the little keyring fascinated me. Who would create such an exquisite miniature and then put it in a cheap plastic frame? I certainly didn't want Mrs Denby to drop it in the bin. I put it in my pocket and went to walk away. "Will you let me know if you want me to walk Archie tomorrow?"

"I will. And I'll make sure the reverend knows how kind you've been. Now, if you'll excuse me, I really must go and sit down for a bit. And you need to get out of those wet clothes."

She closed the door firmly and I heard her footsteps clicking down the echoey hall. The rain, which had eased off for a bit, now started in earnest again and this time I hurried through the churchyard, far more intent on keeping the rain out of my face than to indulge in fanciful thoughts about being watched.

I'd just got home, towelled off my hair and was sneaking past the salon on my way up to my room in case Mum called me in for another spot of unpaid slave labour, when my phone rang. I thought for a moment it was going to be Mitch, asking where my copy was. But the number that came up was Elsie's.

"Is that you, Katie? It's Olive Shrewton here." It was not Elsie but her neighbour bellowing down the phone at me. Olive never had quite got her head around the fact that you didn't need to shout into a phone to make yourself heard. She sounded so agitated that my first thought was that something had happened to Elsie.

"Is everything all right?"

"No. Not really. In fact, to tell the truth, my dear, everything's all wrong. That's what it is. What my sister's going to say when she finds out I do not know."

"Finds out what?" Having a conversation with Olive was a bit like pulling teeth at the best of times. And when she was on the other end of a phone, it was anything but the best of times.

"About mother's blanket," she said. "She'll go mad when she finds out.'

Now Olive was well into her eighties and I was pretty sure her mother had died several years ago. So how was she going to find out whatever it was Olive obviously didn't want her to find out?

"Olive? Is Elsie there?"

"Of course. It was her who said to phone you."

"About what?"

"Mother's blanket going missing. What Millie is going to do when she finds out, goodness only knows. She so wanted that blanket, you know, the one that Mother made. Ever so pretty it is, all crocheted in flowers. Every colour you can think of. But I told Millie that if it was left at the farm, her Abe would probably use it to line the dogs' beds. Or the hen house or something. I told her straight it would be safer with me. And now it's been stolen."

"The blanket's been stolen?" Without meaning to, I found myself shouting back at her and as I did so, Mum opened the door from the salon and frowned at me.

"That's what I was telling you," Olive went on. "I always keep it on the spare bed, you see."

"You mean someone broke into your house and stole it? Did they take anything else?"

"Indeed they did. But not in the house. I'd put the blanket on the washing line first thing this morning because the cat had stolen the skin from my breakfast kipper and taken it on to the spare bed to eat it, the wicked boy. The blanket smelt of fish, so I put it out on the line for an hour or so to freshen it up. And it was such a lovely morning, wasn't it? Before it turned out so bad, of course. Then, just as we were leaving to get our hair done, I realised it was still on the line. Elsie was going on at me to hurry up, so instead of taking it back indoors like I should have done, I left it in my laundry basket in the porch. After we came out of your mum's, Elsie was planning to go straight to the church. She wanted to make sure we had a decent seat and not stuck behind the pillar. But I asked her to save me a seat and went back home to put the blanket indoors as it was looking like rain and the rain will blow in to that porch. Only when I got here, it was gone, along with this morning's bottle of milk. I was that upset, I cried all through Fred's funeral and couldn't bring myself to look my sister in the eye. I phoned the police, but they didn't want to know. So Elsie suggested I phone you."

"Me? But why?"

"Well, she said you're very good at asking questions and you've already solved the odd murder or two."

"Well, not exactly. But..."

"She said this would be a doodle for someone as clever as you."

Now the doodle/doddle bit could well have come from Elsie, but *clever*? That would have been all Olive. No way would Elsie have said such a thing about me.

"But what can I do?" I asked.

"Oh, that's so kind of you, my dear. I knew you'd help out. Elsie said you're far too high and mighty to bother to investigate such a trivial thing. But Mother's blanket is not a trivial thing. My sister will never speak to me again if you

29

don't get it back. I can pay you, you know."

"Pay me for what?"

"You know, for carrying out an investigation, like they do on the telly. *One hundred dollars a day plus expenses.* Isn't that what they say? Although I don't actually have any dollars."

"Olive, I don't want your money…"

"That's so kind of you," she jumped in before I could finish the sentence. "I don't like to go around asking questions of the neighbours in case they think I think they did it, if you see what I mean. I thought maybe you could start your investigation by asking Dave over the road where he was between 10.30 and 11.30 which was when I was at your mum's."

Now if Olive had had a load of underwear stolen from her washing basket, then I could well believe that Creepy Dave was the culprit. But a multi-coloured crocheted blanket? Definitely not his style.

"So you'll do it?" Olive said. "That's so kind. I'll make you a Victoria sponge. With my homemade strawberry jam. If you'd like it."

If I liked? Olive's Victoria sponges were the stuff of legends and had won the best cake in show award at the village Fruit and Produce Show for as long as anyone could remember.

My stomach rumbled at the thought of it. Mum's cooking, never that brilliant at the best of times, had gone from bad to worse to absolutely terrible since Gran K had arrived. The only time I got anything half decent to eat was when I was working at the pub. The idea of one of Olive's Victoria sponges was so tempting and all I had to do was be seen to ask the odd question or two.

"Look, I'm busy this afternoon. Cordelia Hilperton-Jones has deigned to grant me an audience and squeeze me into her busy schedule in order to get some free publicity. "

"Oooh!" Olive's voice rose with excitement. "You'll get to see inside her house. I have to say, I'd love to see what she's done with the old place."

"That's what I thought," I admitted. "Anyway, how about I

ask around tomorrow morning when I pick up Prescott for his walk? I'll come early and ask a few questions. See if anyone saw anything. Will that be ok?"

"You're a good girl, Katie. I always say that when Elsie goes on about you. I knew I could rely on you."

Chapter Five

Cordelia Hilperton-Jones lived in one of the oldest properties in the village, a long low farmhouse situated on a narrow lane that ran parallel to the High Street. At one time the place had been owned by Abe Compton's brother, Arthur, who'd let it get totally run down after his wife Mabel died and there was no longer anyone to nag him about keeping it up together.

Arthur had now gone off to live with his daughter in Weston-Super-Mare and had been more than happy to have sold the place, at almost twice what it was worth, to someone with, he reckoned, 'more money than sense.'

I must admit that even though I wasn't interested in Cordelia's murder mysteries I was more than a little curious to see what she'd done to the interior of the house, which had been swathed in scaffolding and polythene for months. The outside looked unchanged, apart from the freshly painted windows and the front door had been stripped of the peeling white paint and taken back to its original wood. A definite improvement, I reckoned.

But when Cordelia opened the door, the change in the interior was so extreme, the word was out before I could stop it.

"Jeez!"

The last time I'd been in the house, back when Mabel was still alive, the front door had opened into a long, narrow, and incredibly dark hallway. Heavy oak panelling, which over the years had darkened to the colour of peat, added to the gloom and the area was lit, whatever the time of day, by a small dim lightbulb covered with a battered cream lampshade that looked as old as the farmhouse itself.

Now the small, dark rooms at the front of the house on the ground and first floors had been swept away, and the whole area opened right up to the roof, exposing the beams. Even on a dull November afternoon, light poured in through the glass roof tiles that had replaced some of the old slate ones.

It was spectacular, but the sort of space you expected to find in the reception area of an office block or an upmarket hotel, not an old farmhouse that dated back hundreds of years. The steel and glass staircase in the far corner completed the swanky office block feel of the place. It didn't quite go with Cordelia's country gentlewoman look, either.

"You like my improvements?" she asked, watching me closely.

What could I say? I wouldn't exactly call them improvements. But what do I know?

"Yes. It's very…" I paused as I scrabbled around for the right word. "Very bright."

I wanted to ask her who got to change the light bulbs on the ultra-modern, pendulum cluster that was suspended high above our heads. But she'd already turned and began walking across the mirror-like tiled floor.

"Come along in, Katie. I've got the press pack all ready for you."

Without giving me the chance to remind her I preferred to be called Kat, she led me to a room that overlooked a carefully landscaped patio area to the side of the house where Arthur's hen houses used to be.

"My study," she said unnecessarily. The two book-lined walls and the desk with a very new and expensive laptop on it were a bit of a giveaway. A third wall was covered in photographs of various stage productions.

"My company," she said proudly as she saw me looking at them. "The Dintscombe Players. I plan to give them a permanent home when the old barn is restored, one of the main reasons I was so desperate to get my hands on this place."

"You're planning on turning the barn into a theatre?" I tried, but failed, to keep the surprise out of my voice.

"Why not?" She looked like someone who had a secret and was bursting to share it. "I have plans. Such plans. But it's all

33

hush hush at the moment and I've had to promise faithfully not to say anything yet. But believe me, it's going to put Much Winchmoor firmly on the map."

I couldn't see it myself. Much Winchmoor was scarcely more than an insignificant little dot on the Ordnance Survey map and it would take more than some converted barn to rectify that.

"But, from what I remember, when Arthur used to keep his cows in it, the barn's not a lot bigger than the village hall," I pointed out.

She tossed her head. "This will be a purpose-built, intimate theatre and concert hall, with facilities for outdoor events as well. It's going to be amazing."

It's going to be expensive, I thought. The late Mr Hilperton-Jones must have left Cordelia very well off indeed to be able to afford such extensive 'improvements'. (Her choice of words, not mine).

"Here you are," she said briskly as she took a folder out of her desk drawer. "I've prepared a media pack for you. Everything you need is here - pictures, reviews of past productions, that sort of thing."

"Thank you. That's very helpful," I said as she handed it to me.

"That's the advantage of dealing with a professional, isn't it? If there's anything else you need to know, please get back to me."

I glanced through it. "It looks like you've covered everything. That's great."

"Would you like to see the barn?"

"Well, I'm in a bit of a hurry at the moment -" I began, but she ignored me.

"I'm afraid you can't actually see inside it at the moment, but you'll be able to see what I mean from the dining room window. And I can show you the plans."

She led me into a room on the other side of the vast hallway which contained a glass and chrome table and the most uncomfortable looking chairs I've ever seen. All very sleek, minimalist, and a million miles away from the heavy oak furniture that Arthur's family had used for generations.

She crossed to the window that looked across the back garden to the old stone barn. "As you can see, the builders have left things in a bit of a mess, and I can't safely get to it today. They're coming back tomorrow to fix it. You can see it then if you like."

I stared in astonishment at the devastation in what had once been Mabel Compton's flower and vegetable garden, its chaos a stark contrast to the clinical minimalism of the house's interior. There wasn't a plant left standing, just a huge mountain of soil which completely blocked off one half of the garden. The other half was split by a large, deep trench.

"What's the point of the big trench across the garden? What's happening there?"

Cordelia's face tightened. "Nothing. They started digging in the wrong place, even though the drawings I gave them were quite specific. It's such a nuisance and has put the whole thing way behind schedule. I was hoping that the barn's inaugural production would be our spring drama. But it's beginning to look as if the village hall will have to do. Once I've spruced the place up, of course."

I could have reminded her she'd have to get past Elsie first, not to mention Olive's late husband's shed. But I was in no mood for village politics.

Instead, I changed the subject by asking something that had been puzzling me ever since I'd first heard that the farmhouse had changed hands.

"How did you find out about this place being on the market? It was quite a shock to everyone when we heard Arthur had sold up. Abe and Milly's grandson would have loved to have taken the place on. Especially as he now has a young family. He'd have been thrilled to be able to come back to the village he grew up in."

She shrugged. "The place was a total wreck. A young man like that would never have been able to afford to spend the kind of money on it that I have."

"But he's a builder. He could -"

She waved her hand dismissively. "Besides, I'm sure his

wife and children prefer to live in a nice modern new build, rather than a draughty old farmhouse."

There wasn't much of the draughty old farmhouse left of the place now. It looked like something out of one of those glossy magazines that Mum never reads but leaves on the table in the reception area of Chez Cheryl because she thinks it gives the place some class.

"I happened on the place quite by chance. I was having lunch with a girlfriend," Cordelia was saying. "And she recommended the *spaghetti vongole* at the Winchmoor Arms. It was, according to my friend, to die for."

"I certainly hope not," I said quickly. "That would put Norina's hygiene rating way down."

She blinked at me. "I hope you're not implying that the pub has a hygiene problem. Because if so…"

"No, no." It was obvious Cordelia and I didn't share the same sense of humour. "Of course not. I was just…"

"Anyway, that's how I came to hear that the house was about to go on the market. My friend knows people in the know, you see. So I was able to snap it up before anyone else knew about it."

"Including Arthur's own family," I murmured, but she gave no indication of having heard me.

"As soon as I saw the barn, I knew I'd found my perfect spot." She glanced out of the window once again and waved a careless hand at the devastated garden. "And, talking of murder mysteries, that trench would make a perfect spot to bury a body or two, wouldn't you say?"

There was something about the way her eyes lit up when she said about burying a body or two that suddenly made me think of Elsie's remarks about the mystery that surrounded the death of Cordelia's husband.

But it was just Elsie and her nonsense, wasn't it?

Nevertheless, when I got home, I googled Cordelia Hilperton-Jones to see if I could find anything about what had happened to her husband. There was an awful lot about her famous mother, acres of stuff about the Dintscombe Players, but nothing about the late Mr Hilperton-Jones.

***

"You're late!" Elsie announced next morning as she opened the door, raising her voice to make herself heard above the sound of Prescott's hysterical barking. "The dog's going mad, waiting for his walk. I've had to shut him in the kitchen so be quick and get inside. That's no way to run a business, you know, keeping your customers waiting."

I could see she was in no mood to be reminded that, as she didn't pay me, she wasn't exactly a customer. But I let it pass.

"I'm sorry," I said. "I promised Olive I'd ask around the neighbours to see if any of them had seen what happened to her blanket yesterday. Only it took longer than I'd expected."

Elsie sniffed. "This time of the morning, some of the old folks around here take forever to answer their doors. I could have told you to leave it until later. Anyrate, it's a waste of time asking. I'll bet none of them saw anything, did they?"

"No."

"That doesn't surprise me because I know who did it."

"You do? Then why didn't you tell me? Or, at least, tell Olive?"

"Because I don't have any proof. But I know it was her."

"Who?"

"That Morag Browne, that's who."

"But how could she? She was with you all morning, first at Mum's salon, then at the funeral."

Elsie sniffed. "She had no rights going to Fred's funeral. It wasn't as if she knew him. Hasn't been in the village five minutes and she's trying to take over. She's as bad as Her Ladyship. Talking of whom, what sort of a mess has she made of Arthur and Mabel's place? I heard you had the royal invite yesterday. Did she serve tea and cucumber sandwiches on the lawn?"

"Hardly. The garden's in the course of renovation," I said, which was one way of putting it.

"I hope she doesn't make too many changes. Mabel Compton has the best greengage trees in the whole of Somerset."

37

I was already late, so I didn't tell her that, even though I had no idea what a greengage tree looked like, I could say quite categorically that there was no greengage tree, or anything else vaguely green in the waste land that was once Mabel Compton's beloved garden.

"Do you know any more about Cordelia's husband?" I asked in an effort to divert her attention from greengage trees.

It worked. "Last time I mentioned it, you didn't want to know."

"I was just curious about him, that's all. And I couldn't find anything about him when I googled."

She looked scornful. "You young people think the interweb has the answer to everything, don't you? Well, let me tell you, it's no match for good, old-fashioned information gathering."

"You mean, gossiping?"

Her button bright eyes bored into mine and she gave a little smile. "And what exactly are you doing, just at this moment?"

"Fair point," I admitted with a grin. "So, what do you know about him?"

"He was something big in the city, I believe. A marching banker or something like that. My son will know. He reads that boring financial paper every day and knows all about things like that. I remember him saying something about it when Her Ladyship moved into the village. Next time I see him, I'll ask him what it was. Anyrate, I can't sit around here gossiping with you all day and that dog needs a walk. And don't you go cutting it short, mind you. Just because you've spent the morning chatting."

I clipped on Prescott's lead and allowed him to drag me to the front door.

But, as always when I was in a hurry, he insisted on stopping to sniff every few inches or yap at anything that moved, from an empty crisp packet bowling along in the wind to a young guy on a bike. He saved his biggest volley of yaps for his all-time favourite enemy, Pitbull, the pub cat.

Suzanne, Finbar's owner, must have been getting anxious about the time because she was waiting by the front door when I got there. Prescott, excited at the prospect of meeting his bestie started barking. Even normally placid Rosie joined in with a few woofs as we walked up the garden path.

"So sorry I'm late, Suzanne," I explained. "I've been hot on the trail of Olive's missing blanket and asking around her immediate neighbours to see if they'd seen anything. I forgot to factor in just how very long it takes any of them to answer the door."

"That's ok." Her voice was little more than a whisper. "Only, do you think you could get Prescott to be quiet?"

"Probably not," I admitted. "He never takes any notice of what I say. But I can try. Prescott! Be quiet!" As predicted, that had absolutely no effect. "What's the problem? You aren't usually bothered by him. Are you ok? No, don't tell me. You've been on Abe Compton's Headbender and have the hangover from hell."

"Hardly." She bit her lip, her forehead creased as if she was trying to make her mind up about something. Then: "It's no good. I'll have to tell you. Because, to be honest, I don't know what to do. Kat, there's a man in the gallery flat."

Chapter Six

Now there are a few things you need to know about Suzanne Sheldon, owner of Finbar, the beautiful Irish Wolfhound and one of my regular dog walking customers.

First, she was seriously well off, having inherited loads of money from her late grandfather who'd owned a shedload of properties in a fairly affluent part of Bristol.

Second, she'd always wanted to own an art gallery, owing to the fact that (a), she loved art and artists, (b), she used to work in an art gallery in Bristol at one time and absolutely loved it and (c), she had 'more money than sense' - at least, that last bit was according to Elsie who said that what Much Winchmoor needed was a post office, not some fancy-pantsy art gallery.

So when the adjoining cottage to hers came on the market a few months before, Suzanne bought it and set about turning the ground floor into Much Winchmoor's first, and probably last, art gallery. The upstairs was being converted into a self-contained holiday flat, or would have been, if the builders had bothered to turn up and finish the job.

"Do you mean an intruder?" I asked. "Or have the builders come back and you don't want Prescott to disturb them in case they go away for another three weeks?"

"Heavens, no. Nothing like that. This poor young man, I found him, or rather, Finbar found him collapsed outside the back door."

"When was this?"

"About an hour ago. I thought for one awful moment he was dead. But he sort of came round as soon as Finbar got close. He was shivering with the cold and looked terrible. I asked if I should call an ambulance, but he said no. He assured me he was fine, even though it was obvious he was anything but. But he got quite agitated when I took my phone out and asked me to promise not to call anyone. He said he was just cold and tired and needed somewhere to shelter for a couple of hours while he recovered. So I said he was welcome to stay in the flat if he could make it up the stairs."

I stared at her. "Is he up there now?"

"Yes. I've been using the place to store some of the new garden furniture, so I set up one of the recliners for him then went into the house to make him a hot drink and fetch him some blankets. But when I got back, he was fast asleep. So I just left the drink and covered him with the blankets. That's why I didn't want the dogs to wake him."

I could hardly believe what I was hearing. Suzanne was normally a quiet, dare I say slightly dull person, who, although in her mid to late-twenties, dressed more like someone a lot older. Nor was she the sort to give in to impulsive actions. And this was the height of madness. "Who is he?"

She shrugged. "I have no idea. I've never seen him around here before. You might know him, though. You've lived here longer than me."

"More the pity. Want me to take a look?" Much Winchmoor had more than its fair share of undesirables, the sort of men you wouldn't want sleeping off their hangovers in your almost refurbished flat, believe me. And that, I imagined, was what had happened to Suzanne's unexpected visitor.

"OK. But don't wake him, will you?"

I crept up the uncarpeted stairs and saw a slightly built man slumped in one of the chairs, Suzanne's blanket around his shoulders. His chin, with its straggly beard, was almost resting on his chest and his dark hair flopped across his face.

"Well?" Suzanne said. "Do you know him?"

"I can't see his face that clearly underneath all that hair. But I'm pretty sure I've never seen him before. He looks like he's been sleeping rough somewhere. Did he smell of drink?"

Suzanne bristled. "Not all rough sleepers are alcoholics, you know. He did tell me his name, though. It's Dan."

"Dan what?"

"No surname. In fact, when I asked, he shook his head and

41

didn't answer."

"That's pretty suspicious for a start. Look, I'll hang around with you until he wakes up. I don't want you here on your own with him."

"Don't be silly. I'll be fine. I assure you, he's a perfectly pleasant young man and absolutely no threat. He looks like a puff of wind would blow him over."

"Then I'll leave Finbar with you."

"Oh no, you can't do that. He really needs a walk and I'm not going to have time to do it today. Don't look so worried. I'll be perfectly ok."

Still I hesitated. But I could tell from her body language she wasn't going to change her mind. And the morning was already slipping by. I couldn't afford to waste any more time as I'd missed yesterday's deadline for the Chronicle.

"Ok, then. But only if you promise to lock him in until I get back."

Suzanne looked horrified. "Indeed I will not. I'll make sure the doors to the house are locked if that makes you feel any better. But how would it be if he woke up and decided to be on his way then found that some mad woman had locked him in, like some Stephen King story?"

I laughed. "It would be a cracker, wouldn't it? But ok, I guess there's no harm in it as long as he stays where he is. I take it there's nothing of any value up there."

"Only the rest of the new garden furniture. But I don't see him making off with that, do you?"

When I got back from walking the dogs Suzanne came out of the gallery and beckoned me in. Dan whatever his name was awake now, Suzanne's blanket still around his shoulders as he tucked into a steaming bowl of soup.

Finbar ran up to him, sniffed him, then sat down at his feet. He gazed up at him with an adoring expression, no doubt hoping such doggy devotion would earn him a share of the soup. Not that he stood much chance of that. The guy was spooning it up like he hadn't eaten for a week.

"Kat, this is Dan," Suzanne said. "Dan Smith."

"Really?" I made no attempt to hide my scepticism.

"I've been trying to persuade him to see a doctor."

"I'm fine. I don't need a doctor." The man's voice was weak. His deep brown eyes stood out sharply against the pallor of his skin. "Look, I'm sorry to have troubled you and I assure you I feel much better. I'll be on my way as soon as I've finished this. You'll never know how very grateful I am to you."

"At least stay for another hour or so," Suzanne said. "You still look terribly pale."

"Thanks but no," he said. "I have to go."

As he spoke, the sound of an approaching siren filled the air and there was a flash of blue lights in the street outside. We all looked up, startled.

"Someone's in a hurry," Suzanne said. "Couldn't see if it was an ambulance or a police car."

It's always a worry when you see an ambulance in a small community like Much Winchmoor, because the chances are you will know who the patient is. I crossed my fingers, just in case.

"Maybe the police are hot on the trail of Olive's missing blanket," I said, trying to lighten the tension that had suddenly filled the room. But I was the only one who laughed. Dan put his dish on the floor and went to stand up. He swayed then sat down abruptly.

"Sorry," he said with a weak smile. "Guess I need to sit it out a little longer. I'm so sorry."

Just then my phone pinged with a text. It was from the Chronicle, asking where my copy was.

"Look, I'm going to have to go," I said.

"Your friend is in no danger from me, I promise you." His dark eyes burned with intensity, willing me to believe him. Then he turned to Suzanne. "You've been too kind and I'm sorry to have put you to such trouble. Sorry, too, for being such a wimp. I just need a little more time and I'll be on my way, I promise."

Suzanne and I left him to it and went back downstairs. "You mustn't worry, Kat. He's fine. I know he is. The trouble with you is that you see crime and criminals everywhere you go."

I wasn't convinced. "Did he say where he'd come from? From his accent, he's not from around these parts."

She shook her head. "He was very careful about what he said and I didn't want to push him. Figured if he wanted me to know he'd tell me. He did say he'd come to Much Winchmoor to see someone, though, and that he wasn't going to leave until he had."

"Did he say who?"

"No. Just said it was someone he used to know, that he had things to discuss with this person. But that was all. He was very mysterious."

"Ok, well, you know what you're doing, I suppose. Make sure you phone me if you have a problem though, won't you?"

She laughed. "What sort of problem do you imagine I would have? Off you go before that delightful man you work for gives you the sack. Or before I talk you into joining the choir."

"No way. How's that coming along, by the way? How's Gino doing?"

Gino was the landlord of the Winchmoor Arms. He was one of the village choir's most enthusiastic members. The only problem was he was also completely tone deaf which was odd considering he was a little bit Welsh and a whole lot Italian. But both nations great talent for singing had sadly passed Gino by. Although he was the only person not to realise this.

Suzanne grinned. "Let's put it this way. I took your advice and, as long as it's not one of Elvis's numbers I can usually keep him in check. I'll see you same time tomorrow, ok?"

"Ok. And don't forget to ring me if -"

"If nothing," she said firmly as she led me to the door.

I checked my watch. There was no doubt I was going to be hard pushed now to get the copy sent to the Chronicle as I was only part way through the report about the litter bins and then there was the item on the potholes. But the piece about Cordelia's murder mysteries was all but ready to go.

As I walked down the High Street, I could see that it had been a police car that had raced through the village earlier and that it had stopped outside the church. No ambulance then, thank goodness. The police car could be there for any number of reasons, although it was a pretty safe bet they hadn't come to check out the vandalised litter bin.

But whatever it was, it could be a story and was bound to be more interesting than a report on potholes and litter bins. And I could always use the 'chasing up a story' line as an excuse for being late filing my copy.

The entrance to the churchyard was marked off with blue and white police tape which brought back some unhappy memories for me.

Be careful what you wish for, Kat, I told myself as I walked towards the churchyard where a policeman stood at the entrance. There was also a small knot of people standing around, including Olive's sister, Millie.

"What's going on?" I asked her.

"Oh, Katie dear. I don't know. It's a complete mystery," she said. "I don't know what to think. I must be seeing things."

"How do you mean?"

"I've just seen a policeman come out of that old stone shed in the corner of the churchyard. You know, where they keep the gardening stuff. And he was carrying something that I swear was Mother's crocheted blanket. But it couldn't have been, could it? I mean, Olive looks after that blanket like it was the Crown Jewels. She'd never leave it lying around in that dirty old shed."

Before I could say anything, there was a rustling behind us, and a girl I'd never seen before squeezed through the gap in the churchyard yew hedge and out on to the pavement. She stood there, looking down at her phone. She was about eighteen, I guessed, with long black hair that reached halfway down her back, heavily drawn eyebrows and black nails that were so long they couldn't possibly be real. She also had a couple of small silver rings through one nostril.

Beside me, I heard Millie give a short gasp and mutter, "Who on earth is that?"

"Hiya," the girl called as she sauntered towards us. "I managed to get a couple of great shots, but then I got chased away. You can't see much from here though."

45

"Of what?" I asked. "What's going on?"

Her sharp, catlike eyes gleamed under the ton of makeup she'd slapped around them. "Looks like they've found a body in the churchyard." She held her phone towards me. "See? When you zoom in you can see it quite clearly."

My stomach flipped. "No, thank you," I said as I turned away.

"Well come on now, Miss Marple." Her jeering voice had the musical lilt of a Welsh accent.

"From what I hear about you, all you need to do is a quick look and you'll be able to tell us who done it and why."

Chapter Seven

"Go on," the girl urged, jabbing a long black painted fingernail at the picture on her phone. "Look at it properly and tell me that's not a body lying there."

Her eyes glittered with barely suppressed excitement. Millie's gaze, however, was riveted on the girl's nose rings that quivered as she moved her head.

I took one quick glance at the picture and turned away. I'd seen enough.

"Who are you?" I asked, although I already knew. The accent was a bit of a giveaway. "And don't call me Miss Marple. It winds me up."

"That's what Aunty Nora calls you. Among other things," she added with a snort.

"You're Rhianna, aren't you?"

"Got it in one, Miss Marple."

Norina had been threatening me with the arrival of her niece from Pontypridd for the past six months. Rhianna was, according to Norina, a 'natural' barmaid and was working towards a qualification in the hospitality industry. She was also, according to Norina, everything I was not. Although according to Gino, she was 'a right little madam.'

Every time I did something that Norina didn't approve of, which was most of the time, she would tell me darkly to 'wait until Rhianna gets here. Then you'll see what's what, young lady.'

And of course I did indeed see what was what. I saw that I was about to lose one third of my 'portfolio' career, that was what. In case you didn't know (and, believe me, I wish I didn't) a 'portfolio' career is recruitment consultant speak for having several rubbish jobs instead of one half decent one.

Norina's 'natural barmaid' had switched her attention (and

her phone camera) from me to the arrival of yet another car with a blue flashing light as it turned into Church Lane.

"Aunty Nora tells me you're also a bit of a journalist," she said as she clicked away. "I'd have thought you couldn't wait to get this on the front page. I can let you have my picture, for a fee, of course."

"Look, can't you show some respect, and put that thing away?" I pointed at her phone. "Someone's had a horrible accident, and you shouldn't have photographed it. It's tacky."

"It's a news story," she said, while from behind me I heard Millie's sharp intake of breath.

"Katie, dear, please say it's not another murder. What's happening to this place?"

She looked so upset I hurried to reassure her. "Nothing's happening to this place, Millie. And of course it's not another murder."

"Another murder?" Rhianna heavily drawn brows lifted. "Cool. I thought it was going to be dead boring here. But a murder ..."

"It won't be a murder," I said sharply. "Like I told you, it's probably just a horrible accident."

Millie gave another sharp gasp and clutched her hand to her chest.

"An accident? Oh, my life, who... who is it?" she said, her filmy grey eyes suddenly wide and frightened. "Could you see? It's not ... Tell me it's not…"

I shook my head. "No, Millie. I couldn't see who it is. But I can tell you this, it's not your Abe."

Beside me, Millie gave a shaky sigh. "I always think, one of these days.... you know, when he's had a few pints, he's not too steady on his feet."

"It's not Abe," I repeated gently as I saw her eyes shimmer with tears and her lips tremble. "Why did you think it might be? Are you saying he didn't come home last night?"

She looked away, her face scarlet with embarrassment. "It's - I'm being silly, I know."

"It's ok, Millie," I said quickly, aware that Rhianna's nose rings were quivering as she followed our exchange with interest. "Come on. Let's go on home, shall we? By the look of that policeman walking towards us, he's going to tell us all to move on anyway."

Which was exactly what he did. Millie and I moved off and, to my relief, Rhianna tottered off in the direction of the High Street, her sharp heels tapping on the pavement as she did so. Millie and I went the other way.

"I didn't like to say in front of that young girl, Katie," Millie said, her cheeks still flushed.

"You don't have to say anything, Millie." I touched her arm as we waited for a delivery van to drive past before we crossed the road. "It's none of her business, nor any of mine."

"You see, Abe and me, we don't - we don't share a bedroom anymore. He snores and I just can't sleep through it like I used to. So he sleeps down one end of the house and me at the other. He's not happy about it. But I told him straight, do something about the snoring and then he could come back."

"Sounds reasonable to me," I said and went to walk on. But Millie wasn't going anywhere. Not until she'd said what she had to say.

"Then, this morning, I didn't even check to see if he was in before I went out to catch the early bus into Dintscombe. I had a 9 o'clock doctor's appointment about the arthur-itis in my knee. Not that he did anything about it. Just said it was something I had to live with and what did I expect at my age? And there's him looking not old enough to be out without his mum, least of all telling me what I must and mustn't learn to live with. I don't know what's happening to our health service and that's the truth. Anyway, where was I?"

"You were saying about Abe."

"Yes, of course. So I left without checking whether he was up or not, and when that young girl said there was a body in the churchyard, and you said that it looked like someone had had a horrible accident, well, my heart just leapt into my mouth. It suddenly occurred to me that it could be my poor Abe. He could have been lying there all night and I wouldn't even have known."

"Millie, I didn't see who it was, but I told you, it wasn't

Abe. I was working in the pub last night and Abe was wearing that old check jacket of his, wasn't he?"

"Well, yes. happen he was," she admitted. "And now I think on it, when I left this morning it was there on the back of the chair in the kitchen where he always leaves it when he comes in after a night out." She gave a long drawn-out sigh, like she'd been holding her breath. "Oh, Katie, love, you must think me all sorts of a fool."

"Of course I don't."

"Well, it's taught me a lesson, I can tell you," she said as we walked towards the junction of the road that led up to her and Abe's farmhouse. "Tonight Abe is moving back into our bedroom. He wasn't too happy about being banished from it in the first place. Starting muttering on about his rights and I have to admit, I missed it too. Do you know, I really miss the way he always kisses me goodnight and then he -"

"Sorry, Millie, but I've really, really got to go," I said quickly, before she could go into any more detail. Talk about too much information. It was bad enough when my mum and dad started dropping coy hints about their love life, but Abe and Millie Compton? No way. Although I had to admit, I'd obviously been wrong about Millie and her lack of romance.

"Now, don't you worry about Abe," I said. "He's safely at home, I'm sure of it." I looked at my watch. "In fact, it's almost midday. He'll probably be on his way to the pub for his lunchtime pint."

As if on cue, we saw the stocky figure of Abe Compton ambling down the road towards us. Millie gave an exasperated sigh and hurried off to meet him and I carried on towards home.

But before I got very far, I stopped, took out my phone and tried Mrs Denby again. It seemed a terrible thing to worry about, given what was happening in the churchyard, but she'd promised to ask the vicar about signing me up to walk Archie on a regular basis.

Seeing Rhianna had seriously unsettled me. I'd always thought her impending arrival was just a threat Norina used to keep me in line, that she would never actually do it. Certainly, if my job at the pub was going to come to an end, I would need to increase my other jobs.

Including, of course, the one with the Chronicle. I took a deep breath. Time to overcome my squeamishness and see if I could find out what was going on in the churchyard. And whose body was it underneath that white police tent they had just set up.

I turned back towards the church. My luck was in as I recognised the man who was getting out of yet another car that had pulled up in Church Lane.

I'd gone to school with Ben Watkins, or Detective Constable Watkins as he was now, and he'd had a massive crush on my friend Jules.

Should I contact Liam? I wondered. *Even though he was on holiday? He'd not be very happy at being called away if it turned out that someone had just collapsed and died of a heart attack or something. And also, he'd want to know who it was lying there. As, of course, did I.*

Time to start behaving like a professional journalist. I didn't mind admitting that Rhianna's little dig had struck home.

"Oh, hi, Ben." I gave him my brightest smile. "What's going on?"

"Hi, Katie. Can't tell you that, I'm afraid. Are you asking as a mere nosy neighbour, or a journalist sensing a story?"

I bristled. "I'm not a nosy neighbour. And I prefer to be called Kat, as you very well know."

"Then you're definitely here as journalist sensing a story. There will be a statement in due course."

"Then there is something wrong?"

"Can't tell you that either."

"I was on my way to the vicarage. Is it ok if I nip through the churchyard, or is it all roped off? Only, it's so much quicker than going round the road."

His eyes narrowed. "What are you going there for?"

"Are you asking as a nosy friend, or in your professional capacity?" I shot back at him.

He grinned. "Both, I suppose."

"I was supposed to be walking the vicar's dog this

51

morning," I said. "Or at least I was hoping to. Only I've been trying to get hold of Mrs Denby, the vicar's secretary, but she's not answering her phone. She –" I stopped dead as a horrible though occurred to me. "Oh no. The body on the ground. Don't say it's Mrs Denby."

He frowned at me. "How did you know there's a body on the ground? Were you here when it happened?"

"Oh no, no. It's just, well, someone happened to take a picture and she showed it to me. That's all."

His frown deepened. "A picture? Who?"

I hesitated. Rhianna hadn't actually done anything illegal. Just tasteless and tactless. But I didn't want her getting into trouble about it.

"It was just some stranger to the village," I said, which was, after all, the truth. "I'd not seen her before. She showed me the picture on her phone and left soon after. It wasn't a very clear picture and I hardly glanced at it. I couldn't even see if it was a man or a woman lying there. So, come on, Ben, please. Could I just go through to the vicarage if I stay on the other side of the church?"

"Sorry. The forensic boys will be there for some time. I'm afraid it's the long way round for you today." As he spoke, his radio crackled into life and he moved away.

"Ben?" I called after him. "Please tell me it's not Mrs Denby lying there."

"It's not a woman, Katie."

"Then who?" I began, but he'd already moved away.

I stood there, undecided for a moment, looking around to see if I could see anyone else to talk to. But although the churchyard was now swarming with more policeman than on the opening night of the Glastonbury Festival, not one of them looked in my direction.

I tried Mrs Denby yet again, but there was still no answer. Where was she, and why wasn't she picking up?

I turned away and, as if on cue, saw Mrs Denby herself coming across the churchyard towards me. Her normally round cheerful face was as grey as the lichen on the church wall.

"Mrs Denby?" I called and hurried across to her. "Are you ok?"

"Oh, Katie. Katie, it's terrible. Terrible." Her eyes welled with tears, and her round face crumpled in on itself, like a collapsing balloon. "I just can't ..."

I put my hand on her arm, thankful that Rhianna wasn't around. "Come and sit on the bench. You look as if you're about to keel over."

"No. No. I can't..." Her breath came in short, panicky gasps. "I can't stay here. I've got to get away. I can't ... The police said I could go home."

"Would you like me to walk with you?" I offered her my arm which, to my surprise, she took.

"You're a good girl, Katie." She gave me a grateful smile and leaned heavily on my arm as we walked in silence until we reached her cottage, although I was dying to ask what had got her so upset.

As she went to open the gate, she turned to me. "Thank you, my lovely. I'll be ok now. I just need to get indoors, sit down, and have a nice cup of camomile tea. It was the shock."

Once again, her face threatened to crumple and the tears slid down her cheeks. "Look, you might as well know. Goodness knows, nothing stays secret in this village for very long."

"You don't have to tell me, Mrs Denby. Not if it upsets you."

"It'll come out all too soon. On my way through the churchyard this morning I saw what I thought was a pile of old clothes lying on the path. I went to pick them up, grumbling away at myself about people leaving their rubbish all over the place for others to pick up. Only - only when I got there, it - it wasn't a pile of clothes. It was the reverend."

"The vicar?" I gasped. "That was him lying there on the path? What happened? Did he have a heart attack?"

She shook her head. Then a strange thing happened to her face. It turned bright red and her tear-filled eyes flashed with fury.

"It was no heart attack," she said fiercely. "No accident

either. It was murder. Cold blooded murder."

My heart missed a beat or ten. "What makes you so sure?"

"Because there was a note. I found it."

"A note? Well surely that points to suicide?"

"Not this note. It was next to his body. Pinned to a teddy bear, of all things. And it said - as God is my witness, I don't think I will ever be able to get it out of my head. It said something about how abseiling is only the second fastest way down a church tower."

A shiver snaked down my back. "You mean he - he fell from the tower?"

"I mean he was pushed from the tower." She took a deep shuddering breath. "And I think I know who did it."

Chapter Eight

This couldn't be happening. Another murder in Much Winchmoor. Mrs Denby was joking surely?

But one look at her ashen face told me she was deadly serious.

"You say you know who did it?" I asked. "Who?"

"There's Anna, for a start. You heard her yesterday, didn't you?"

I shook my head, thinking maybe the shock was making her talk nonsense. "I'm sorry. I've no idea who you're talking about. Anna who?"

"Anna Fairweather. The reverend's ex-wife." She spoke slowly, deliberately, as if to a small child who was having trouble keeping up. "You were there. You heard her threaten the reverend, didn't you?" She closed her eyes and whispered, "God rest his poor soul."

"The woman at the vicarage? That was the vicar's wife? But you told me -"

Mrs Denby pressed her tightly clasped hands into her stomach. "Yes, well, I was trying to be discreet, wasn't I? The reverend doesn't like anyone and everyone knowing his personal business. Especially a member of the press." She looked at me, her normally placid expression replaced by a much fiercer one. "And you're not to write about this, promise?"

"Mrs Denby, please believe me, I will treat anything you tell me in strictest confidence," I hurried to reassure her. "Although it sounds like you should be telling the police this. Not me."

She sighed. "Yes, I'm going to have to, aren't I? They're sending an officer around later to take a full statement from me. I'll tell them then. I should have told them before," she went on. "But…" Her voice trembled and her eyes filled with tears. "But I wasn't thinking straight. Heaven help me, I will never get that picture out of my head. The poor, poor man." Her voice had sunk to a whisper.

I knew exactly how she felt. Will and I discovered a body once and although it was a couple of years ago now, the memory was as fresh and horrible as if it had been yesterday. I still woke up in the night sometimes with flashbacks.

Before I could come up with anything to say that might comfort her, she looked up, her eyes swimming with angry tears. "And then when I saw that awful girl taking photos on her wretched phone. You just can't believe some people, can you? I don't know who she is. Certainly no one I'd ever seen in the village before with her short skirt, ridiculous shoes and black nails. She looked like a leftover from a Halloween party. I don't suppose she was from that paper you write for, was she?"

"No," I said quickly. "She's definitely not from the Chronicle."

Mrs Denby flushed. "Well, whoever she is, she needs to learn some respect." She shook her head. "He was still lying there, God rest his poor soul and there she was, snapping away. It made me feel really sick, I can tell you."

Her face had gone a horrible grey colour again and she looked on the point of collapse.

"Would you like me to come in and make you that cup of tea?" I asked. Mrs Denby lived alone. There had been a husband once, according to Elsie, but he left years ago when Mrs Denby 'got religion.'

I was uneasy about leaving her on her own, but she shook her head firmly.

"No. I'll be fine, I promise you. But thank you for asking, lovely. I do appreciate it. You're a good girl. Thank you for all your kindness."

She took her key out of her bag and had just put it into the lock when I called her back.

"Mrs Denby, what's happening about Archie?"

She stopped, then turned to face me. There was a hunted

expression in her eyes as she dragged her hand through her normally neat hair. "Archie! I hadn't even thought about him. He'll still be in the vicarage. I can't go and get him. I just can't face going there. Not at the moment."

"Would you like me to get him?" I asked.

"Would you, lovely? That would be such a help. I've got a spare set of keys to the vicarage in the kitchen. Hang on while I get them. Yes, he can't stay there on his own, can he? He'll be wanting to go out soon. Oh dear, this is all such a terrible worry. What a thing to happen. I just - just can't think straight. And then there's the police will be here any minute to take my statement. I don't know, that's for sure."

She disappeared inside and came back a couple of minutes later with a key. "That's for the back door. If you could bring him here, I'll sort him out. Although what to do with him, goodness only knows." She sighed. "I'll get on to the animal rescue place right away. It will give me something else to think about."

"You're sending him to a rehoming centre?" I was horrified.

"What else can I do? He's a very popular breed, so I'm told. He'll be rehomed in no time. It's for the best. I can't keep him. My cat hates dogs."

So did mine. But that was beside the point.

"Look, don't you worry about Archie. I'll have him for now," I said, trying not to think of the time I brought Prescott home with me and Cedric (that's our dog hating cat) left the house and didn't come back for a fortnight. And goodness only knew what Gran K's Max would have made of him.

But I couldn't bear the thought of poor, sad little Archie being sent to a rehoming centre. He was depressed enough as it was. "Look, I've got a friend who might be able to help. She was talking the other day about getting another dog. I'll speak to her."

Mrs Denby looked doubtful. "Your friend will have to go through the proper adoption channels," she said firmly. "I'm only thinking of the dog's best interest. But I'll sort it out tomorrow when I'm feeling a bit more myself. I'm just not up to coping with that right now."

I pocketed the key and set off in the direction of the vicarage, taking the long way round to avoid going through the churchyard which I assumed was still cordoned off.

Archie didn't seem particularly pleased to see me. But then again, he never looked pleased about anything. He certainly was one depressed little dog. I collected his lead and took a last look around the kitchen. A copy of the day's Times lay open on the table, folded at the crossword. I swallowed hard and looked away, blinking back the tears.

The poor man. No one would finish that crossword now. No one would read the brightly coloured post-it note that was stuck to the calendar on the wall by the window. No one would wear the reading glasses that were next to the newspaper or put on the worn-down slippers that stood by the back door.

I clipped Archie's lead on, glad to close the door of the gloomy old vicarage firmly behind me, trying to forget the sight of the rinsed coffee mug on the draining board that Rev Fairweather would never use again.

***

"Well, Archie," I said as we set off down the long, winding Vicarage drive, with him trotting along quietly behind me, his head and tail down as always. "I know what I said to Mrs Denby but that was to stop her doing something she'd probably regret tomorrow. But what on earth am I going to do with you? Mum will go mad when I bring you home and Gran K will probably have a fit of the vapours." My spirits lifted slightly as a thought occurred to me. "But maybe that might be just what's needed to persuade her now would be a good time to go back home."

We'd just passed the clump of rhododendron bushes where we'd leapt for our lives the day before when I heard a car engine and saw a flash of yellow coming up the drive towards us. Talk about *déjà vu*. I recognised the car immediately and prepared to dive back into the bushes again. This time, however, it was travelling much more slowly and drew up at the sight of me. A thin, pale faced woman, light brown hair pulled back in a careless ponytail, got out and started to say something. Only I couldn't hear what she was saying because at that moment, Archie appeared to go mad.

This dog, who until that moment, had been content to trot listlessly behind me, head down and silent, suddenly pulled so hard the lead was wrenched from my hand. At the same time he began making this really weird noise, a cross between a yelp and a howl. What was the matter with him? Was he having some sort of fit? I made a mental note to brush up on my doggy first aid.

The woman, who I guessed was in her late thirties, was wearing faded jeans and a washed-out sweater that looked a couple of sizes too big for her. She stood as if turned to stone as Archie hurled himself at her. I expected her to recoil in horror and have a go at me for failing to control my dog. Instead, she knelt down and wrapped her arms around him.

"Archie. Oh Archie, Archie. It is you, isn't it, baby?" Her voice was muffled as she buried her face in the dog's fur, while he squirmed in her arms and reached up to lick her face. "It really is you. But I thought - I thought you were dead. I thought Lionel ... they told me...." She looked up at me, the tears streaming unchecked down her face. "I thought Archie was dead."

I'd never seen Archie so animated and I had no doubt of the reason why.

"You're Anna, aren't you?" I said. "Anna Fairweather."

She nodded, still hugging the dog who was smiling up at her with doggy adoration in his amber eyes, his whole body a mass of wriggling, squirming delight.

"You were here yesterday," I said. "In fact, you drove off so fast Archie and I had to jump for our lives, into the bushes."

She bit her lip. "I did? I'm so, so sorry. I was - I was not myself. I was upset and angry. I thought - I thought Archie had been -" She pulled him closer to her, kissed the top of his curly black head and rocked him as if he was a small child. "I thought he was dead. But I must have misunderstood. I was pretty wound up before I even knocked on the door, to be honest and was more concerned about saying what I had to say

59

to Lionel. I was desperately upset when I found he wasn't here that I wasn't really listening to what Mrs Denby was trying to tell me. And you say you were in the bushes as I drove past? Oh, how I wish I'd seen you both."

"Why would you think Archie was dead?"

She smoothed back her hair and shrugged. "Like I said, I was in a state. I'd driven all this way to see Lionel, only to be told that he wasn't at home and to come back tomorrow, even though he'd known I was coming. And when I asked about Archie, Mrs Denby said -" She broke off and shook her head. "She must have said that Archie wasn't here."

"Which he wasn't as I'd taken him for a walk."

She nodded. "I don't know why I jumped to the wrong - the worst conclusion. I told Lionel I'd be back for Archie one day. I thought that was why he'd run away for the day, that he couldn't face me telling me that Archie was ... that he was dead." She picked up Archie's lead. "Look, I'll take him back to the vicarage and Lionel and I will sort it out."

I stared at her. "You don't know, do you?"

"Know what?"

"I'm sorry, but I'm afraid Lionel was found dead this morning. In the churchyard. I've just come to collect Archie."

Her eyes widened with horror. "Lionel's dead? But he can't be. He was always so fit, always took such great care of himself. I can't believe it."

I cleared my throat as I remembered what Mrs Denby had said about finding that horrible note on his body. What to do? I'd probably already told her too much. Certainly Mrs Denby had no doubt that she'd done it and, indeed, I had heard her threaten Lionel yesterday.

And yet, she'd looked so shocked when I told her he'd died. That had looked genuine enough. Surely she couldn't have been acting.

"The police are treating his death as suspicious," I said and watched her reaction carefully. If anything, she went even paler. Her hands dug into Archie's fur and she held him so close, he wriggled free. She didn't even seem to notice he'd gone or that I'd picked up his trailing lead.

"Are you staying in Much Winchmoor?" I asked when it looked as if she wasn't going to speak. "Only I think the police might want to talk to you."

"To me?" Her eyes were wide now. "Why?"

"You threatened him. I heard you. So, too, did another witness."

"Witness? Oh, you mean, Mrs Denby? Yesterday afternoon. She knows I didn't mean it. I was angry with Lionel, yes. I'd come back for Archie and the rest of my things and to have it out with him about..." She paused, as if debating whether to confide in me. Then obviously decided against it. "We- we had things to discuss. When I..." She swallowed hard. "When I left, I wasn't able to take any of my things with me, including stuff that belonged to my parents who are both dead. I didn't have anywhere to keep them. But now I have and contacted him to say I was coming to collect them and, of course, Archie. Only when I got here, I found that Lionel had got rid of all my things. Burnt them on the bonfire. And didn't even have the courage to face me." Her eyes flashed angrily. "I couldn't believe he would do such a terrible thing."

"Perhaps you got that wrong as well," I said, feeling sorry for her in spite of everything. She sounded in a very confused state, and if Mrs Denby was right, then she needed help.

"I was angry with him, yes. I still am. But I didn't kill him," she said. "I wasn't even in Much Winchmoor last night. I stayed at a guest house in Dintscombe. I was going to drive back to - to where I'd come from but Mrs Denby phoned and said he'd promised to see me this morning and explain everything. You can ask her and, of course, the people in the guest house."

"And you left there at what time this morning?" I asked.

"Just after 9.30."

I glanced at my watch. "It doesn't take an hour and a half to drive here from Dintscombe."

"My car broke down. Luckily, someone came along and got it going for me." She frowned at me. "Why are you asking all these questions?"

Because I'm just plain nosy, I could have said. But before I could say anything, the sound of a siren split the air, causing rooks in the nearby beech trees to spiral upwards in alarm. She backed away like a spooked pony.

"I've got to go," she said as she turned towards her car.

"Please don't. It's much better to stay and sort this out."

"But I had nothing to do with this. I've only just this minute arrived here. I'm sure I'll be able to prove that. Maybe find the man who stopped to help me fix my car." She held out her hand. "If you'll just give me Archie. I've got plenty of room in the car now there's nothing of mine left in the vicarage."

"I'm sorry, but I can't let you take him."

"But he's my dog. You must be able to see that."

I could indeed. I'd never seen Archie so animated. As I hesitated, the sirens sounded ever closer. She froze for a second, then jumped back into her car, and wound down the window.

"Then, please, look after him for me," she called. "I'll be back. I promise. But for now, I have got to go. It's really, really important. This isn't just about me, otherwise I'd stay and sort things out. Because I swear on anything you want me to swear on, I did not hurt Lionel. I haven't seen him since - since the day I left."

"But if you drive off now, it will look even more suspicious."

"Not if you don't tell anyone you've seen me," she said, looking at me with the same sort of pleading expression that Rosie the labrador uses when she's after a treat.

Only Anna wasn't after a treat. She was after her freedom.

"Have I just let a murderer get away?" I asked Archie as we watched her do a neat three-point turn. He responded with a quiet little whimper as Anna's car disappeared down the vicarage drive. His tail went down, his shoulders sagged, and he was back to his normal, depressed self.

And yet, I believed her when she said she had nothing to do with Mr Fairweather's death.

But then, I'd been wrong before, hadn't I?

Chapter Nine

While I dithered about what to do, my phone rang. It was Will.

"What time shall I pick you up this evening?" he asked.

"Pick me up?" For a moment I couldn't think what he was talking about.

He sighed. "You've forgotten, haven't you? We agreed the other night that I was going to book a table at the King's Head. It's curry night. You know how busy it gets. "

My heart sank. "I'm sorry, Will. I'm not really in the mood for a curry. Not tonight."

There was a small, tense silence on the other end. "Fair enough. No worries," he said, although he didn't for one minute sound like he meant it.

"I'm sorry. I didn't mean it to come out like that. It's just - well, there's been some bad news in the village. It's the vicar. He was found dead this morning."

"Yeah, I heard. But please tell me you weren't the one to find him, Katie." His tone was sharp, like I was some naughty kid who'd lost my lunch money or something.

"Of course I didn't." My tone was as snippy as his. "I don't make a habit of going around finding dead bodies, you know."

"You sure about that?"

"I'm not even going to dignify that with an answer, William Manning."

"Fair enough, Kathryn Latcham."

"My name is -"

"Yeah, yeah. Katie."

"Kat."

That was one of the things I loved about Will. We have argued and bickered all our lives. And both thoroughly enjoyed it. And most of the time, I won, or at least I got the last word, which amounted to the same thing.

But the laughter died in my throat and I felt guilty that just for a second in the cosy familiarity of bickering with Will I'd almost forgotten the poor vicar.

"Oh, Will. It was Mrs Denby who found the body. She's in a terrible state and is pretty sure he was murdered."

I heard Will's sudden intake of breath. "What on earth makes her think that? Sounds like she's been spending too much time with Cordelia Hilperton-Jones and her crackpot murder mysteries."

"Mrs Denby found this note next to his - his body. He - he fell from the church tower, and when she found him, there was this note that said something about abseiling being only the second fastest way down a church tower. Isn't that awful?"

"It's certainly sick. Not to mention a totally weird thing to do."

I was about to tell him how Mrs Denby thought it was Anna who'd done it. Suddenly I really wanted - no, *needed* to talk it over with him. Will always had this way of making me see things in perspective.

"Do you know, I think I might be up for a curry after all," I said. "It will be good to get away from this place for a bit. That is, if I can work out what to do with Archie."

"Who's Archie?"

"The vicar's dog. He was all on his own in the vicarage and I couldn't leave him there, could I? Do you think your dad would have him?"

"No way. You know what Tam is like around other dogs."

Tam was Will's wild-eyed sheepdog who was no fonder of his own species than he was of any other. Will and his dad, John, were the only people he got along with. He always looked at me like I was a stroppy ewe and he was just dying to give me a nip on the ankles to keep me in line.

"Fair enough. I'll have a word with Suzanne," I said. "She'll probably have him for a couple of days. She's always saying Finbar's lonely and that she's thinking of getting another dog. So, I'll see you later then?"

"That's great." He sounded so relieved that I felt guilty for having been so reluctant in the first place. "I'll confirm the booking then. You know how rammed the place gets on curry night. And Katie... I mean, Kat...?"

My heart gave an anxious leap. I never trusted Will when he remembered to call me Kat. It usually meant he was going to say something that he knew I wasn't going to like.

"What?" I said and instantly regretted it. I hadn't meant it to come out so grumpy. But it had been a truly awful day and it wasn't over yet. I still had to find somewhere for Archie to go. Otherwise, it would be me, Will and Archie up for curry night at the King's Head.

"Nothing. Just don't be late. I'll pick you up at 7.30, ok? I've even given the Land Rover a good clean in honour of the occasion."

And before I could ask him what occasion, he rang off. Now I was seriously worried. The last time Will had cleaned the Land Rover had been for his cousin's wedding. And that was six years ago.

And I had a sinking feeling I knew what the 'occasion' might be.

***

"Thanks, Suzanne," I said as she handed me a mug of coffee. She made the best coffee on the planet. Or rather, her machine did. It was bigger than my mum's kitchen and made a noise like a jet engine psyching itself up for take-off. But you put the beans in one end and out came a cup of perfect coffee at the other. Exactly what I needed at that moment.

Well, that and the chance to talk things over with someone.

"I'm really grateful to you for having Archie tonight. Mum's not really a dog person, and Gran's cat will probably terrify the life out of the poor creature."

"Like I said, it's no bother. Archie's a sweetie and he and Finbar get along fine. It's Prescott who has the problem with him."

"Prescott has a problem with anything on four legs and most things on two legs. Except Finbar, of course."

"You sounded a bit wound up on the phone just now," she

said. "Everything all right? Apart from the awful news about the vicar, of course."

"Yes. No. Oh, I don't know. And that's the problem."

"Sorry, Kat, but you're going to have to be a tiny bit more specific than that."

I bit my lip. Normally I'd talk things through with Jules, but she has known me and Will forever (Jules and I started at the village primary school at the same time) but she tends to get a bit judgey where my relationship with Will is concerned. She thinks I should stop 'messing him about and get on with it.'

And, of course, she's right. Only...

While I dithered, Finbar padded across and laid his huge head on my lap. I smoothed his bristly fur and said, as much to the dog as to Suzanne, "It's Will. He wants to see me this evening. Says it's very important. So much so, he's cleaned the Land Rover in honour of what he calls The Occasion."

"And that's a problem because?"

"I'm pretty sure he's going to propose. He's been dropping all sorts of hints recently."

Suzanne gave a puzzled frown. "But I thought he already had. It was the talk of the village at the time and the choir was buzzing that much about it I couldn't get them to settle. Not by the time Elsie Flintlock had finished telling everyone how Will had stood stark naked in the village pond with a rose between his teeth and said he wasn't coming out until you agreed to marry him."

"He wasn't naked," I said quickly. "Not completely. Only the top half. And it was a sort of joke. Will and I are always winding each other up."

"So you didn't agree to marry him?"

"Well, yes. But that was to get him to come out. He was gathering quite a crowd."

Suzanne, whom I'd always thought of as quite a refined person gave a very un-Suzanne like snigger. "So I heard. So, what's your problem? Don't you want to marry Will? Don't you love him?"

"That's just it. I love him, of course I do. But..." I broke off.

"Go on," she prompted.

"I still think that one day I'm going to leave Much Winchmoor. I had a taste of city life and I loved it."

There. I'd said it.

"You loved it?" Suzanne pulled a face. "I hated living in a city. I love it here and wouldn't want to live anywhere else."

"But it's so claustrophobic. Everyone knows everyone else's business. If someone sneezes at one end of the village, someone down the other end will have said who they'd been with and what they'd been up to, to catch the cold in the first place. It's like living in a goldfish bowl."

Suzanne gave a wry smile. "You're not wrong there. But most of the time it's because they care about you. It's better than living somewhere where you don't even know your next-door neighbour."

I wasn't so sure about that. But as she was doing me this huge favour by agreeing to look after Archie while things were sorted, I didn't want to upset her by arguing with her.

"So how long have you and Will known each other?" she asked.

I shrugged. "Forever. His mother and mine were best friends, and we're both only children, and more or less grew up together. More like brother and sister than anything else. Until a few years ago when things changed between us. But I sometimes wish..." I let my voice trail away and shook my head because, to be honest, I didn't know what I wished.

"Is there someone else?" Suzanne asked, her voice soft, her eyes kind.

"No! Of course not." At the sound of my raised voice, Finbar lifted his huge, grey head. Now they were both looking at me. "I love Will," I said simply. "I can't imagine life without him."

"Do you think he'd leave Much Winchmoor?"

Will, leave Much Winchmoor? There were probably Mannings up at Pendle Knoll Farm when Judge Jeffries was rampaging around the West Country, hanging, drawing and quartering rebels who'd taken up arms against the King back in the seventeenth century.

"No way," I said firmly. "He's as much a part of the place as the village pond. Only he smells a lot nicer. Unless, of course, he's been muck spreading."

"So what are you going to do?" Suzanne asked.

"I'm going to say yes, of course." I said quickly. "I love him. He loves me. That's all there is to it. It's that simple."

She continued to watch me carefully, a small frown creasing her forehead. "Don't say yes out of a sense of duty, Kat. Will's a good man. He deserves better than that."

I put my coffee cup down. She was quite right, of course. Will was a good man and he did indeed deserve better than me.

"Anyway, I'd better go." I said briskly. "I've got tons to do this afternoon. Thanks so much for agreeing to take Archie. It's only until we can sort out what to do with him. Mrs Denby thinks he should go to a rehoming centre. But I hope it won't come to that."

"He gets on well with Finbar, so he'll be no trouble. Might as well look after two dogs as one. And as I said the other day, I think Finbar is lonely. He'd love another dog in the house."

"And your temporary lodger?" I asked. "I take it he's now moved on like he said he was going to?"

Now it was Suzanne's turn to squirm.

"No," she said, looking not at me but down at her hands. "He's still far from well, and he's really no trouble up there in the flat. I said he could stay for as long as he needs in exchange for a few odd jobs around the place. He's really good in the garden apparently. And look." She went across to the kitchen table and picked up a piece of paper. "Look what he drew for me. As a thank you for letting him stay. He really is a very talented artist, you know. I might not have any artistic talent myself, but I can recognise it when I see it. Even in a rough sketch like this."

She held out a pencil drawing of Finbar. He'd caught the dog's character perfectly. But I refused to be impressed. Instead I stared at her.

"You're letting him, a total stranger, stay in your house? Are you mad?"

She flushed. "He's not in the house. He's in the flat which is completely self-contained. Now that the builders have almost finished, it's good to have a non-paying guest stay there, to try it out before I start letting it as a holiday cottage."

"But surely you've heard about the vicar, haven't you?"

"Yes, of course. It's awful, isn't it? Some terrible accident, I understand."

"No, Suzanne. It was no accident," I said fiercely. "They're saying there is evidence that he was murdered."

Before Suzanne could respond, a sudden crash made us both jump.

Suzanne's 'house guest' stood in the kitchen doorway, a broken coffee cup shattered in tiny fragments at his feet. His face was as white as Suzanne's uber expensive kitchen units.

Then, before either of us could move, he fell into a crumpled heap and landed with a thud among the broken crockery.

Chapter Ten

Suzanne reached him seconds before I did.

"Stay there for a moment," she said when he showed signs of struggling to get up. "Are you hurt?"

He shook his head. "No. No. I'm sorry." He gave a weak smile. "I came over a bit faint, that's all. I'm fine."

"Then let me help you up and come sit here," she said and put her hand under his arm as he got to his feet. I began to collect up the broken cup before one of the dogs stepped in it.

"I'm so sorry," he said. "I feel all sorts of a fool. I'm fine now."

"Did you eat the sandwich I gave you?" she asked.

"It was very good, thanks," he muttered.

"And when was the last time you ate before that?" she asked. "And I don't mean the soup I gave you earlier."

He shrugged. "I'm not really sure."

"Would you like another sandwich? Or some more soup? I was going to make myself some for lunch. You're welcome to share it."

I put my hand on her arm and drew her to one side. "What are you doing?" I hissed. "You don't know him from Adam."

"I'm not Adam," he said with a flash of a smile.

"So who are you?" I asked. "And what are you doing here?"

As he hesitated to answer, Suzanne jumped in. "You don't have to answer that."

"Yes, he does," I said firmly. "For goodness' sake, Suzanne. There's been a murder committed here this morning. The place is crawling with police and you're harbouring someone who looks as if he's been sleeping rough for goodness knows how long."

I turned towards him. "Where did you sleep last night?"

"I - I'm not really sure," he said.

But I was.

"You slept in the shed in the churchyard. That's what Olive's blanket was doing there, wasn't it? It was you who took it out of her laundry basket."

"For goodness sake, Kat, one minute you're almost accusing him of murdering the vicar, the next he's nicking washing," Suzanne said. "Which is it?"

"Maybe both," I said.

"I didn't murder anyone," he said. "But I admit, I did sleep in the shed last night. And, yes, I 'borrowed' a blanket which I will have cleaned and returned to the rightful owner."

"You can't," I said. "The police have taken it for evidence."

"You slept in the shed in the churchyard?" Suzanne said. "No wonder you're unwell. It was freezing cold last night and that shed has no windows."

"And that shed," I pointed out, "is also just twenty feet from where the vicar's body was found. I think we should call the police."

"Do I look as if I'm capable of climbing up the church tower, least of all pushing someone off?" he asked.

"How do you know that was how the vicar died?" I was quick to ask.

There was a long silence broken only by Finbar's heavy breathing.

The man took a long steadying breath and pushed his hands through his dark untidy hair. "Ok, I'll tell you. When I got here yesterday, I was exhausted. I think I must have passed out as much as slept when I got in the shed. I came to this morning to the sound of a dog barking somewhere nearby. While I was still trying to work out where I was, I heard this thud like something heavy hitting the floor. I was about to go out and see what it was when I heard footsteps so I hung back and after a few minutes I heard the footsteps go away again. So I crept out to see what was what and saw someone lying face down on the path. I could tell, from the way he was lying, there was nothing I could do for him and figured that whoever I'd heard had gone to get help. So I legged it."

"You ran away?" Suzanne asked.

"I'm ashamed to say I did. But I knew it would look bad for me if I was found hanging around. I hurried out, desperate to get away before the emergency services arrived. I would have kept going but I felt really rough. And then I collapsed. The next thing I remembered was you, bending over me." He looked at Suzanne. "I'm really grateful. And I've no right to ask you to believe me but I promise you, whoever pushed that man off the church roof, always assuming he was pushed, of course, it was not me."

Suzanne nodded. And, funnily enough, I believed him as well. But then, I'd believed Anna Fairweather, too. What was happening to me this morning?

"I'd best get going," I said to Suzanne. "If you're sure you're going to be ok?"

"I'm sure," she said. "And don't worry about Archie. He'll be fine."

He looked anything but fine, sitting as he was with his head bent, his shoulders hunched. I thought of how animated he'd been around Anna and could hardly believe it was the same dog.

I put my hand in my pocket to give him a dog treat. I always carried plenty as it was the only way I could get Rosie the labrador to keep going past every litter bin and empty crisp packet she came across. As I put my hand in, my fingers closed around the exquisite little sketch encased in its bulky plastic frame. I took it out and laid it on the palm of my hand.

"Is this yours?" I asked, looking at the pale faced man in front of me who was staring, not at me, but at the sketch.

"Where did you find this?" he asked, his voice hoarse.

"Yesterday afternoon," I said. "At the vicarage. I thought you said you hadn't been there."

"I haven't," he said. "And no, it's not mine. And that's the truth."

Before I could say any more, my phone rang. It was Ben Watkins.

"Just thought I'd let you know the TV cameras have arrived and my boss is going to make a short statement in about fifteen minutes. Thought you might like to be there."

"Thanks, Ben. I'm on my way." I turned to Suzanne. "That was Ben Watkins, the local policeman." I added for Dan's benefit. "I'm just going to meet up with him."

"Kat? Please, don't say anything," Suzanne begged.

"I won't for the moment," I said as I turned to her guest. "But in return, when I get back you can tell me who you are and what you're really doing in Much Winchmoor. Because I don't believe you came here by chance."

***

It sounded a great exit line, didn't it? But, as it happened, it was rubbish. Because I never made it to the churchyard to hear Ben's boss give his statement.

As I hurried off, I called Mitch to keep him up to speed.

"Just to let you know the police are about to make a statement about a suspicious death in Much Winchmoor," I told him. "I'm on my way there now."

"Don't bother," he said. "It's already covered."

"Don't say Liam came back early."

"No, not Liam," he said. "But somebody on the ground who's got a bit more gumption than you. She's on the scene right now and has already sent in some cracking pictures. She told me about the police statement and offered to cover it. And if past experience is anything to go by, they won't say anything anyway, so I said she could. She's sharp, that one. And she's got a good eye for a story. I could do with more people like her."

"Don't tell me. Her name's Rhianna, isn't it?"

"Something like that."

And before I could say anymore, he'd rung off, leaving me standing in the middle of the road, staring down at my phone and feeling that, given the right circumstances, I could easily have committed murder myself.

"Katie?" A voice rang out from the other side of the street. "I've been trying to call you. Why do you never answer your phone?"

It was Norina, standing in the pub doorway. "I just looked out the bar window and there you were, chattering away. You young girls are never off your phones, are you?"

"What did you want?"

"I need you to come and give a hand," she said. "The pub's packed. The word's got around about the murder and you know what happens then. The world and its mate come to gawp and gossip. But it's good for trade, so I'm not complaining. I'm just making an extra load of bolognese sauce and Gino's sorting out the cellar."

"What about Rhianna?" I asked, even though I knew the answer. "I thought she'd be around to help out."

Norina shook her head. "She's off on some business of her own. Besides, she needs training up a bit before I'd let her loose on a busy lunchtime crowd. Look sharp then, young lady. There's a bunch of media people booked in for 12.15. I'm assuming you're up for an extra shift?"

I was indeed. I was going to get nothing out of the police statement now that Rhianna had beaten me to it, although I didn't for a moment believe Mitch would dare use that horrible picture she'd taken.

"Well, go on then. Hurry home and change. Can't have you behind the bar looking like you've been pulled through a hedge backwards now, can I?"

Not only did I look like I'd been pulled through a hedge backwards, I *felt* like I had. I hurried home to change, not looking forward to my shift. At least it would be busy, which would make the time go quicker.

But I was just in the mind to flatten the next person to call me Miss Marple.

Chapter Eleven

I got dressed with particular care that evening, as if I was going on a proper date. Ok, we were only going into the King's Head, one of the few pubs in Dintscombe that hadn't been turned into a housing estate, but anywhere that wasn't the Winchmoor Arms got my vote.

"You look - um..." Will said when he picked me up that evening.

"Weird? Washed out? Fed up?" I suggested when it looked as if he wasn't going to finish the sentence.

"All three," he said. "But you look pretty good as well. Come on, I've booked the table for 7.30."

I smiled at him as I got in his battered old Land Rover, which, I couldn't help noticing, had been thoroughly cleaned on the inside. Usually there was enough straw and stuff to line a hen house and I once ruined a perfectly good pair of boots by putting my foot in something unpleasant that had been lurking in the footwell.

It was still early so the pub was quiet. I was touched to see that there was a reserved sign on our favourite table, the one in the corner by the fire. I leaned back in the chair and watched Will as he went up to the bar to order our drinks and pick up a couple of menus, even though we both knew we'd have tonight's special, the lamb rogan josh.

He was laughing and joking with the girl behind the bar and I felt a momentary flicker of annoyance at the way she smiled up at him and tossed her long blonde hair back. Will had a thing about blondes, which was the only colour my hair has never been.

"I thought I was going to have to come and bail you out there," I said when he eventually returned with our drinks.

"She certainly was very chatty."

Chatty wasn't the word I'd have used, but I let it go. For now.

"She's just moved into the area and was asking me where all the fun places were," he said as he picked up his pint and nodded. "She pours a good pint, I'll give her that."

"I hope you told her there aren't any fun places around here," I said, still smarting at the way she moved with the grace of a ballet dancer, her silky blonde hair swaying as she did so.

He put his glass back down and looked across at me, his face suddenly serious. "Katie, the thing is..." He picked up a beermat from the table and began tearing it into small, neat pieces. "There's ... there's something I need to say."

"Like it's my turn to get the next round in?" I suggested when his voice trailed away.

"Course not. Look, I'm just going to come out with it, ok?"

He put his hand in his pocket and took out a small leather box. And I forgot to breathe.

"I - I want you to have this," he said. "I've had a word with Dad and he's ok with it."

Confused, I stared at him, then down at the tiny box that sat on the table between us. What had his dad got to do with what I thought this was?

"Go on. Open it," he urged as he pushed it closer.

I picked up the box, flipped it open and found myself looking at three beautiful diamonds on a gold band, nestling on a cushion of blue velvet. They were winking up at me, catching the flickering firelight, and sending tiny little rainbows flashing and dancing towards me.

"It's ... it's beautiful," I said, then realised where I'd seen this particular ring before - and why Will had spoken to his dad about it. "But, Will, this is..."

"Mum's engagement ring," he said, his voice soft. "She'd have wanted you to have it, Katie. You know how your mum and mine were planning our wedding from the day you were born."

Will's Mum, Sally, died a few years ago now. She was one of the sweetest, kindest women I've ever known and during

76

my growing up years I spent more time at her house than my own, back when Mum's salon was a lot busier than it is now.

Sally was a brilliant cook and the kitchen at Pendle Knoll Farm was always filled with the scent of baking. She made the best meat and potato pie I've ever tasted and was the only person in the village who gave Olive a run for her money when it came to Victoria sponges.

"Yes," I said. "But... -"

"And Dad was all for it. In fact, it was his idea. He's very fond of you."

"This was your dad's idea?"

"No, of course not. I meant he was all for me asking you to marry me, I mean properly this time, not mucking about like that time in the pond. I think he thought this would hurry things along a bit."

I sat watching the diamonds twinkling away in the firelight and didn't have a clue what I was going to say next. Or how I felt.

He groaned. "You hate it, don't you? I knew this was a bad idea." He went to take the box away, but I stopped him.

"No, Will. I don't hate it. It's just - just a surprise, that's all. I - I wasn't expecting it."

"Well?" His lovely dark eyes, with those long sweeping lashes that I'd always told him were wasted on a guy, were serious. "Will you?"

I swallowed. "Will I what?"

"Look, don't worry about the ring. Tomorrow afternoon I'll take you into town and you can choose whatever you want. It was a dumb idea."

He looked so anxious, so uncomfortable, so many millions of miles out of his comfort zone that my heart melted. I picked up the box and looked down at the ring.

"Well, go on then." The lump in my throat made my voice croaky. "Do it properly."

"Will you marry me, Katie?" he asked.

"Kat," I corrected him, although I didn't say it with my usual conviction.

"Kat", he said with a shaky sigh. "Look, I'd rather not go

down on one knee in front of the whole pub but if you insist..."

"No. No," I said quickly as he stood up. "Of course I don't want you to do that, you idiot. On the contrary. I'm walking out if you do. So please sit down. You're making me nervous."

"Everything all right?" asked a cheery voice behind us. It was the blonde bombshell herself. "Ready for refills?"

Once more there was a toss of her silky blonde mane and, to my mind, she got a bit too close to Will as she leaned across to take his glass.

"Everything's more than all right," I said as I picked up the box and held it towards her, "Will has just asked me to marry him."

"Oh right." Her cheery voice dipped a little and her smile faltered. "Well then, congratulations to you both. How romantic."

And yes, it was romantic which was not like Will at all, or, to be honest, me. It still brought me out in a heat rash, just thinking about the time he stood in the middle of the village pond, dressed only in his boxer shorts, with a rose between his teeth. And that had just been a joke.

This was for real.

I gave him the box and held out the third finger of my left hand. Watched him as he took the ring out and slipped it on my finger. Held my breath.

I looked down at his mother's ring, moving my hand so that the stones caught the firelight. It was beautiful. Will was a great guy and I've loved him all my life. Couldn't imagine life without him.

And yet... and yet....

"When shall we tell them?" Will asked. "Shall I come in with you when we get back?"

I shook my head. "Gran K will still be up. And I'd rather tell them when she's not there, if you don't mind."

"Don't leave it too long then," he said. "Because Elsie Flintlock probably knows already."

"Yeah, you're probably right." I glanced around the now busy bar, as if expecting Elsie to suddenly emerge from the crowd.

When I got home, Mum, Dad and Gran K were still up. I shoved my hand deep into my jacket pocket. I'd tell them tomorrow. Mum would only go into overdrive and start looking for wedding planners, meringue style wedding dresses and mother of the bride hats the size of cartwheels.

I wasn't ready for all that. If I'd ever be. That was the only reason I was reluctant to tell them about the engagement.

At least, that's what I was telling myself.

Chapter Twelve

I woke next morning with a pounding headache and a sick feeling in my stomach that had nothing to do with last night's lamb rogan josh, most of which I'd pushed around my plate and eaten very little.

I'd hardly slept because every time I looked at the clock (which was, on average, every forty-five minutes), I would see the little leather box standing on the broken stool that pretended to be my bedside table and a thousand butterflies would start yomping around in my stomach.

Sally's ring, and it was no good, it would always be Sally's ring, was too big for me, so that would be reason enough to leave it in the box, at least for today. But after today, what then?

I put the box right at the back of my underwear drawer and went downstairs. Dad had already left for work, and Mum was alone in the kitchen. She was standing at the stove, peering into a saucepan and stirring vigorously. This was always a worrying sign. Believe me, my mother is no domestic goddess. She is to cooking what Nigella Lawson is to mud wrestling.

"You're just in time," she said without looking up. "Fetch another dish, love. I've made chia porridge. Supposed to be a wonderfood."

"It's ok, Mum, thanks. I'll pass. I'm not really hungry."

She looked up and waved her wooden spoon at me. "You're looking peaky. This will make you feel better."

I doubted that very much. In fact, going on Mum's past record, it was virtually guaranteed to make me feel a whole heap worse.

"No thanks. I'm still full from last night."

"So, how did it go?" Her face was alight with happy expectation.

I was going to make some flippant comment about the curry not being up to its usual standard, but I knew that wasn't what she was asking about. Had she, too, noticed the unusually clean state of Will's Land Rover and put two and two together and made fifteen and three quarters? She was very good at doing that. Maths had never been her strong point.

"It's…" I took a deep breath. "He - he asked me to marry him. Properly, this time. I mean, he asked me properly this time. Not that…"

"I hope you said no, Kathryn." Gran K's voice made us both jump as neither of us had heard her come into the room.

"Now why would you say that, Mother?" Mum whirled round to face her, two spots of red high on her cheeks. "You don't even know Will. He's a lovely boy and just right for Katie." Her eyes shone with tears as she turned back to me. "I'm really, really happy for you, love. Sally would have been too. It's what she and I had always hoped for."

Gran K tossed her head, then pulled out a chair and sat down opposite me, her face stern. "I say that because Kathryn can do so much better for herself than marry a simple farmer."

"Will's not simple," I said, bristling with indignation.

"That's as may be," she said, dismissively. "But what are you thinking about, tying yourself down at your age? You should be out there in the real world, Kathryn, using the skills you've been trained for, doing the sort of job you spent three years at university (and costing the country and your parents goodness knows how much) working towards. Not stuck on some mud encrusted farm in the middle of nowhere, milking cows and feeding pigs."

"Will doesn't have any dairy cows on the farm," Mum said. "Or pigs."

Gran K ignored her and fixed me a gimlet stare, her perfectly made-up eyes steely and intent. "Well, Kathryn? Am I right?" she barked. "Do you really want to spend the rest of your life mucking out chickens or driving a tractor?"

I could have told her that Will wouldn't allow me within a mile of his precious tractor which he looked after far better than he did the Land Rover. Instead, I looked from Mum back to Gran. Mum seemed as if she was holding her breath, the chia porridge forgotten on the stove.

"Yes," I said firmly. "I love Will and I want to spend the rest of my life with him. It's as simple as that."

"Then you're a bigger fool than I thought," Gran snapped while, at the same time, Mum dropped the spoon. She rushed over and gave me a big hug.

"I'm so happy for you. Will's a lovely, lovely man and Sally and I always used to say the two of you were made for each other. It just took you both a while to realise it. Have you set a date yet? Not too soon, I hope, because there's such a lot to arrange."

How had that happened? I was going to talk with Mum, quietly and calmly, about my misgivings. How, yes, I loved Will, but was far from certain I was ready to settle down yet and that everything was moving a bit too quickly.

But she'd looked so down when Gran K was going on about how I was wasting my life in Much Winchmoor that I just came out with it. And it was true. I did love Will and I really couldn't imagine life without him. And yet... and yet...

But Mum was in full flight. "I'd better go and see John Manning. Maybe we could have a marquee on the farm. That would be better than the village hall, wouldn't it? But first, of course, you must go and see the vicar and - oh!"

She stopped and clapped her hand to her mouth. "I'd forgotten. Oh, how awful is that? How could I?"

"I'll just have some toast this morning, thank you, Cheryl," Gran K said, tapping on the table as if she was summoning a waiter. "I'm feeling a little fragile this morning. Awake all the night with the pain from my wrist. And if you could do my hair for me this morning. I'm going out this afternoon. Thought I'd check out the Floral Art Society, although I don't imagine they're up to much."

For once in my life I was grateful to Gran K for diverting Mum's attention.

"I'm a bit booked up this morning, Mother," she said. "And I'm single-handed, now that Sandra has left."

She gave her a long stare, but Gran K shrugged her bony,

elegant shoulders. "I did you a favour, Cheryl. You're better off without the woman. She's not a very good advert for your salon, is she, with a hairstyle that went out with The Beatles, and forever showing all she's got? And while we're talking about people not being a good advert..." she turned her attention back to me. "What have you done with your hair this morning, Kathryn? Do you even own a hairbrush? And what on earth are you wearing? You're surely not going out dressed like that. You look like a female Worzel Gummidge."

"It's my dog walking gear. Talking of which, I've got to go. I've arranged with Elsie to pick Prescott up early this morning as I'm going to have to get in two lots of dog walking this morning as there's no way I can walk Prescott and Archie at the same time."

"Archie?" Mum said.

"I told you, the vicar's dog. Or rather, his wife's dog."

Mum sighed. "Poor Mr Fairweather. I still can't quite believe it. I hope you're not going to get yourself involved."

"Of course I'm not." I tried not to think about how I'd let Anna drive away from the vicarage yesterday. I had certainly shied away from getting involved there and I didn't feel very good about it. "Anyway, I'd better go. Norina's offered me yet another lunchtime shift today so I'd best crack on if I'm to get in two dog walks before then."

"But it's pouring down out there," she protested.

"Dogs still have to be walked, whatever the weather," I said as I grabbed my waterproof and hurried out before she could say anymore.

"And it will be good practice for you for when you're getting the cows in," Gran K called after me as I left the house.

Chapter Thirteen

"You'd best come in," Elsie said as she opened the door to me. "Prescott's going to need his waterproof on this morning. Once I can mind where I put it, that is. Only, don't go dripping all over the hall carpet. Come along into the kitchen."

"It's ok," I said. "I'll stay out here. I'm in a bit of a rush this morning, as it happens."

"I shan't keep you long."

I followed her into the kitchen where she opened one of the kitchen drawers and began rummaging around.

"Well?" she said as she busied herself dumping handfuls of assorted gloves, hats and an astonishing number of folding umbrellas on the kitchen table while she continued to rummage.

"Well what?" I asked as the eighth umbrella landed on the table. How many umbrellas does one little old lady need?

"Well, have you found out who the murderer is yet?" She stuffed everything back in the drawer and started on the next one. "Olive and I have been talking and we reckon -"

But before she could tell me what she and Olive reckoned, Prescott started barking so shrilly it made my ears ring.

"That'll be her now," Elsie said. "I can tell from his bark."

"What? He has a different bark for each of your visitors?"

"He's a remarkably clever dog. Let her in, will you?"

And she, or rather, Prescott, was right. Olive stood on the doorstep, clinging to her umbrella as if it was about to take off and swoop her, Mary Poppins-like, up into the stormy grey sky.

"Katie, I thought I saw you," she gasped, as she carefully shook her umbrella before stepping into the hall. "My life, what a terrible morning. You're surely not going to take that poor little dog out in that?"

That 'poor little dog' didn't notice if it was raining, hailing or whatever.

"He's got his waterproof," Elsie said. "Or he will when I can find it."

"Well, you know what my Geoffrey always used to say on a day like this, don't you?" Olive said as she peered out of Elsie's kitchen window. "He'd say, *Olive, my dear, if you can see the Mendips, it's going to rain. And if you can't see the Mendips, it's raining already.* He was always a joker, was my Geoffrey."

I looked over Olive's shoulder towards where the Mendips, a range of hills into which Much Winchmoor nestled, should be but wasn't. It seemed the late Geoffrey Shrewton had it right again. You couldn't see the Mendips and it was indeed raining.

Although the Mendips is a designated Area of Outstanding Natural Beauty, I've never had much time for it, to be honest. I always thought of the range of hills as more as the barrier between where I was (Much Winchmoor) and where I wanted to be (Bristol). Not that I wanted to be back in Bristol, you understand. Not now I was engaged to Will.

"And she said the two of you were looking all loved up, whatever that meant."

Elsie was looking at me and I realised I'd drifted off again.

"Sorry? Who was looking all loved up?" I asked.

"You and Will Manning, of course. Millie's granddaughter ... what's her daft name, Olive?"

"Whitby," Olive said. "So named because her parents were on holiday in Whitby when she was... well, you know."

Olive's voice trailed away, as two spots of colour appeared high on her cheeks.

Elsie tutted. "All I can say, it was a good job they didn't holiday in Basingstoke that year. Or Swindon," she chuckled as she continued to hunt among the chaos of her kitchen drawers. "Or Piddletrenthide. Or -"

"Look, Elsie…" I cut in before she could work through the entire Dictionary of Weird English Place Names. "I really am in a hurry this morning. Couldn't we just leave Prescott's coat?"

"No. I'll find it any moment now. Anyway, as I was saying, Millie's granddaughter with the daft name works in the King's Head, and she told Millie that you and Will were looking all loved up last night. I think that was what she said, wasn't it, Olive?"

"Have you had chance to talk to your son yet?" I asked Elsie, in an effort to divert her attention. "About the late Mr Hilperton-Jones?"

"No. He's away on a conference this week to drone on about debits and credits or whatever chartered accountants talk about when they get together. But Olive and I have worked out who murdered the vicar."

"And who do you think it was?"

"His wife." Elsie and Olive exchanged triumphant glances.

"Anna Fairweather?" My heart lurched. I really, really hoped they were wrong. "No way. She's not a murderer."

"And how would you know?" Elsie's eyes narrowed. "She was only here for a couple of years or so and you were away for all that time. So what makes you so certain Anna Fairweather is not the murderer?"

"What makes you so sure she *is*?" I countered.

Elsie closed the drawer with a sigh and began to rummage around in the next one. "It's as often as not the spouse. Inspector Barnaby always says that and he's solved more murders in Midsomer than you've had hot dinners."

"Perhaps we should send for him then," I suggested.

Elsie gave me a stern look, but Olive jumped in. "Oh no, dear. Inspector Barnaby isn't real. He's on the telly. Ever so good, he is. You should watch it some time. You might learn something that would help you in your investigations."

Elsie snorted and I turned towards her. "Ok, then. Why do you think Anna Fairweather murdered her husband? Have you seen her hanging around the village?"

"Haven't seen her since the day she left. It's just a feeling I have and I'm not often wrong, am I? What about the last time there was a murder here? I got it right then, didn't I?"

"Only because at one time or another you reckoned almost everyone in the village had done it."

Elsie wagged her bony finger at me. "I'll tell you this much. The vicar should never have married her in the first place. I said so at the time. The two of them were totally incombustible. He was much older than her for a start and a bit stuck in his ways."

"She was such a shy little thing, especially when she first came here. But she loved her music and playing seemed to bring her out of her shell," Olive said. "She could make that wheezy old church organ sound lovely. It's not sounded the same since she left."

"Every day, come rain or shine, she'd be there in the church, practising her playing," Elsie said. "When it was my turn on the church cleaning rota, I always made sure I timed it to be there when she was."

"But he should never have made her do the Christmas crib service," Olive said. "I'd never have believed the vicar could be so cruel if I hadn't heard it with my own ears. It was so unlike him."

"Cruel?" I stared at her. I'd always thought Rev Fairweather was a kind, gentle man, if a little on the vague side. Yet yesterday Anna was telling me he'd burnt all her possessions, and she'd believed he was capable of having poor little Archie put to sleep just to hurt her. Now Olive, too, was saying how cruel he'd been?

Elsie sniffed as she moved on to drawer number three. "It just goes to show, you never really know someone, do you?"

It did indeed.

"It was a couple of days before the crib service for the little ones," Olive went on. "I was in the church doing the flower arranging. They didn't know I was there. Mrs Fairweather was practising the carols. Oh, and they were lovely. I was really enjoying humming along to them while I did the flowers. But then she got part of the way through *Away In A Manger* and stopped. 'It's no good, Lionel,' I heard her say to him. 'I can't play that.' And when he asked why not, that she managed perfectly well with the other carols, she said that she kept thinking about their baby and how she should have been there."

"They had a baby?" I asked.

A shadow passed across Elsie's face. "The poor soul had a miscarriage a couple of months earlier," she said quietly and, unusually for her, said nothing more.

Olive went on with the story. "I could hear the tears in her voice, but the vicar told her, very sharp he was, that she was just being silly. It was, after all, he said, only a carol. One that she'd played many, many times. And it was an integral part of the crib service and couldn't be left out. And, of course, he was quite right. It was the bit the children all look forward to. You must remember, Katie."

I did indeed. It had been a tradition in the village church since long before I was born. There was a stable scene made up in the church to the side of the lectern and, during the carol, specially chosen children who could be relied upon not to be silly (which was why I never got to do it) would walk up to it and place the figures of Mary, Joseph and the shepherds around the crib while the congregation sang *Away in a Manger.*

"She said she'd arrange someone else to play in her place but he was insistent. She had to be there. The dean was coming specially to hear her, he said and she'd be letting him down if she didn't do it."

"What happened? Did she play at the crib service?"

Elsie closed the final drawer with a bang and sighed. "She tried. But she got part way through *Away In A Manger*, just as the little ones were walking up the aisle to place the figures round the crib when she suddenly stopped playing, stood up and ran from the church. One of her fellow teachers from St Philadelphia's was in the congregation and he took over the playing and after a while everyone else joined in. But we never saw her again, certainly she never returned to the church organ. We heard that she'd taken to her bed."

"She taught at St…" I almost said Philadelphia's, but corrected myself in time. "St Philomena's?"

That was where Suzanne went to school, I realised. They must have known each other.

"For a short time, yes," Elsie said. "Taught music."

"And when did she run off with the organist?" I asked.

"A few weeks after Christmas," Elsie said. "And he wasn't

88

really the organist. He was the one who took over from her at the crib service. A fellow teacher at that school. She ran off with him, left everything. Even that silly little dog of hers that she doted on."

"The vicar was quite heartbroken after she left," Olive said. "Mrs Denby said he didn't eat for a week. She was quite worried about him. It seems a shame, him getting killed now, just when we all thought he'd maybe found happiness again."

"How do you mean?" I asked.

"Didn't you know?" Her eyes sparkled, the way people do when they are about to pass on a particularly good piece of gossip. "Him and Mrs Hilperton-Jones, they were in love."

"So you say," Elsie said scornfully. "I couldn't see it myself."

"Oh, Elsie. You only had to see the way he changed when she came on the scene and they became friendly. Don't forget how he took her to the Deanery dinner a few weeks ago. And he stopped wearing those sleeveless jumpers that made him look so much older than his years. I even caught him whistling in the churchyard one day last week. It wasn't a hymn, either, but something jazzy and modern. What was it now?"

"Look, I really am in a bit of a rush this morning..." I tried to say, but I should have saved my breath.

"Oh, I know," Olive said. "It was *Mama Mia*, that was what it was. He sounded so cheerful and he had quite a spring in his step." Her eyes suddenly swam with tears. "It's so sad, isn't it? Just when they'd found each other and this awful thing has to happen."

"Unless she was the one who did it, of course," Elsie said bluntly. "Don't forget, a police car was seen outside her house yesterday afternoon, just hours after the murder."

"That doesn't mean she's a suspect," Olive said. "I heard her little dog went missing yesterday. I expect that was why they were there."

I thought it very unlikely the police would bother about a missing dog in the middle of a murder investigation, but I'd wasted enough time that morning and couldn't afford to waste any more.

I picked up Prescott's lead, glanced across at his bed in the corner of the kitchen and saw a flash of red under his blue fluffy blanket.

"'Would this be what you're looking for?" I asked Elsie as I picked up the shredded remains of a little red doggy raincoat.

Prescott, it appeared, had had the final word on rainwear for dogs.

"Never mind," Olive said. "It looks as if the rain might be stopping soon."

***

But Olive had got that wrong. If anything, it was raining harder than ever by the time Prescott and I finally set off to collect Rosie for our walk.

So when my phone rang, I almost didn't stop to answer it, until I saw that the caller was Will, who hardly ever used his phone. Worrying.

"Is everything ok?" I asked.

"Why wouldn't it be?"

"It's just not like you to phone at this time of the day. Or any time of the day, come to that."

He laughed. "Yeah, well, this is not just any old day, is it? How are you feeling this morning? No regrets?"

"Of course not," I said quickly. Too quickly, maybe?

"Just calling to see if you're still on for going into Dintscombe with me this afternoon, to have the ring altered."

"I'm working a shift at the pub lunchtime. I told you, remember?"

"That's fine. I'll pick you up from there, shall I? At about 2.30? Got to go. My phone's about to die. Catch you later."

"Yes, but, the thing is, Will..."

I never did get to tell him what the thing was as the call ended abruptly. Just as well though, as I had no idea how I was going to find the right way to tell him that I didn't want to get Sally's ring altered.

Chapter Fourteen

I walked on, head down against the driving rain, and gave up trying to work out what I was going to say to Will. That went into the 'too difficult to think about right now' category. Instead I focussed on the fact that Suzanne had probably known Anna Fairweather. If I hadn't had Prescott and Rosie with me, I'd have gone straight to her house and asked her about it.

But that would have to wait until I'd walked these two, neither of whom seemed any more in the mood for a brisk walk that morning than I was. And given the weather, who could blame us? I did remind Prescott that he used to have a perfectly good waterproof coat, which was more than I did.

As we passed the pub, Prescott strained at his lead and made a high-pitched rasping sound in his throat that sounded for all the world as if I was strangling him.

I wasn't strangling him, of course, as his lead was attached not to his collar but to his harness. It was all done for effect as he was on high alert, looking for his arch enemy, Pitbull. But Pitbull had more sense to be out and about in such awful weather. More sense than us, that was for sure.

"Come along, Prescott," I urged him. "Nothing to see."

But that was where I was wrong because at that moment the pub door opened, and Rhianna stepped into the porch. She beckoned to me. "It rains here even worse than back home," she said. "Jeez, this is a dreary dump, isn't it? It's the back of beyond and then some."

I bristled. It's one thing for me to criticise Much Winchmoor, but quite another for someone who hasn't been in the village five minutes to do so.

"I've lived in worse places," I said defensively and hoped she wouldn't ask me to name one.

"Hey, your boss is a lively one, isn't he?" she said.

"By my boss, do you mean Liam, the editor? Or Mitch?"

"I haven't met Liam ... yet. Although from what I've been told, that's something I've got to look forward to. Quite tasty, by all accounts. No, I meant Mitch. Well impressed with my pictures, he was. Especially the one of the body."

I stared at her. "But he's not going to use it, surely? He could find himself in all sorts of bother if he does. As, of course, could you. You're not going to post it on social media, are you?"

She shrugged. "Mitch says it's ok as long as nobody's been charged. They haven't been, have they?"

"How would I know? You were the one at the press briefing." That still stung. "The responsible thing would be to hand the picture over to the police. It could be evidence."

"Yeah, well, see, I don't really do responsible. And how can it be evidence? You can't see anything."

A thought occurred to me. "Did you see a note on the body?" I didn't want to mention the teddy bear. I still couldn't quite bring myself to believe it.

"You what?" She gave a puzzled frown and the rings in her nose trembled.

"A note. Someone said... well, I heard there was a note on the body."

"What? Like a suicide note? You think the vicar jumped off the church tower?" Her black-rimmed eyes widened.

"Well, no." I was about to say that it sounded as if the note had been placed there after the body had landed on the path by whoever had pushed him off the roof. But why? What was the point of the note?

I assumed the police had it. Unless, of course, there was no note because Mrs Denby was so shocked by the whole thing, she was imagining things. It was possible. She'd looked pretty shaken up.

"Thanks, Katie -"

"Kat." I reminded her, but she ignored me.

"Thanks, *Katie*. You've just given me an idea for a follow up. A note, you say? Mitch is going to love this. He says I have

92

a natural nose for a good story. And, he said, a way with words. Unlike some, he said, he could name but wouldn't. I'd stick to the dog walking if I was you. See you."

A nose for a good story? Her nose looked better suited as a makeshift hoopla stall at the next church fete. If, of course, there ever was another one.

But before I could say anything, she turned and went back inside, slamming the door as she did so.

***

The river Winch ran through the village, via the pond and the leat that fed Winchmoor Mill, before winding its way around the surrounding fields like a snake chasing its tail. It crossed the lanes where I was walking the dog that morning not once but twice. These crossing points were imaginatively named Long Ford and Short Ford.

I had just reached Short Ford and, while the dogs were enjoying a drink and a splash about, phoned Mitch.

"I was just about to call you," he said before I could speak. "About this murder mystery plaything you sent me."

"You got my amended copy, did you? Only there's been a change of venue and I thought -"

"No point," he cut in. "I'm not using any of it. Why would people want to read about a murder play when they've got the real thing right on the doorstep? I've got all the copy I need." He gave a wheezy laugh. "You should see this week's front page. It's a cracker. I'm going to have to order a bigger print run."

My heart sank. So it was true then and not just a question of Rhianna winding me up.

"Mitch, tell me you're not using Rhianna's picture. Surely, it's evidence or something. Have you shown it to the police?"

"They'll just have to buy a copy of the Chronicle like everyone else." He gave another throaty wheeze that was probably a laugh. Only I didn't feel like laughing.

"Have you spoken to Liam about it?" I asked, raising my voice to make myself heard above the wheezes.

"Why should I? It's my paper, not his."

This was turning into the day from hell. First there was Gran K giving me advice on my love life and touching a raw spot as she did so. Then came the worry over Sally's ring. And now Mitch, wheezing and spluttering like he'd just told the funniest joke ever. Not.

The tide of anger that had been simmering away all morning finally broke through the sand bank of my limited self-control. "It's really tacky, not to mention downright bloody stupid," I snapped, making both dogs pause in their hedge snuffling and look up at me in alarm. "There's his family to consider, as well as people in the village who really cared about him. They'll be desperately upset to see something like that. You can't publish it. It's cruel."

"And there will be lots more who'll be lining up to have a see for themselves. People are ghouls, Katie. Haven't you worked that out for yourself yet?"

I thought of the hordes of people who'd packed into the pub yesterday lunchtime with nothing else to talk about but the murder, and to speculate on who'd done it and why. It was as if they thought they were bit players in one of Cordelia's murder mysteries, not in a real-life tragedy affecting real people.

"I think that's horrible," I said. "That isn't what people buy the Chronicle for. Added to which, you're going to be in all sorts of legal trouble if you print it. You could -"

"Just you hang on there a minute, young lady," he growled. "First, I don't appreciate being called stupid. Or tacky. Or being told how to run my paper by someone who's just out of school."

"Not exactly just out of school," I began. "And I remember from my training that -"

"Training!" His voice was thick with scorn as he cut in. "Total waste of time. You don't have the stomach to be a proper journalist. Stick to your potholes and jumble sale reports. That's all you're fit for. I'd have sacked you months ago if it hadn't been for Liam."

I'd had enough. "Well, I can save you the bother of sacking

me. Because I quit."

But if I thought that was going to make him back down, I'd got that wrong.

The day from hell suddenly got a whole heap worse.

"Fair enough," he said. "That Rhianna, she's smart. She knows a good newsy picture when she sees one. Something she didn't get from going to college. You could learn a thing or two from her."

And with that, the line went dead and I was left staring at my phone, and wondering why I'd just talked myself out of one third of my job portfolio.

I really hoped Norina would have a few extra shifts for me, but I wasn't holding my breath. Chances were, Rhianna was about to take that from me as well.

Chapter Fifteen

By the time I'd finished walking the dogs, my brain ached. I didn't want to think any more about Will, or the implications of the phone call with Mitch. Working for the Chronicle wasn't the best paid job in the world, but it earned me more than the dog walking and bar work put together, most of the time at least. And I'd just thrown it away.

So I did what I always do when things get difficult. I shoved them to that part of my mind labelled 'To be thought about later', a little trick I'd borrowed from Scarlett O'Hara. (*Gone With The Wind* was one of Gran Latcham's favourite films, and we'd watched it again and again when I should have been doing my homework).

So instead of thinking calmly and sensibly about things that were my concern, I focussed instead on those that weren't. I took Prescott and Rosie back to their respective homes and headed for Suzanne's, determined to find out who her unexpected guest really was. I'd already had a suspicion, but a quick call to Millie had confirmed it. This was one thing, at least, that I'd got right.

***

As I approached Suzanne's cottage, I saw him, a little further along the path that led to the back garden. He was bent over as he worked on a downpipe that had pulled away from the wall.

As Suzanne opened the door, my hand closed over the tiny, framed sketch I'd picked up outside the vicarage the day before.

"Hi. I'd almost given you up this morning," she said, then added with a grin. "What happened? Did Will keep you up too late last night? That's sounding promising."

Her teasing smile faded as she saw my expression.

Instead of answering, I turned towards the man who'd called himself Dan. "Could you come here a moment please, Rob? That is your name, isn't it?"

"Kat?" Suzanne frowned at me. "What's all this about?"

"The identity of your 'houseguest', Suzanne," I said. "You're Anna Fairweather's brother, Rob, aren't you?"

He straightened up slowly, put down the screwdriver he'd been holding and wiped his hands down his jeans.

"I don't know what your surname is, but I'll take a bet it begins with the letter L," I went on when he didn't answer. "Am I right?"

He looked from me to Suzanne, then back to me again, his dark eyes wary and uncertain. Then he nodded. "It's Lovell," he muttered.

"And you're Anna's brother?"

Another nod. "Yes," he said, his voice low. "It was the keyring picture, wasn't it?"

I nodded. "Millie Compton said what a talented artist Anna's brother was, and how he'd given her a drawing of their house. And when I asked her if the picture had been signed, she said it had. RL, the same initials that are on the sketch. So come on, Rob Lovell, time for the truth now. Where is Anna?"

"How do you mean?" He looked bewildered. "She's at the vicarage, of course. Where else would she be?"

Suzanne found her voice at last. "Anna left the vicarage, and the vicar, over a year ago now. You didn't know?"

"She left him?" Rob dragged his hand through his long dark hair. "Well, I'll be ... Where did she go?"

Suzanne didn't answer.

"According to village gossip she ran off with a teacher from the school." I turned to Suzanne. "The one *you* went to. You may well have known him. He taught physics, I think. Oh yes, and he was really into music."

"Mr Chappell?" Suzanne's voice rose an octave. "Mrs Fairweather ran off with Mr Chappell? Never in a million years."

I shrugged. "It may not be true, of course." Elsie and Co, aka The Much Winchmoor Grumble and Gossip Group, had a habit of filling in the blanks of their knowledge with whatever they thought would make the juiciest story. "Did you know either of them?"

"Of course I did. Mrs Fairweather was only there for my last year and I really liked her. She was one of the reasons I settled on Much Winchmoor when we - when I was looking to buy a place in the country.

"I'd taken part in a Christmas concert she'd organised in the church here and I fell in love with the place. But when I moved in here, I went to the vicarage hoping to catch up with her again. For some reason I got hold of the wrong end of the stick, because the vicar... I thought he'd said she was dead. But what he'd really said was something like she was no longer with us, or something like that. It was some time before I learned the truth, that she'd run off with the organist. But I didn't think for a moment they meant Mr Chappell. No way. He'd never do something like that."

I shrugged. "People do strange things for love." Even as I said it, I realised how lame that sounded.

We both turned to Rob and spoke at the same time. "You mean you really didn't know?" Anna asked him, while I said: "When was the last time you spoke to your sister?"

"No, I didn't know," he said. "And I've never heard of this Chappell guy. If you must know, the last time I spoke to my sister was just before the police arrived to cart me off to prison, and she stood by and let them do it. Look, do you mind if I sit down? I'm still feeling a bit woozy."

I tried not to look at my watch where the big hand was galloping way too quickly towards the lunch opening time at the pub.

"Let's all go into the kitchen and I'll make some coffee," Suzanne said.

"No," he said firmly. "No coffee, at least not until you've heard my story. Then you can call the police or whatever you want. I just need you to hear my side of it first, ok?"

Pity about the coffee. I could really have done with a cup,

but I didn't want to do anything to stop him now he was opening up a bit so I nodded. As did Suzanne.

"Anna and I grew up in Stargate Bay, a little seaside village not too far from here on the Dorset coast. We lived in this lovely old house on the cliff with a great big garden and wonderful sea views."

"The big house on the cliff," I said. No wonder the place had seemed familiar.

"You know it?"

"I certainly do. Stargate Bay's one of my favourite places. We go there a lot. But please, go on."

"My dad's business failed and rather than sell the house which she loved, Mum turned it into a B&B. She worked all hours of the day and night and it was really successful. Something my father resented. People booked from year to year, and there were several mentions in Sunday supplements and travel magazines. But she died very suddenly of cancer when I was fifteen and Anna sixteen."

He looked down at his hands, twisted tight in his lap. "Our father didn't handle it very well. He shut himself up in his study with his books and his whisky and left Anna to get on as well as she could with running a busy B&B and coping with a grieving angry teenager, while she was herself trying to deal with her own grief.

He unclasped his hands and rubbed one across his straggly beard. "I went off the rails a bit. Dad and I had never really got on and with Mum no longer around to keep the peace, things went from bad to worse. But eventually Anna made me see that art college was my ticket out of Stargate and so I worked my socks off to get a place." His face darkened. "She didn't get the chance to finish her education and go to uni. Instead, she stayed at home to look after Dad and to run the business that Mum had started.

"That was how she met Lionel Fairweather. He'd been coming to Bay View, that's the name of our house, for years. He and my father were both very keen chess players and would spend ages over a game. He was the only guest Dad ever bothered with.

"And then, when I was in my second year at art college, Anna found Dad collapsed in his study. Dead from a massive heart attack. Helped on, no doubt, by the amount of whisky he consumed every day. Lionel was staying there at the time and he was very supportive, so she says." He scowled. "Personally, I thought he was taking advantage of someone who was very vulnerable."

"Oh, surely not. Not Mr Fairweather," I murmured. "He was such a kind man. I'm sure he was only acting from the best of motives."

That earned me a murmur of agreement from Suzanne, but a glare from Rob. He obviously had quite a chip on his shoulder where the vicar was concerned.

And yet... and yet... I couldn't help thinking back to the story Olive and Elsie had told about the way the vicar had treated Anna in the church that Christmas. It certainly didn't add up to the kindly, quite inoffensive man who, although he had probably been in his early forties, looked a lot older, with his old-fashioned lace up shoes, flappy trousers that were a tad too short and that endless succession of fairisle jumpers.

Although now I thought about it, Olive had been quite right. Recently he had indeed stopped wearing the jumpers which, for reasons best known to herself, Olive had taken as proof of his attraction to Cordelia.

I dragged my attention away from the unfathomable workings of Olive's mind and focussed instead on Rob's story.

"I heard everyone was very surprised when he came back from his holiday that year to announce he was getting married," I said. "As you can imagine, it really set tongues wagging."

Rob glowered. "I'm not surprised. I didn't go to the wedding. I was mad with the pair of them. I knew she was making a mistake, but she wouldn't listen. She closed the house up, put it into the hands of a letting agent, and moved to Much Winchmoor. She said I was welcome to stay at any time, but I said no. Why would I want to bury myself in a draughty old mausoleum in the middle of nowhere?" He glanced at me. "No offence."

I shrugged. I was getting a bit fed up with people having a pop at Much Winchmoor. But I let it go.

"Instead I got in with a bad crowd, started doing drugs and stuff and dropped out of college. Ended up in court and got a suspended sentence because it was a first offence. But I needed a permanent address and Anna had let the house in Stargate, so I had no choice. I had to come to Much Winchmoor. Nowhere else to go."

"And how did that work out?" Suzanne asked.

"Not good. Lionel and I had never got on. To be honest, I think I scared the life out of him. Wouldn't surprise me if he locked the bedroom door at night when I was around. He knew I didn't think he should have married my sister. I made no bones about that. I stayed with them in the vicarage in return for some gardening and odd jobs and had a room, not in the main house but in a poky flat over the old stables, which suited me fine. I didn't want to stay in the house with them anyway.

"But even so, I could see all was not well between them even though Anna denied it when I asked her. She crept around looking like death warmed up most of the time. As for Lionel himself, he seemed to spend more time locked away in his study or playing chess with that crony of his from the posh school where Anna used to work. He reminded me so much of my father that I actually accused Anna of marrying a father figure." He gave a short bitter laugh and raked his fingers through his hair again. "I can tell you, she didn't take that very well. She has a sharp tongue on her, my sister, when the mood takes her."

I thought back to how furious she'd been the afternoon she'd confronted poor Mrs Denby at the vicarage.

"You mean, she has a temper?" I asked.

Something flickered in the back of his eyes. And a flush of colour came to his too pale face.

"No. Nothing like that," he said indignantly. "She wouldn't… she'd never..."

I glanced at my watch and tried not to see how close to opening time it was getting. Now he'd started talking, I didn't want him to stop.

"Go on," I prompted. "What happened to make you leave the vicarage?"

"You mean you don't know? In that case, you're the only person in this village who doesn't."

"I was living away at the time."

He sighed. "Ok. One afternoon I was working in the garden, pruning some rose bushes, when the knife slipped and I cut my hand pretty badly. I went to see if Anna was around. I was bleeding all over the place. As I went past, I peered in the kitchen window to see if she was there and nearly frightened that secretary of his to death. Can't think of her name just now. Dumpy little woman who was always either knitting or running around after Lionel as if she was his hand maiden."

"Do you mean Mrs Denby?" I asked.

"Is that her name? I could never remember. We weren't exactly on friendly terms. She always looked at me as if she was afraid I was going to steal the very chair she was sitting on. And anything else that wasn't tied down. Anyway, when I looked in through the window, she was working at the kitchen table, piles of money spread all over it. At the sight of me, she jumped like she'd seen a ghost and I suppose I did look pretty grim, dripping blood everywhere. By the time I got in the kitchen, the table was cleared and she bustled around trying to find the first aid box.

"She got me cleaned up and sent me on my way as quick as she could. It was opening time at the pub by then, and I took myself off there for a pint or two, as I used to do once I'd finished work for the day. Then I went back to my little room above the garage and crashed.

"Next thing I knew, the police were banging on my door, accusing me of stealing the money she'd been counting. The proceeds from some church fund raising bash, I think. And that was it. Because I was on a suspended sentence and had, they said, broken the terms of my probation, I was carted off to prison. Talk about innocent until proven guilty. That's a laugh.

"I wrote to my sister. I told her that I had nothing to do with the money going missing and asked her to find out what really happened to it, but she didn't even bother to reply."

"From what I heard about that time," I said, "your sister was quite ill."

He shrugged. "Yeah, well, I didn't know that, did I? I'd been in prison a few months when she applied for a visitor permit. But I was still feeling very bitter towards her and prison was…" His voice faltered, and he closed his eyes briefly. Then he cleared his throat and spoke again.

"Anyway, I refused to see her. She wrote a couple of times, but I didn't open them. After that, she stopped writing."

Chapter Sixteen

"So what brought you here after all this time?" Suzanne asked.

"I was released from prison early, on account of my good behaviour." His laugh was bitter, his eyes hard and cold. "I stuck it out in a hostel for a while, but that was almost as bad as being back in prison, so I moved on and lived rough for a month or so. That was ok until the weather turned. A couple of days ago I decided to head back to the house in Dorset. I figured that at this time of the year there wouldn't be any holiday lets and there'd be plenty of places around Stargate Bay where I could doss for the night. Even the house itself, if it was empty.

"But when I got there, it was obvious the place hadn't been let for ages. The house that our mother had worked so hard to turn into a lovely home was a wreck. I peered through the windows and it looked as if squatters had been in and trashed the place."

"Was that the house in the picture you were working on this morning?' Suzanne asked.

He nodded. "It's what I do when I'm trying to get my head around something. I'm not very good with words so over the years I've learned to put my emotions into my sketches. I couldn't understand how Anna had let things get into such a state. And then I thought maybe they'd sold it without telling me and that some developer was letting it fall into disrepair so he could knock it down and build a housing estate on the plot."

"It's a very powerful sketch," Suzanne murmured. "You have a serious talent. "

He didn't answer her but went on. "I was exhausted. I had a blister on my heel that hurt like hell. I hadn't eaten in over twenty-four hours and I ached with the cold that had seeped into my very bones. Then, as if things weren't bad enough, it started to rain.

"I still had my front door key, so I fished it out. I could hardly hold it, my hands were that cold. And then I found they'd changed the locks, which didn't help my mood any. The summer house I'd planned to stay in if all else failed had completely collapsed, so I smashed the downstairs toilet window and got in that way. I dossed down on the floor of what used to be my old bedroom. I've slept in worse places over the last few months and at least it was dry.

"I woke the next morning to the sound of a car pulling up. I was astonished to see it was Anna. All the old anger and resentment I felt towards her came rushing back. And then some. So they hadn't sold the house after all. How dare she and that sanctimonious husband of hers let it get in such a state. That house belonged to me by rights, or at least *half* of it did.

"I thought she was going to come in. I waited for her to do so instead of rushing out and challenging her. I wanted to see the shock on her face when she saw me. But I could have kicked myself when, instead, she got back into her car and drove off. I was livid. That was when I decided that, even though I'd vowed never to set foot in this place ever again, I had to come to Much Winchmoor and have it out with her once and for all.

"Only by the time I eventually got here, I was feeling really rough. No comfy heated car for me. I'd had to hitchhike and spent more time hiking than hitching. People don't often stop for the likes of me. But thankfully one guy did, an old farmer who lives not far from here gave me a lift in the back of his pickup. Not the most comfortable way to travel, but I was grateful to him.

"Anyway, by the time I got here, I was feeling like death. I couldn't remember the last time I'd eaten. I was shivering, my legs were like jelly, my blistered foot hurting like hell and I knew I was in danger of passing out. As I passed what looked like old folks' bungalows, I noticed a bottle of milk on the doorstep that hadn't been taken in. There wasn't a soul about, so I went to take it and as I did so, I saw this basket tucked inside the porch. It contained a blanket. Food and warmth at a stroke. So I took both, and snuck along to the churchyard. I knew there was an old stone shed where they keep the lawnmower and stuff, and was never locked. I thought that if I waited there, I'd be bound to see Anna on her own.

"She always came to the church, you see, every day, to play the organ. I wrapped myself up in the blanket, drank the milk and went to sleep. Next I knew it was dark but beginning to get light. It must have been around six in the morning and I was numb with the cold. I tried to stand, but my legs had gone. I spent the next few hours drifting in and out of consciousness, listening out for Anna, only she didn't come. The rest is like I told you. I woke again to the sound of a barking dog. Then the thud. Then the footsteps walking away. A man's footsteps."

"How do you know they belonged to a man?" I asked.

He gave a wry grin. "Well, if it *was* a woman, she was wearing a pair of size ten hobnail boots."

It couldn't have been Mrs Denby then. Which meant, of course, that the footsteps he'd heard must have been those of the murderer.

"You sure you didn't see who it was?" I asked.

He shook his head. "I'm afraid not. I'm not proud of myself. I waited until I was sure he'd gone before venturing out and going across to see. I'm no medic, but even I could see the poor guy was beyond help."

"You didn't recognise him?" I asked.

He shook his head and closed his eyes briefly, as if to shut out the memory. "He'd fallen on his head. His own mother wouldn't have recognised him. I knew that if anyone saw me, they'd have me down as suspect number one and I'd be back inside." He shivered and wrapped his arms around his thin body. "I can't go back there," he whispered, as much to himself as to us.

Suzanne and I exchanged glances. There was something about the way he spoke, the haunted look in his eyes, that convinced me he was telling the truth. And it was obvious Suzanne thought so too.

"When you did go up to - to the body," I said, "did you see anything?"

His head shot up, eyes blazing. "Of course I did. I saw him, lying there, dead. What is it with you? Do you want all the graphic details? Want me to draw you a sketch?"

"Of course not," I said quickly. "I just wondered if there was something else by the body. You know, like a note."

He stared at me for a long moment. "Are they saying he committed suicide?"

"No. Nothing like that. It's just … well, someone said they thought they saw something by the body." I wasn't going to tell him about the teddy bear. "But they'd probably got it wrong. You know, shock can play terrible tricks with your mind when you see something like that."

His hand shook as he dragged it across his face. "Tell me about it. I mean, I didn't like the guy. I'll make no secret of that. But he didn't deserve that."

"No, he didn't. And -" But before I could say any more, my phone buzzed with a text. It was Norina.

Where R U? It read. *Shd have bn here 15 mins ago!!!*

***

I reached the pub in record time. The place was heaving again. The presence of the police and press vehicles in the village ensured that.

"So happy to see you, Katie," Gino beamed. "We're so busy here and -"

"Then stop hanging around chattering," Norina boomed as she crashed through the swing door that led from the kitchen to the bar. She never pushed it quietly like everyone else did but always swooshed through it like a whomping whirlwind, barking orders as she did so. "Katie, we'll have that talk about your bad timekeeping later. But for now, start taking orders from the two tables by the window, they've been waiting for ages. Gino, get behind the bar, there's customers waiting."

"But where's Rhianna?" I asked and Norina's face darkened.

"If I knew that, I wouldn't have had to ask you to come in

107

early, would I now?" she snapped. "First off, she spends most of the morning chatting to the builders in my new dining room, wasting their time and stopping them from getting on with their work, like they aren't far enough schedule already. As for Ed Fuller, if that wife of his could see the way Rhianna makes up to him, he'd be in big trouble."

Knowing my friend Jules, who was the wife in question, Norina was probably right. Ed was one of these guys who didn't have to go looking for trouble, it found him. This time, apparently, in the form of Rhianna.

"Honestly, that girl is more hindrance than help," I heard Norina mutter to herself as she stalked off to the kitchen which made my day that little bit brighter and this particular part of my portfolio career a tad safer.

As I took the menus across to the table by the window, I couldn't hide a grin at the thought of this 'natural barmaid' being found wanting when the chips were down.

As I was taking their order, I heard someone call my name across the crowded bar.

"We'll have three pensioners' specials, please, Katie." It never ceased to amaze me how someone as small as Elsie could have such a loud voice when she chose to raise it. On a foggy day, she could be used to direct shipping in the English Channel.

She, Olive, and Morag were at Elsie's favourite table by the fireplace. "Three steak and mushroom pies, and be sure to tell that Norma that we want more steak than mushrooms this time, and not to hold back on the chips."

"But what are you doing in here?" I couldn't help asking. "It's Friday. You usually come in on a Tuesday."

"That'll be me," Olive said. "Morag here, being new to the village, wanted to try out the pub, only she didn't feel comfortable coming in here on her own."

"Where I come from, it's not the done thing for women to go into a public house on their own," Morag said with a sniff.

"So I said, why not come with me and Elsie when we come in for our pensioners' lunch on a Tuesday? Really good value for money, isn't it?"

"But today's Friday," I pointed out.

Olive's voice took on the tone of someone talking to a very young child. "That's because Tuesday is fish and chips day and Morag doesn't do fish and chips on account of her irritable bowel."

The look on Morag's face suggested her bowel wasn't the only part of her that was irritable. But Olive, it seemed, was the only one of us not to notice that.

"Anyway," Olive said, "she suggested we came here today instead. She said she had some news to share with us." She turned to Morag. "And you were right, weren't you? As soon as we heard, we knew we had to come and find out if it was true. But you are a dark horse, aren't you, Katie? Why didn't you tell us when we saw you earlier, you naughty girl?"

"I couldn't believe it when you said you didn't know anything about it, Elsie." Morag's usually sour face creased into what looked more smirk than smile. "From what I've heard, it's not like you to miss out on a bit of gossip."

Before I realised her intention, Elsie's bony fingers wrapped around my left wrist. "You see? She's not wearing a ring. What did I tell you? You don't want to believe everything you hear, Morag Browne."

"What exactly did you hear, Mrs Browne?" I asked, as Elsie looked triumphant.

"It was in your mother's salon. I'd come in to make an appointment for my perm when that strange looking woman who lives in the little cottage by the mill -"

"Do you mean Dilys Northcott?" I asked. "She's not strange looking."

Morag scowled. "I still can't sort out who's who in this place. Anyway, she was in there having her hair dyed. It's not her natural colour, you know, she's quite grey at the roots. And she asked your mother if it was true what the postie had told her about the engagement. Well, your mum hummed and hawed a bit. Then the woman said that of course it must be because the postie had heard it from the groom's father himself."

John Manning. I should have known. Will had said he was pretty happy about the news but to share it with the postman!

That man could have given Elsie a run for her money in the gossip spreading stakes.

"So, is it true?" Elsie demanded. "And if so, why aren't you wearing a ring? You don't look like someone who's just got herself engaged."

"Oh, I don't know," Olive murmured. "I thought this morning there was a glow about her."

"That came from having to run from one end of the village to the other, Olive," I assured her. "I've been playing catch up all morning and if I don't get a move on, Norina will be after me again. She's already had a go at me for being late."

As I turned to hurry away, Olive called me back.

"There was someone in here earlier looking for you. You've just missed him."

"He didn't look too pleased either," Morag said. "Went out and slammed the door behind him."

"Who was it?" I was puzzled. If it had been Will, they'd have said so.

"Such a handsome young man," Morag said. "With a lovely Irish accent. If I'd been a few years younger..."

"Liam was here?"

Elsie nodded. "He's her boss, from the newspaper," she told Morag.

"He wasn't too happy when we told him," Olive said.

"Told him what?"

"About you and Will getting engaged. He looked really put out, I can tell you," Olive went on. "Honestly, Katie, I do believe that young man is carrying a torch for you, my lovely. He looked that upset."

That gave me my first real laugh of the day. Now that was one thing I could put Olive right on.

"He's not carrying a torch or anything else for me, Olive. He'd have been here to give me the sack. Or he would have done if I hadn't already resigned."

I almost laughed at the expressions on their faces. "And that," I said as I hurried off towards the kitchen with the food orders, "is another bit of gossip you've missed out on."

Chapter Seventeen

It was a long, difficult shift. The place got busier and busier, which should have pleased Norina. Instead, her mood went from bad to worse to absolutely foul, and by the time the food orders were beginning to wind down, she made Cruella De Vil look like Little Miss Sunshine.

But it wasn't just the kitchen where things were dark and stormy. There was a weird atmosphere in the bar as well. I reckon it was because now the initial excitement was wearing off, people were beginning to realise just how horrible it is to have a murder (and, of course, a murderer) in your midst, especially when the victim is someone everyone knew and loved. Well, maybe loved was too strong a term. But everyone liked Rev Fairweather. He had a sweet smile and a continually slightly bemused expression as if he could never quite work out what was going on.

But he was kind and did his best for everyone. And he had the loudest, most out of tune singing voice you've ever heard. He even managed to make Gino sound like he was singing in tune.

He and Anna would have made a very strange couple, that was for sure. But then, who's to say who's suited to whom? Look at me and Will. We'd been lined up for each other since we were toddling around in nappies apparently. And yet we're complete opposites. He's quiet, calm and thoughtful. And I'm ... let's just say I'm none of those things.

But we were made for each other. At least that was what everyone always said.

"It'll be lovely to have something to look forward to, Katie," Olive cooed at me as she, Elsie and Morag left, somewhat unsteadily after a second round of port and lemons. "After all the nastiness there's been in this village these last few years."

"But we haven't set a date yet, Olive," I reminded her.

"No, but I think your mum's right. There's something special about a June bride. Me and my Geoffrey were married in June, you know."

A June bride? No doubt by the time I got home Mum would have ordered the flowers and made a start on the cake.

By the time I'd cleared up behind the bar and managed to avoid Norina's little talk about my timekeeping, I was well steamed up and ready to have a go at my mother. A June wedding indeed! I strode off down the High Street like I was in training for the London Marathon.

"Katie?" Mrs Denby's voice was breathless as she hurried to catch up with me. "My goodness, dearie, you're in a hurry today. You rushed straight past me. Didn't you see me beckoning to you?"

"I'm sorry, Mrs Denby. I didn't see you there. How are you today?"

Her eyes, red-rimmed and puffy, told of a sleepless night. She looked down at her hands. Her fingers worked as if they still had a pair of knitting needles in them. "Not very well, I'm afraid. I kept waking up in the night. Seeing him lying there. And seeing that horrible, horrible teddy bear. I don't suppose you've had any more thoughts, did you?"

"About what?" I prompted when her voice trailed away.

"Thoughts of who might have moved it. There was a young girl taking photographs, wasn't there?"

"There was someone, yes," I said cautiously.

"Did you recognise her?"

"She was a stranger to the village," I said, which was almost the truth. Rhianna was indeed a stranger to the village.

"If you do find out who she is, you will let me know, won't you?" Mrs Denby went on. "You see, I'm not sure the police believed me. About the teddy bear and that awful note."

I chose my words with care. "You know, Mrs Denby, when you've had the sort of traumatic shock you've had, your mind can play cruel tricks on you. I found a body a few years ago and I don't mind saying, it did my head in for quite a while after. I found in the end that it really helped to talk with someone."

112

Her busy fingers stilled. "You don't believe me either," she said, her voice flat.

"Yes, yes, of course I do. I believe you thought you saw something. But you'd just had a terrible shock and -"

"Where's Archie?" she said with an abrupt change of subject. "I've just come off the phone to the rehoming centre. That's why I was so keen to catch you. They're very interested in him. I showed them his picture and they assured me he's a very popular breed. They have several people lined up already who'd love to adopt him. I said I'd be over with him this afternoon. The sooner the poor little chap gets settled, the better."

"But you can't do that," I protested. "What about the vicar's wife? Didn't you say he was her dog? Perhaps we should get in touch with her and find out before doing anything so drastic as take him to a rehoming centre? Do you know where she lives?"

Mrs Denby looked at me as if I'd taken leave of my senses - which I probably had. I didn't want to tell her - or anyone else, come to that - how I'd met Anna at the vicarage on the morning of the murder. And had stood back and let her drive away.

"I've already told the police how she threatened the reverend that day and it's my belief that she came back to the village the next day, followed him to the top of the church tower and pushed him off."

"But that doesn't make any sense," I protested. "What was he doing up there anyway?"

"He had a meeting with the Health and Safety people from the council later this week to make sure all the right precautions were in place ahead of the Teddy Bear abseil. And knowing him, he'd have wanted to get along and check it all out for himself before they arrived. And now, of course, the Teddy Bear abseil will be cancelled. Along with so many other things." She shook her head. "I really need to get my head around things and go back to work. But ..."

"If there's anything I can do to help," I said.

"Well, you can tell me where the dog is for a start. That will

113

be one less thing for me to worry about."

"Archie's with Suzanne. You know, the girl with the big Irish Wolfhound called Finbar. He and Archie get on really well and I think Suzanne would really like him to stay."

She frowned. "That's the woman who's bought Mrs Foster's cottage and is converting it into an art gallery, isn't it?"

"Yes. I think it will be an asset to the village once it's up and running."

"And she's letting the upstairs as a holiday let, I hear."

"I believe so."

"I see she's got someone in there already," Mrs Denby said. "I saw the curtains moving only this morning when I went past."

You see what I mean about this place? When I lived in Bristol, I didn't even know what the person in the flat across the landing from mine looked like, least of all be able to track his or her whereabouts. And yet here in Much Winchmoor, the twitch of a curtain was enough to set tongues wagging.

"Oh, I wouldn't know about that. I expect that was Suzanne hanging some new curtains or maybe even cleaning the windows," I said quickly. Too quickly, because the look Mrs Denby gave me told me she didn't buy that for one moment.

"Maybe I'll go and have a word with her," she said. "And see what's what with poor little Archie. Well, it's been nice chatting to you, Katie, but I mustn't stand here all day. I've got a hundred and one things to do this afternoon."

And with that, she bustled off back into her cottage and I carried on home, still intent of having it out with my mother.

When I got home, Mum was busy in the salon, and I realised our little talk would have to wait. I was on my way upstairs when I heard the murmur of voices coming from the kitchen. It could have only been Gran K, but who was she entertaining?

I heard her give a soft girlish laugh. Whoever it was had done the impossible if she was laughing. Ever since she'd first descended on us, unannounced, with her arm in plaster and her

114

cat in a basket, her face had been set in a permanent scowl. Or sneer. Or sometimes both.

The only time I'd seen her come close to a smile was when Dad was coming back from his allotment, with a box of freshly harvested vegetables, and tripped over the cat. As he fell, potatoes and tomatoes went skittling across the front path and ended up bobbing around in his precious fishpond.

I was halfway up the stairs when I heard a man's voice. And recognised it.

Liam. Great. That was all I needed.

"What are you doing here?" I demanded as I pushed open the door, to see Gran K and Liam cosied up either side of the kitchen table. A pot of tea and a plate of tastefully arranged chocolate Hobnobs (my chocolate Hobnobs) between them.

"Really, Kathryn, that's no way to talk to a guest," Gran said sharply, no trace of the girlish giggle now.

"Kathryn, is it now?" Liam's eyebrow lifted and there was a smile dancing at the corner of his mouth, just waiting to break out. I sent him a warning glare. Just let him try.

"What are you doing here, Liam?" I repeated.

"I've come to tell you I've had a word with Mitch and he says that he will forget all about it – once you apologise, of course."

"Apologise?" Gran K was on it faster than Prescott down a rabbit hole. "And what is it you've done for which you need to apologise? Something to do with the inappropriate way you dress, I imagine."

"I've done nothing to apologise for," I said quickly, then turned back to Liam. "And you could have told me this by phone."

"Ah yes, but then I'd have missed out on the pleasure of Amelia's delightful company. Not to mention her grand biscuits."

Gran simpered. She actually simpered! And smoothed her already smooth hair with an immaculately manicured hand. Mum had obviously found some time during her busy morning to fit her in for a blow dry and manicure.

"I don't usually serve my guests biscuits," Gran said. "I'm

an accomplished baker, you know, and it's been suggested many times that I would walk *Bake Off* if I entered. But TV shows are not really my thing. Do you like lemon drizzle cake, Liam?"

"My absolute favourite," he assured her.

"It's my speciality. When my wrist has recovered sufficiently," she tapped the cast on her arm, "- it's my whisking wrist, you see - I will bake one especially for you. I think you'll agree that's much better than shop bought biscuits."

My 'shop bought' biscuits. She might not approve of them, but I noticed there weren't many left in the packet.

"Would you like a cup of tea, Kathryn?" she went on. "I think there might be some left in the pot. Liam kindly made it for me." She gave a dainty shrug. "I really have no strength at the moment. Everything is so difficult one handed. You have no idea."

"No tea for me, thanks. I'll have a couple of biscuits, though. Didn't have time for lunch at the pub today, we were that busy."

"Nothing like a murder to bring everyone out in droves," Liam said. "I bet the landlady is delighted. Anyway, Mrs Kingham -"

"I told you, it's Amelia," Gran said, with another of those rare smiles that she never wasted on the likes of us. In fact, the only one she smiled at was at Max. And now, it seemed, Liam.

"Amelia," Liam said, making her name sound like something really special. Then he stood up and crossed to the window.

"Hello, what's on? That looks like yet another police car going through the village," he said as he turned to me. "Shall we go and see what's happening, Kath-" he paused just in time and added: "Kat? You coming? Thanks again for the tea and biscuits... Amelia."

He didn't wait for an answer, and I had just time to grab the last of the chocolate Hobnobs before following him out of the door.

As we turned into the High Street, my heart almost stopped

as I saw where the police car was parked.

"Would you know who lives there?" he asked, then grinned. "Silly question. Of course you do."

"It's my friend, Suzanne," I said, my heart thudding. What on earth would they want with her?

But that question was soon answered, more the pity.

Liam and I watched as two policemen came back to their car - with Rob sandwiched between them, his face white and set. He didn't look back as they drove off.

"Who was that?" Liam asked as he took a photo of the back of the car.

But before I could answer, Suzanne came out, her eyes blazing, her face scarlet with fury. She saw me and was about to turn and go back into the house without speaking when she changed her mind. She came towards us, her fists clenched in fury.

"How could you, Kat? I'll never forgive you for this. Never."

Chapter Eighteen

"Suzanne, please," I said quickly, trying to shut her up before she said something in front of Liam that she'd regret. "This is –"

"This is hardly the time for introductions." She bristled with fury. "I trusted you. Rob trusted you. How could you do it just for a cheap headline?"

"Rob?" Liam's eyebrows lifted. "Was that the name of the guy we just saw being taken away?"

"Suzanne!" I was almost shouting. "This is Liam. He's the editor of The Chronicle. He does all the crime stuff." I laid particular emphasis on the word 'crime'.

There was a small silence then Suzanne went back into the house and shut the heavy front door with a slam.

"So what was all that about?" Liam asked. "Who is this guy Rob? Is he anything to do with the murder?"

"Of course not," I said quickly.

He gave me a straight look. "You'd better be right about that, Kat Latcham because last time I looked impeding a police enquiry was a criminal offence."

"I'm not impeding anything," I said. "Although you are impeding me."

His face darkened. "I've got it. You're doing it again, aren't you? I'll bet on my sweet mother's head that this guy has something to do with the murder and that you are planning to beat me to a story again. Like you did before. Was that what your friend (or should I say ex-friend?) meant about a cheap headline?"

"I didn't–"

"We're supposed to be on the same team, you know. Or rather, we were. I can't work with someone I can't trust. And I don't trust you. As for this Rob whoever he is, I have a contact in the police. I'll soon find out who he is and what their interest in him is."

And with that, he stormed off down the street and I turned back to Suzanne's. This time she was going to hear me out.

I rang the doorbell four times before she finally answered it, and that was probably only because Finbar and Archie made such a racket every time I rang the bell. She was worried about upsetting the neighbours, but not, it seemed, worried about upsetting me.

"Don't shut the door on me again, Suzanne," I said when she opened it a mere three inches. "I didn't tell anyone, least of all the police. You, however, have just told the editor of the local paper. Now, if you want me to stand here on the doorstep and have every ear in the village tuned in to our conversation then that's your choice. But you will listen to what I have to say, whether it's in your nice warm kitchen or out here in the middle of the High Street. Your call."

She was about to close it again when she paused, then stood aside to let me in. The two dogs slunk back into their beds with long sighs. Finbar because he realised I hadn't come to take him for another walk and Archie because I wasn't Anna.

"I'll just say what I've got to say then I'll leave you in peace," I began. "I promise you I didn't tell anyone that Rob was staying here. But you're forgetting one thing. You're living slap bang in the middle of what has to be the nosiest village in the country. Even Mrs Denby, who's not known for gossiping, was speculating about who was staying in your gallery flat because she'd seen the curtains opening and closing. I tried to tell her that it was probably you changing the curtains but then she went on to say that you'd only hung those curtains a week ago. If I'd given her long enough, she could probably have told me where you bought them and how much you paid."

I was relieved to see a flicker of a smile chase across Suzanne's pale face.

"I'm sorry, Kat," she said with a sigh. "You're quite right. I should have thought it through. But I was so panicked about seeing him taken away. He looked so frightened. He was only telling me this morning how he'd rather die than go back to prison. I felt I'd let him down by letting you question him the way you did."

"And then you went and blurted it out in front of Liam, who is the coldest, most calculating and least trustworthy journalist I know," I said, then wished I hadn't as I saw her go even paler.

"Don't beat yourself up about that," I added. "He'd have found out anyway. He has some very good contacts among the local police."

Finbar left his basket and padded across to place his large bristly head in her lap. "I've made a bad job worse, haven't I?" she said, as she gently smoothed the dog's rough coat. "Mrs Denby was here earlier, you know."

"She was?"

"She'd heard I was interested in adopting Archie and wanted to warn me that we had to go through what she called the proper channels. She said the rehoming place she contacted has someone who's very interested in him. But that if I could hang on to him until then, she'd be very grateful as her cat hates dogs."

"But I asked her to hold off on that," I said, then without thinking added, "and I promised Anna I'd look out for him until she could come back for him."

"Anna? As in Rob's sister?" Suzanne's eyes darkened with suspicion. "You didn't say you'd met her. When was that?"

I had no choice but to tell her. Besides, telling someone would be a relief.

"Yesterday morning. She'd come to the vicarage. Honestly, Suzanne, I swear she had no idea Mr Fairweather was dead. She looked absolutely stunned when I told her."

"What was she doing there?"

"She'd come to see Mr Fairweather and have a go at him about the state of the house at Stargate, I suppose. It all fits in with Rob's story, doesn't it? He said he saw her there."

"You mean Anna was actually here in the village at the time

of the murder? Have you told the police?"

"Well, no. But –"

"And you had the cheek to lecture me about harbouring what they would call a 'person of interest' in a police enquiry. For goodness sake, Kat. What were you thinking of?"

"Like you with Rob, I believed her," I said simply. "Either the two of them are extremely accomplished actors or ..."

"Or we are both gullible," Suzanne added as my voice trailed away. "And you're forgetting something. Even Rob said his sister had a bit of a temper."

I thought of the way she'd threatened the vicar. The set of her face as she'd driven away after confronting Mrs Denby. Even though I'd only caught a glimpse of her face that day, it was very different from the shocked and upset person I'd seen on the day of the murder.

"We need to find her, don't we?" I said. "If for no other reason than to let her know what's happened to her brother."

"And how do you suppose we do that?" she asked. "Rob told us they'd lost touch ages ago. Do you think Mrs Denby could help?"

I shook my head. "I'd prefer not to involve her. The fewer people who know the better. Mrs Denby's no gossip, but things have a habit of getting out in this village. Besides, I've a pretty good idea of where Anna will be."

"You do?"

I pointed to Rob's picture still on the kitchen table. "I think she may have gone there, back to their house in Stargate."

"But Rob said the place was a wreck."

"And yet, he slept there, didn't he? He said he slept so well, in fact, that he only woke when Anna drove up. Do you fancy a trip to Stargate? It's only a little over an hour's drive from here, although it would probably take me four hours on my scooter, and there's this lovely little cafe that does the most gorgeous cream teas."

Suzanne shook her head. "I'm sorry, but I really need to be here, for when Rob gets back. I promised him he could come back here when they let him go. As they will."

It was then that I thought of Will. Yes, we had planned to go into Dintscombe this afternoon to see about getting my ring made smaller. But he would surely jump at the chance to go to the coast instead. He hated shopping.

But to my surprise, he didn't seem at all keen when I suggested we went to Stargate instead of Dintscombe.

"Why the change of plan?" he asked.

I shrugged. "I just fancy getting away from this place for a bit. How about it? You know you always feel better for a walk along the beach. And we could have tea and cakes in the cafe there. My treat."

He didn't look too excited about that either.

"Are you ok?" I asked. "Because we can go to Dintscombe if you prefer."

"No. Stargate it is," he said and, before I could say anything else, he reached across and started the Land Rover, after which conversation became impossible above the rattles and wheezes of the old vehicle.

I thought it best not to tell Will that the real reason I wanted to go to Stargate was to check if my hunch was correct and Anna was indeed at Bay View. He'd only have a go at me for getting involved with yet another murder and I wasn't in the mood for any more lectures from anyone. Least of all him when he was in what appeared to be a particularly grouchy mood.

It was a cold, blustery afternoon. The wind was coming straight off the choppy sea and into our faces. We walked along the shingly beach then up the steep cliff path which would take us close enough to Bay View to be able to see if Anna's distinctive yellow car was there. As we walked, I was trying to work what I was going to say to Will if it was. But I needn't have bothered because there was no sign of either the car or Anna.

It had been a long shot, that was for sure. Although someone had indeed been there. I could see a newly boarded up window and assumed it was the one Rob had broken to gain entry to the house a few nights ago.

But there was nothing else to see. I was going to suggest we walked along the path to the top of the cliff to see if we could spot any peregrines, but I could tell he wasn't in the mood and I was getting fed up asking him what was wrong. Each time I did, he just grunted that there was nothing wrong with him apart from the fact that I kept on asking what was wrong.

But at least we'd had a blast of sea air although it didn't seem to have done Will much good. He was as quiet and moody as he had been when we set off. He even refused my offer of a cream tea in the little beachside cafe and said he really had to get back.

When we got back to Much Winchmoor he stopped outside our house. We both got out and when I asked him if he wanted to come in he shook his head. Then he turned towards me, his face more serious than I'd ever seen it.

"You asked me what was wrong," he said. "And I didn't like to say while we were out and about. It would have made the drive home a bit awkward."

"Like it wasn't already?" I asked, seriously worried by an expression in his eyes that I'd never seen before.

He gnawed at his thumb nail. "The thing is, Katie," he began. But at that moment my phone rang. It was Suzanne.

"Go on," I said to Will. "I'll call her back later."

He shook his head. "No worries. Answer it. What I have to say will keep."

"I'll just see what she wants." As I answered the call, I could hear what sounded like a sob. "Suzanne? Are you ok?"

"No, Kat. I'm not. I'm really not." Her voice was shrill, panicky. "Can you come round please?"

"It's a bit tricky at the moment," I began, but Will had already begun to walk away. He gave a little see-you-later wave, got back into his Land Rover and drove off.

"Ok," I said to Suzanne, trying to swallow down the bad feeling I had as I watched him drive away. "What's wrong?"

"It's Archie. I went up to Rob's room just now and he came with me. He started to rummage around underneath the bed and pulled out Rob's rucksack. Before I could stop him, he'd got it open and had his head inside."

I laughed. "If he's anything like Prescott that will be

because Rob had left some food in there."

"It wasn't food." I could hear Suzanne take a deep steadying breath. "He - he pulled out this - this really odd thing. It was an old teddy bear. But the thing is, Kat, it had this strange note pinned to its fur. It says…"

But even before she read the words, I knew what they were going to say.

'Abseiling is only the second fastest way down a church tower.'

Chapter Nineteen

The old teddy bear lay on the kitchen table. It was such an innocent little thing. Only about six inches tall, it showed obvious signs of having been very well loved in its time. Its fur was worn away around the nose, and one ear was missing.

"You shouldn't have touched it," I said. "It's evidence."

"But I had to get it away from Archie. I had quite a tussle. He wasn't keen on letting it go."

"And I think I know why. I reckon that bear belongs to Anna which is why Archie went mad for it." I thought of his sad face as he'd watched her drive off without him. "Poor little fellow. He really misses her."

"But what's it doing in Rob's rucksack? And what about this strange note? I don't understand."

I took a deep breath. She had a right to know. "When Mrs Denby discovered the body yesterday morning, this bear was near it with the note pinned to its chest. But by the time the police got there, the bear and the note had disappeared. She was desperately upset when she realised the police didn't believe her and that they thought the shock had made her imagine things."

Suzanne looked down at the note and shivered. "But who'd do such a horrible thing? And why?"

I shrugged. "As to the who, I'm not sure yet although there are one or two possibilities. And why? I think it was someone's idea of a sick joke. I don't know if you've seen the posters that have been all around the village but there was to be a teddy bear abseil from the church tower as a fundraising event. The children had all paid £3 a head for the vicar to lower their precious bears, one at a time, off the church tower."

Suzanne's face went pale. "Come on, Kat, you saw Rob yesterday morning. He could hardly stand up least of all climb

125

up to the top of the church tower and push the vicar off. That would take the sort of strength he doesn't have."

"He doesn't," I murmured. "But his sister does. And I don't think Rob put the bear there. But I think, in fact I know, that he took it away."

"But why?"

"Because he thought Anna had left it there."

Suzanne stared at me. "And is that what you think now?"

"I don't know. Or perhaps someone put it there to make it look as if she did."

"What are we going to do? If we take it to the police, they'll think they have an even tighter case against Rob and not bother to look any further. And he's hardly going to implicate his sister. If he'd been going to do that, he'd have done so by now, wouldn't he?"

I looked at my watch. "There's no point doing anything for the moment. I'm afraid it looks as if Rob's going to have to spend a night in the cells. I've got to go because I'm working in the pub again tonight. But tomorrow I'll have a quiet word with Mrs Denby and see if she has any idea where Anna might be."

When I walked into the pub that evening, things were not good. Gino was scuttling about, smiling too much and singing '*Are you lonesome tonight*' at the top of his out of tune voice, in an effort to drown out the sounds from the kitchen where pots and pans were being banged and crashed around.

Norina was working up a perfect storm, her mood even worse than it had been at lunchtime.

At the far end of the bar was a group of about a dozen kids, late teens, early twenties, most of whom I didn't recognise apart from a couple of lads from the next village that I'd seen around. I was pretty sure some of them were employed by the builders who were working on Norina's precious dining room. Or, as was more often the case, not working.

Certainly the Winchmoor Arms wasn't their usual haunt. They were very loud but loudest of all, and bang in the middle of them was Rhianna, who didn't look in any hurry to take her

126

place behind the bar.

"What's going on?" I asked Gino who'd come to the end of his song and paused for breath.

"Is Rhianna," he whispered, casting an anxious glance at the door into the kitchen where the pots and pans were working themselves up into a crescendo that rivalled the bit in Tchaikovsky's 1812 Overture when the cannons wake everyone up. "Norina she's about to explode."

I didn't like to tell him that, by the sound of it, Norina already had exploded. Instead, I nodded for him to continue.

"That girl," he sighed. "She is nothing but trouble and the way she is making the eyes at Ed... do you see?"

I looked across. I hadn't even noticed Ed Fuller was in the middle of the noisy crowd.

"If his wife's brother comes in - you know the man I mean?"

"You mean Ryan?" Jules' brother was built like a tank. More to the point, a tank with a very short fuse, if you'll excuse the mixed metaphor.

"He'll be in later, for sure, and if he see her and Ed ... well, you know how protective he is about his sister and how handy he is with his fists." He gave an unhappy sigh and another worried glance towards the kitchen. "And if there is trouble, I will get blame. I've tried to get her to leave him alone and I've tried to get Ed to go home. But you know what he's like."

I did indeed. Ed was harmless and I didn't for a moment think there was anything going on between him and Rhianna. At least not as far as Ed was concerned. But if Jules got to hear about it, his life wouldn't be worth living. And if her fist happy brother got to see it - it didn't bear thinking about. Gino was quite right to be worried.

"That girl's nothing but trouble," I grumbled at Gino. "I don't know why Norina puts up with her. It's not like she pulls her weight in the pub."

Gino gave an unhappy shrug. "Is complicated, Katie *bach*. You see if you could have a word, would you? She never listen to me."

I was pretty sure she wouldn't listen to me either. But I

knew someone who would. Not that I'd give him any choice.

"Ed?" I called as I marched up to the group. "There's a call for you. Over there."

His face paled. But he got up and went across to the phone in the corner of the bar.

"Don't worry. It's not Jules," I said.

"Then who?"

"No one. I just wanted to ask you what the hell you think you're playing at? Ryan usually comes in around this time. If he sees that girl pouring herself all over you the way she was just now, there's going to be hell to pay. You know what he's like."

Ed shook his head miserably. "I know. And I'm trying to get away from her, Katie, honest I am. She just - she won't take no."

"And of course, you're trying really, really hard, aren't you?" My voice crackled with sarcasm. "Look, why don't you go home? I'll say you've had an urgent call from your wife if anyone asks. You did tell her you had a wife, I assume? And two children?"

I took the look on his face as a no. Or, at least, a 'not exactly' and breathed a sigh of relief as Ed shrugged on his coat and headed out of the door. That, at least, was one major incident avoided. This time.

The noise from the group in the corner quietened as Rhianna left them and sauntered across to the bar.

"They'll have the same again," she said.

"Then you'll have to do it, won't you? You are, after all, supposed to be on this side of the bar this evening. I'm busy. I need to get the order from the couple in the window who look as if they've been waiting for ages. And Gino says if you've got five minutes, could you top up the crisps and peanuts. There's a couple of new boxes in the storeroom."

I knew there was no way she was going to do that. But I didn't hang around long enough for her to tell me that. Instead, I picked up an order pad and went across to the window table. As I did so, I glanced across at what we called the settle table to see if they, too, were waiting to order.

The settle was a high-backed wooden seat with cushions that had a habit of sliding off if you wriggled around too much. My heart sank as I realised that the man sitting on the other side of the table was one of my least favourite people. Gerald Crabshaw.

Overbearing, pompous and far too full of his own self-importance for someone who used to be one of Much Winchmoor's big cheeses - or so he thought when he was a District Councillor. But a couple of years ago that all came crashing down after what he called 'a little business misunderstanding' but what most people called fraud.

He only avoided prosecution because he resigned his position on the council. He was not even a little cheese anymore. More a 'past its best' mouldy old Cheddar.

He now spent his time cooking up Full English Breakfasts at Winchmoor Mill, the guest house that he and his wife Fiona ran. While she, in a complete reversal of roles, was elected to Much Winchmoor Parish Council and now spent most of her time wandering around the village with a ruler and clipboard measuring potholes.

Fiona! Why hadn't I thought of her before? Elsie had told me that Fiona and Anna had been friends, or 'thick as a pair of hedge sparrows,' was her way of putting it. (And no, I didn't know what she meant by that, either.)

But perhaps Fiona would know how to contact Anna, always assuming I could ask her without Gerald overhearing.

As I waited for the lady at the window table to decide whether she wanted chips or jacket potatoes with her fish (she'd asked for new potatoes, but I didn't think Norina was in the mood to allow someone to go off menu) I glanced across at the settle. But it wasn't Fiona across the table from Gerald. I couldn't quite see who it was, but Gerald certainly never smiled and smarmed like that at his wife.

They were certainly getting very cosy across the table, their heads almost touching. They were so caught up in their conversation that they didn't notice me edging closer, dying to see who the unfortunate recipient of Gerald's cringe-making charm was.

"So, you'll do it?" I heard her say, in a low, sexy drawl. "Oh Gerald, that's marvellous. I knew I could rely on you. Here, let me give you this. Only you have to promise, on your honour, that Elsie Flintstone, or whatever the wretched woman's name is, will never know that I have a spare key to the village hall."

I'd know that cut-glass accent anywhere. It was Cordelia Hilperton-Jones, the so-called grief stricken almost-widow of poor Reverend Fairweather. Not that she looked very grief stricken as she cosied up to Gerald.

"Dear lady, I will sleep with it under my pillow," he said as he took the key, kissed it lightly, and put it in his pocket.

Yuk! I doubt Elsie would want the key after Gruesome Gerald had slobbered all over it. But what was Cordelia doing with it?

As if on cue, Gerald asked almost the same question. "But how did you come by it? Elsie Flintlock guards the key as if it was the Crown Jewels."

"Lionel had a spare one cut a while back, when Elsie was down with the flu or something and Mrs Denby had to step in. He felt, quite rightly, that it was a health and safety risk to only have one key holder. He kept it, along with all the other keys, on a hook in the vicarage kitchen." She sighed. "Dear man, he would do almost anything to avoid a confrontation and people like Elsie Flintstone took advantage of that. I'm forever in your debt, Gerald. And yes, of course, I'll be sure to tell my mother how very helpful you have been. Maybe even get you a ticket for -"

"Can I tempt you to join me in a bit to eat, dear lady?" Gerald cut across her as he finally caught sight of me. "I see *spaghetti vongole* is on the menu tonight. And a little bird told me that's a particular favourite of yours. I know we agreed one quick drink but there is that other small matter to discuss. Besides I'm in no hurry to go home. My wife's at another damned council meeting. And she's left me cold chicken and salad for dinner. What sort of a meal is that for a man on a cold November evening? So, I'm going to eat here and you are very welcome to join me. As my guest, of course."

I glanced back at the bar where there was a small queue

beginning to form and, needless to say, Rhianna was nowhere to be found.

"Look, shall I come back in a minute?" I said quickly.

Cordelia flashed me a smile. Gerald didn't. Our relationship, such as it was, didn't extend to smiles. Just the occasional glare.

I allowed myself a little smirk at the thought of Fiona Crabshaw taking herself off to council meetings. She threw herself into her role with more enthusiasm and commitment than her husband had ever done when he was a councillor.

When I went back to take their order, Cordelia was looking flushed, her eyes shining as she looked up at Gerald, who was preening like a peacock - although, to be honest, he was more pigeon than peacock.

I was surprised at Cordelia. I'd have thought she'd have more sense - not to mention better taste - than to be taken in by Gerald Crabshaw's smarmy ways. And what was Gerald doing that was going to earn him her undying gratitude and perhaps a seat at the RSC's next production?

As for Cordelia, she wasn't exactly grief stricken, was she? Elsie's words worried away at the back of my mind. Suspicious death. Wealthy widow but not a grieving one. And hadn't Mrs Denby hinted that there'd been a bit of a scene between the vicar and someone a few nights ago? Had that someone been Cordelia?

It was probably all nonsense, of course. Just Elsie having a go at someone who dared to challenge her over the way the village hall should be run.

They gave me their orders - s*paghetti vongole* for her and a meat feast pizza for him.

"And we'll have a nice bottle of merlot to go with it, Katie," Gerald said. "Not that cheap Italian plonk the landlady gets from the cash and carry that tastes like battery acid."

He gave Cordelia a wink as he said this, but his grin faded as I muttered, "Serve a lot of battery acid to your guests, do you, Gerald?"

But before he could reply, Cordelia leaned across and touched his arm. "Talking of wine, why don't we have our next village hall committee meeting at my house? I've got some really nice burgundy that would -"

"Later, my dear," he said, glaring at me, then added with an attempt at a French accent that wouldn't have been out of place on *'Allo, 'Allo'*. *"Pas devant les domestiques. Comprenez-vous?"*

She might not have understood. But I did, in spite of the accent. Not in front of the servants? Before I could think of a suitable come back, Gino started warbling again. He was now on to *'Heartbreak Hotel',* a sign that things were not going well.

I couldn't work out what it was for a moment. The noisy group had upped and left, thank goodness. And then I saw it.

Rhianna had upped and left with them.

"Did she say where she was going?" I asked.

"She say nothing," Gino said unhappily. "I went to take more wine to the table by the window and when I get back, she is gone. And her bag and coat which she hangs in back room is gone too. Norina, she going to go mad. She promise her sister - that's Rhianna's mother - she'd look out for her."

"Look, Gino, she'll be fine. Rhianna seems pretty streetwise. And those kids she was with look harmless enough. In fact, I know a couple of them."

"You do? Could you call them? Ask her to come back?"

"I don't know them that well. But what's the big deal? The bar's quietening down now and we're really not that busy."

"Is not that. Ok, I'll tell you. But don't tell Norina I tell you, no? Rhianna, she come here so we can keep an eye on her. She was in with bad crowd in Pontypridd. Her mother felt she'd be safer here."

"I shouldn't worry about her, Gino. She'll be back. You'll wake up in the morning and there she'll be, acting as if nothing has happened. She'll probably be sitting on the doorstep waiting for you to open up."

And at the time I really believed that.

Chapter Twenty

Next day I denied myself my usual Saturday morning lie-in because I knew Fiona Crabshaw always walked her little dog, Harvey, about 9 o'clock. I often thought it was one of those little ways she got back at Gerald, leaving him to clear up after the guests had all had their breakfasts.

I also knew Fiona was a creature of habit and did the same walk every morning. It was far too early for Prescott to be walked so I put my running gear on and headed out along the lanes that circled around the back of the village, past Short Ford and out on to the moorland beyond.

Sure enough, I was only about a mile into my run when I saw her and Harvey, a cute little Highland white terrier, coming towards me. It was just as well I hadn't brought Prescott with me. He was a feisty, over-opinionated little character who thought he was leader of the pack. Harvey, on the other hand, was also a feisty little character but didn't give two hoots who was the leader of the pack.

He was a gorgeous dog, cute, good natured and gentle with people. Prescott was the complete opposite. He was one of those dogs whose bite was definitely worse than his bark and he would always bite first, ask questions later. When I was out walking him, I spent half my time apologising for him. The other half trying to get him to shut up.

At least being without him meant I was be able to hold a conversation even if Fiona, as always, wasn't very keen. We've had a few run-ins over the years and Fiona, like far too many people in Much Winchmoor, had a very long memory.

"Good morning," I said, bending down to greet Harvey, who came up to me, his little stumpy tail wagging furiously. "It's a lovely morning."

"Is it?" Her curt reply made it very clear she was in no

mood to stop and chat. "Come along, Harvey. We'd best get back. Lots to do."

"I'm glad I bumped into you. There's something I want to ask."

She frowned at me. "Is this for the paper? In which case I've nothing to say to you. Last time I did, my words - and, indeed, some words that I didn't say - ended up splashed across the front page of that rag you work for."

"Only I don't," I said quickly. "I mean, I don't work for the Chronicle anymore. I resigned yesterday. Editorial differences," I added before she could ask.

She looked slightly mollified at that. "What was it you wanted to talk about? Only I really am in a rush this morning."

"Then I'll walk back with you," I said. "I wanted to ask you about Anna Fairweather."

It was like a shutter had come down. "I prefer to walk alone, if you don't mind."

"I understand you were friendly with her when she was at the vicarage and I was wondering if you knew how to get in touch with her. It's very important."

"What do you want with her? Are you sure this isn't for some newspaper or other? Raking up all that old dirt? It's what you usually do."

"Nothing like that, I promise. I need to find her. It's about her brother, Rob. I don't know if you know this, but I suppose it'll be public knowledge soon enough. He's been arrested in connection with Mr Fairweather's murder."

She stopped abruptly, her eyes wide with shock. "I don't believe you. The last I heard he was still in prison."

"He was released a couple of months ago. He came here trying to find Anna and didn't know that she'd left the vicar. I understand Anna and Rob were estranged."

"Through no fault of Anna's."

"That's as maybe." I wasn't sure how fond I'd be of a sister who'd stood by and let me be accused of a crime I didn't commit and who'd deliberately let our family home fall to rack and ruin. "Anyway, he has no way of getting in touch with her. And believe me, he really needs her help now."

134

"But if he's the murderer -"

"I don't believe he is," I said. I took a deep breath and decided to trust her. "I think Rob is covering up for his sister."

She stared at me. "You surely don't think Anna murdered Lionel? But that's ridiculous. Anna is the gentlest of souls and wouldn't hurt a fly."

She looked so indignant I could see I was in danger of losing her, so I tried another tack.

"Or maybe someone is trying to make it look like she did? Rob found something on - on the body that he thought would implicate her. And he took it. To protect her. I just need to talk to Anna again."

"Again?"

I nodded. "I saw her the morning of the murder and, if what she was saying is true, she has an alibi - if the police bother to check it out. She stayed the night in a guest house in Dintscombe and was having her car fixed at the time the vicar fell to his death."

Fiona looked hurt. "But why didn't she stay with me?"

"I saw her that day. She didn't look like she was thinking straight. She thought ..."

"Go on. You might as well tell me now you've started."

"She thought Lionel had had her dog Archie put to sleep. She was dreadfully upset, apparently."

"But why on earth would she think that?" Fiona looked shocked. "That's crazy. Lionel would never have done such a terrible thing. He thought the world of that dog. And of Anna. Had a funny way of showing it sometimes, but that's men for you, isn't it?"

"Probably." For someone who claimed to be in a hurry, she was showing no sign of it now. "So, do you know how I can get in touch with her? I'm sure she'll want to know what's happened to her brother."

Fiona shoved her hands deep in her pockets and nodded. "She probably will. She has a house. Somewhere on the Dorset coast. She always used to say she wanted Rob to make a life for himself there. The chances are she's there. I'm not quite sure where it is though."

"That's ok. I know where it is but she's not there. She had been because Rob saw her there a couple of day ago although he didn't get to speak to her. I thought she may have gone back there so I went there yesterday but there was no sign of her. Although someone had been there very recently and boarded up a broken window."

"Then she probably went back to London. When she left here, she went to work in a homeless shelter there that was run by Ben Chappell's sister, Rachel. I could give you Rachel's number, I suppose. Although whether she'll tell you Anna's whereabouts is another matter. She's very cautious, as you can imagine, in her line of work. They work with some pretty vulnerable people, many of whom are there to escape abusive relationships."

"Are you saying Mr Fairweather was an abusive husband?"

"Goodness, no. Nothing like that. He thought the world of her, in his own way. But he was such a confirmed old bachelor, they should never have married in the first place. They were so ill suited."

I could have said that was exactly what Elsie Flintlock thought too. But I didn't think Fiona would appreciate being of the same mind as Elsie.

Fiona took out her phone, scrolled through and then read out the name and number of Ben Chappell's sister. Then she called Harvey, who by that time had lost interest in us and was wading through a ditch. When he came out, the muddy water had left a tideline. He looked like he was wearing mud-coloured waders on all four feet.

"Oh, will you look at the state of him! Come along Harvey. Straight home and a bath and it serves you right," Fiona said as she hurried off.

I watched them go, then called the number she'd given me. It rang and rang and after a while went to voicemail. I didn't leave a message but turned back and continued my run, hoping that the exercise would clear the fog in my mind.

I still didn't really think Anna had murdered her husband. But what did I know? I'd been wrong before. However, I thought she'd want to know her brother was back in police custody.

By the time I got back to the village, I was feeling a bit more optimistic and decided to try Rachel Chappell again.

This time, my call was answered after just a few rings.

"Hello?" The woman's voice was quiet and guarded.

"Oh hi. You don't know me but my name's Kat Latcham. I'm from Much Winchmoor and I'm trying to get in contact with Anna... I suppose she still calls herself Fairweather. I believe she works with you?"

There was such a long pause that I thought we'd been cut off until I heard sounds in the distance.

"Hello?" I said.

"What do you want with Anna?"

"I just want to speak to her. If you could give me her number?"

"I can't do that."

"No. I don't suppose you can. Well, look, how about I give you my number, you tell her I called and ask her to call me. Would that work?"

"I'd still want to know what you want with her."

"Ok. Well, the thing is, Anna already knows this, but her ex-husband's been murdered. And I think she'll want to know that the police have arrested her brother, Rob. Only I don't think he did it. He-"

"It couldn't possibly be Rob. He's -" She hesitated, then went on. "He's not around at the moment."

"But he is. He was released from prison a couple of months early and came to Much Winchmoor hoping, I imagine, to see his sister."

There was another long pause. A burst of shouting from somewhere inside the building, then, "Ok. Give me your number and I'll pass on the message. I can't make any promises though."

"Thanks. I appreciate that. Because I don't think it was Rob any more than I think it was Anna. But someone may be trying to make it look as if it was one or both of them."

I ended the call and made my way back to the village. As I jogged down the High Street, Norina was standing outside the pub, looking up and down the road, her face taut with anxiety.

"Katie?" she called. "I'm glad I've seen you. I'm out of my mind with worry, that I am."

I had a pretty good idea what or rather who she was worried about. "Rhianna?"

She nodded. "The little madam didn't come home last night. I've tried ringing her but her phone's turned off. I don't suppose you've seen her? Or know where she might be? Gino says you know one of the lads she left with last night."

"I can't say I know him exactly. But you do too. He's one of the builders. You know, the spotty, lanky one who's always sniffing."

Norina pulled a face. "Oh, him. Honestly, that girl. I'll swing for her, I will. Do you know where he lives?"

"No idea. He's not from Much Winchmoor. But won't he be working today?"

Norina snorted. "On a Saturday? You've got to be joking. I have trouble getting them to turn up during the week, least of all on a weekend."

"Well, can you phone the boss? He's sure to know where he lives."

She scowled and mumbled something I didn't catch.

"Sorry?"

"I said they've blocked my number," Norina snapped. "Accused me of harassing them. Me? I ask you. I don't go around harassing people, do I now?"

I didn't think she was expecting an answer to that, which was just as well.

"Ed Fuller will know where he lives, won't he? I pass their house on my way home. I could ask him if you like?"

"Would you? Thanks." She gave me a rare smile. "You're a good girl, Katie."

It's a pity you don't say that more often, I thought.

Then as if she could read my mind, she went on: "Your job was never in danger, you know. I was only saying what I did to keep you on your toes. Let's face it, Rhianna is pretty damn useless as a barmaid. No interest in the job whatsoever."

"Then why?" I began but thought better of it. Norina wasn't big on sharing confidences. But to my surprise she carried on talking.

"Why do we put up with her?" She shoved her hand through her hair. "I might as well level with you, seeing as how you're doing me a favour. Only don't go spreading this around. Promise?"

"I promise."

"See, my sister, Rhianna's mother, lent us the money for the dining room conversion. On condition that we had Rhianna. She'd got in with a bad crowd and my sister wanted her out of the way for a bit. Now it sounds as if she's gone from one bad crowd to another. "

"I doubt it. From what I know about him - I think his name's Dylan - he's pretty harmless. I'm sure she's fine and will come tottering down the street any moment."

"Well, let's hope so. And let's hope, too, she's got the hangover from hell. It would serve the little madam right. Ok, I have things to do. Can't stand here nattering. You let me have that boy's number as soon as you can." She turned to head back indoors but paused. "I'll see you later then. Oh, and Katie?" she called after me.

"Yes?"

"Don't be late."

Norina had reverted to type already.

Ed was in the front garden as I went past, trying to straighten out the front wheel of a bright pink bike, with silver tassels hanging from the handlebars.

"What happened there?" I asked.

Ed shook his head. "Kids, eh? That's our Kylie for you. So busy chatting to her friend she didn't see the lamppost. Went straight into it."

"Oh dear. Is she ok?"

"She is. Can't say the same for the lamppost. Or the bike," Ed said with a grin. "You want Jules? She's just sorting Kylie out. As you can probably hear. That girl is such a drama queen."

"Takes after her mum." I smiled. "Anyway, it's you I want to see."

His eyebrows shot up. "My lucky day."

"In your dreams. Actually, I wondered if you had Dylan's number."

He frowned at me. "Really? I'd say he's a bit young for you."

"And I would say Rhianna's a bit young for you, Ed Fuller," I shot back at him. "He left something in the pub last night, that's all. I wanted to make sure he comes in to collect it."

Ed looked around as if expecting Jules to suddenly appear at his elbow. But from the yells that were coming from the house, she was still fully occupied at the first aid station.

"It's all right, I won't say anything," I said. "Not if you stop messing me about and give me his number. Or, failing that, the number of your boss so I can pass it on to Norina."

"I'll give you Dylan's number. But don't you go giving it to Norina, will you? She'll be on the phone to him day and night, like she did with the boss. Promise?"

"Ok, I promise. But if you all turned up and did your job when you said you were going to, then she wouldn't have to, would she?" I said as I handed him my phone for him to type in Dylan's number.

"Thanks, Ed. Tell Jules I said hi but I'm dashing home to get a shower. I hope Kylie's ok."

I wasn't having much luck with phones that morning because when I called Dylan's number it rang and rang. I was about to give up when a muffled voice answered.

"Yeah?"

"Is that Dylan?"

"Yeah."

"It's Kat Latcham here. From the pub."

"Yeah."

"You were in the pub last night. With Rhianna."

"Yeah?" The only way I could tell he was engaging with the conversation was the slight inflection at the end of the last 'yeah'.

"The Welsh girl," I said. "Black nails. And tattoos."

"Oh, yeah."

"You left with her."

"Yeah."

I sighed. This was going to take for ever. "Is she still with you?"

"What?"

"I said is she still with you? Simple enough question."

"No. No. She's not."

"Do you know where she is?"

"Back at the pub I s'pose."

"Where did you all go last night when you left the pub?"

"To a party. Friend of ours, his dad has a barn. Got some music and some drink. It was epic. We left there about 4 this morning."

"And Rhianna?"

"I took her back to the village."

"You mean you dropped her outside the pub? You saw her go in?"

"Nah. She said to drop her on the corner. Said she'd walk the rest of the way."

"But she never reached the pub, Dylan," I said. "Her bed wasn't slept in last night. I assumed she stayed with you."

Dylan swore. He was fully awake now. "Then where is she?"

That was what I wanted to know.

There was a bad feeling in the pit of my stomach. A young girl was missing. And there was a murderer still at large in the village.

How on earth was I going to tell Norina?

Chapter Twenty-One

"For goodness sake, Dylan," I snapped. "How could you let a young girl go staggering off on her own at that time of the night."

"She wasn't staggering. She actually seemed quite sober. But she said she wanted to creep in quietly and didn't want the noise of my old banger waking her aunt up. I tried to argue with her." He paused as he searched for the word. "But she can be very stroppy when the mood takes her."

He wasn't wrong there. In the short time I'd known her, she seemed to be in a permanent strop.

"And you didn't see anyone hanging around, I suppose," I said.

"Nah. Who would -" he began to say, then stopped. "Hang about. I did see someone as it happens. It was that batty woman with the yappy little dog. Lives in the old farmhouse that's just been done up. My boss says she was properly ripped off and that she should have employed a decent firm of builders like us. As for that so called barn conversion she's having done, the boss was saying -"

"Do you mean you saw Cordelia Hilperton-Jones when you dropped Rhianna off?" I said, pulling him back to the matter in hand.

"Is that her name? I wouldn't know. She keeps coming in the pub, banging on about her murder mystery evenings and getting in everyone's way. She was coming down the road after I dropped Rhianna off. I remember wondering where the hell she'd been at that time of night. Or rather morning."

It certainly made me wonder too. "Well, thanks Dylan. You've been a great help."

"Yeah, right. Hey, you will let me know, won't you? I mean, I'm sure she'll turn up and all that. She's a tough cookie, is

Rhianna. I'd say she can take care of herself."

"Yeah, I'm sure you're right." I certainly hoped he was, and that the sick feeling in my stomach was due to the fact that I hadn't had any breakfast that morning rather than a premonition that something awful had happened to her. But my breakfast would have to wait. I had this sense of urgency that just wouldn't go away.

Rather than go back home, I headed to the other end of the village to where Cordelia lived. I rang the doorbell and, just when I thought she wasn't in and was about to turn away, the door opened.

She looked terrible. Like she hadn't slept for a fortnight. Certainly nothing like the smartly dressed woman she'd been in the pub last night. Nor even the tweeds and pearls country gentlewoman look we'd got used to seeing around the village.

"Yes?" Her voice was tinged with impatience.

"Hi, Cordelia." Now I was here I had no idea what I was going to say to her. "It's a lovely morning, isn't it?"

She stared at me. "You woke me up to tell me that?"

"No. Of course not. Sorry. It's about your plans for the barn. I'd like to do a follow up to the piece I did last week." I hoped she hadn't heard that I no longer worked for the Chronicle. "And know how keen you were for me to see it. I was just wondering if the builders have now made it easier for you to access the barn and, if so, whether I could take some pictures. For the article."

Her smile, which had started when I mentioned doing a follow up piece vanished abruptly.

"That won't be possible," she said sharply.

"I was hoping to be able to tie it in with a piece I'm doing about Suzanne and her art gallery which is due to open any day now. She told me how you and she were making plans for a Much Winchmoor Festival of the Arts next year. It would be a shame if people thought she was the one who came up with the idea."

Cordelia looked indignant, as indeed I'd hoped she would. For a moment I thought she was going to step back and invite me to come through to see the barn, but she shook her head.

143

"No, I'm sorry. It's still impossible to access the barn. It's a shame but there you go. I'll be having words with the builders about leaving the garden is such a state when I eventually catch up with them."

The garden had indeed looked like a bomb site and I reckoned it was just as well Mabel was no longer around to see what had become of her precious…

"Mabel's flower and vegetable garden!" I said. "Arthur used to put his cows in that barn sometimes. There's no way on earth Mabel would have allowed them through her precious garden."

Cordelia raised her eyebrows. "Your point being?"

"There has to be another entrance to the barn. From the field. It is your field, I suppose."

"Why yes. Although it's let to a local farmer which is why there's a padlock on the gate."

"Do you mind if I go and have a look?"

Cordelia frowned. "I've already told you, the gate's locked."

"So?" I grinned. "I learnt to climb gates before I learnt to walk. There isn't a gate in this village I haven't climbed over at some time or another. Including that one. I could go down and have a look for you? Maybe even take some pictures. Just so you can see what's going on."

Something flickered in her eyes. Was it annoyance? Was she running out of patience with my questions?

Or was it something else?

"Indeed you will not," she said firmly. "Besides, if there is an entrance to the barn from the field, it's not accessible. The brambles that have grown up around the barn must be three feet thick. That was what the builders were supposed to have cleared for me, not the garden. By the time I realised what they'd done it was too late. They say they will restore it, but -"

"It's the Dunning Brothers, isn't it?" I said. "They've got a bit of a bad name, I'm afraid."

"Nothing that can't be sorted," she said briskly. She moved as if to close the door, intimating that the conversation, such as it was, was at an end.

I tried to think of a way to steer the conversation to Rhianna but couldn't. In desperation I just came out with it.

"I don't suppose you've seen Rhianna recently, have you?"

She looked puzzled. "Rhianna who?"

"Norina's niece. The one with the black nails."

"And the nose rings." She shuddered. "Honestly, it makes you wonder what happens when she gets a cold, doesn't it?"

"So, have you seen her?"

"Well, yes. I saw her in the pub last night as you well know. She was in the middle of that noisy group of youngsters. I was glad when they left."

"And you didn't see her after that?"

"Why would I?" She looked surprised.

"Someone said they dropped her off in the village at around 4 o'clock this morning. Only she never made it back to the pub."

"How odd."

"Indeed. Norina's out of her mind with worry. She's only just turned 18, you know, even though she looks a lot older."

"But why are you asking me?"

"I'm asking everyone."

"You're going door to door to every house in the village?" Her eyes widened. "Does that mean you think something awful's happened to her?"

"Of course not. I'm sure she'll turn up safe and sound with a perfectly reasonable explanation of where she'd been and with whom."

"Judging from the way she was behaving last night, I'd take a bet on the whom being young and male," Cordelia said firmly. "Now, if you'll excuse me, Princess Persephone will be wanting her breakfast. She's still not recovered from her trauma of the other day."

"What trauma would that be?"

"She escaped. The postman must have left the front gate open and she ran off. Apparently, she was seen right down by Long Ford and must have fallen in because when I finally found her, she was soaking wet. Poor little mite. I think she has a chill now. Anyway, I've already kept her waiting long enough."

I thanked her for her time and she nodded curtly, then closed the door firmly. She hadn't looked that surprised that Rhianna was missing. And she was probably right. The girl was with one of her friends from last night. It made sense.

But meant that either Dylan lied, or Cordelia had. The question was, which one?

I hadn't got very far when, to my surprise, she called me back.

"You say it was around 4am this boy says he dropped her off?" she said.

"Yes. Did you see her?"

"No. I've already told you that. But I saw what could well have been him. Or rather, I saw - and heard - a rackety old car."

"Where was this?"

"On the lane that leads down to the village from the main road. I couldn't sleep. I suffer dreadfully with insomnia, especially if I've had a heavy meal and a glass or two of red wine. And Gerald Crabshaw would insist on me trying Norina's chocolate fondant which I did, even though I knew it would cost me a night's sleep. As indeed it did. So, rather than lie in bed fretting about not being able to sleep, I got up and went for a quick walk. It's what I always do. Once around the village usually does the trick. I came back, had a cup of camomile tea and went out like a light. Didn't wake until I heard you banging on the door."

She sounded very convincing. But then she knew she'd been seen. I shouldn't have told her about Dylan. So, had she seen Rhianna?

And why, when she'd been so eager for me to see the barn, was she suddenly being so cagey?

As I rounded the corner into our road, I was surprised to see Will's Land Rover in the parking space opposite our house. Usually if he turned up when I wasn't there, he'd wait indoors. We'd virtually grown up together and were used to treating each other's houses as our own.

I walked up to the Land Rover and tapped on the window.

He gave such a startled jump I wondered if I'd woken him up.

"I can think of better places to take a nap," I said with a laugh. "Are you coming in or what? Mrs Chinnery will think you're casing the joint if you stay there much longer."

Mrs Chinnery, who lived in one of the bungalows opposite us, watched far too many episodes of NCIS and saw spies and criminals in every vehicle that came down the road and had been known to take down their registration numbers if they stayed too long.

When he showed no sign of getting out, I went around to the other side and climbed into the passenger seat.

"It's freezing in here," I said. "Why didn't you wait for me indoors?"

Then I looked across at our kitchen window and saw the answer. Gran Kingham.

"Ok. Fair enough." I laughed. "I can see why you'd choose to sit in a cold, smelly old Land Rover rather than endure the third degree from the grandmother-from-hell."

But Will didn't share my laughter. His face was so serious, much like it had been during out trip to Stargate. And it was beginning to worry me.

"William Manning. Are you going to tell me what the hell is eating you up or do I have to beat it out of you?" I punched him lightly on the arm. "Because, if you remember rightly, that's something I am quite capable of doing. Remember at junior school when you told me there was no such country as New Zealand? I believed that for ages and felt a right idiot when I found that you'd -"

"Katie. Please." He slammed the flat of his hand against the steering wheel. "For once in your life, just shut up and listen. You're not making things any easier."

"And you're not making sense. Why didn't you come to the pub last night? You said you were going to."

"I wasn't in the mood. I did text you."

"For pity's sake, Will, if you've got something to say, then come and out say it. You're beginning to freak me out."

"I'm sorry. I don't mean to. It's just - I - I don't know how to say it." His hand, which he'd slapped against the steering

147

wheel, was now gripping it so tightly his knuckles were white. "I've been going over and over in my mind, trying to find the best way to put it. I'm not clever with words like you are, Katie. And that's the trouble. Or part of it."

I've got this problem. When things get really, really bad, my mind tends to shut down and words come tumbling out of my mouth that should never have been in there in the first place.

It's just nervousness. Coupled with the urge to stick my head in the sand and hope that whatever is happening will go away. Or happen to someone else (which I realise isn't a very nice thing to wish for. But, like I said, I'm not at my best when I'm nervous.)

So instead of prising his hand off the wheel and asking him quietly and calmly to say whatever it was he had to say I gave a short and totally unconvincing laugh and said, "What? You want me to do your English homework again, is that it? After the last time when you moaned because I only got you a B+ I vowed I'd never do it again. So, you can -"

"This isn't working," he cut in, his face pale, his eyes troubled.

The smile, such as it was, froze on my face. "What isn't?"

"Us."

"What do you mean?" Now, along with my frozen smile, my tongue acted as if it had stuck to the roof of my mouth.

"You and me."

"I know what us means," I mumbled. "What are you on about?"

"It's not working. You and me. We should never have - I should never have ..." His voice trailed away. "I'm sorry."

"Are you saying we should never have got engaged?" My voice had sunk to a whisper, like I was afraid Mrs Chinnery might hear.

"We were ok before, weren't we? I mean, we've been mates for ever. But recently -"

"This isn't about the ring, is it?" I said quickly. "Because I love it, Will. I really do. I've just not been wearing it because it's a bit too big. And I'm frightened I'll lose it. I'm sorry

148

about yesterday when you were all set to go into Dintscombe and I wanted to go to Stargate instead. I had a really good reason for wanting to go to Stargate. It wasn't that I didn't want to go to the jeweller's and get it made smaller."

"It's not about the ring. You can keep that. Mum would have wanted you to."

You can keep that.

Finally, the reality of what he was trying to say hit me.

"Are you saying we should break up?" My voice came out all stiff and squeaky, from the effort of biting down the bellow - half pain, half rage - that had started way down in my stomach but was now working its way up to my throat.

He nodded. "We both want different things. It's for the best."

"But I want you, Will!" I cried. "I love you."

And then I saw his face.

He pushed his fingers through his hair, the way he does when he's really stressed. "I love you too." His voice was so quiet I had to strain to hear him. "But not - not in that way. I - I think we both gave in to pressure from other people. Like I said, I love you, Katie. I always will. Just -" I saw him swallow. Hard. Then he finally released his death grip on the steering wheel and bent his head as he scratched at a mark on his jeans. "Just not in that way. Not in the way you deserve to be loved. I'm sorry."

I could hear the drone of a tractor in the distance. I could hear Mrs Chinnery's TV. I could hear the dull thud of my own heart.

"Is - is there someone else?" I forced myself to ask, even though I didn't want to hear the answer.

He shook his head.

"Will. Look at me. Is there someone else?"

"No."

Then I saw it in his eyes. In the way he'd hesitated. In the flush on his cheeks. I've known him for too long. I could always tell when Will was lying and he was lying now.

There was someone else. *Will. Had. Someone. Else.*

I sat there, stunned, as I tried to work out what to say or do

149

next. Wondering whether to thump him hard or just walk away. Or maybe both.

But I can act every bit as well as Cordelia when I have to.

"Well," I said lightly. "It's just as well we found out now before Mum bought the meringue dress and cartwheel hat, isn't it? And, like you said, Will, it would never have worked out between us. I'll make sure you get your mum's ring back. It wouldn't be right to hang on to it."

I clambered out of the Land Rover and walked across the road with my head held high. I could see Gran K hovering around in the kitchen but went straight upstairs to the sanctuary of the bathroom and closed the door quietly behind me.

Then I took my clothes off and jumped in the shower. Only when the water cascaded over me, did I give in and let the tears go.

I would have stayed there until the water went cold and my skin turned to the texture of a prune had my phone not started ringing.

I jumped out of the shower and snatched it up, my heart pounding.

It was Will. It had to be him. Phoning to say he'd been winding me up. That he hadn't really meant it and that he'd see me as usual tonight.

But it wasn't. It was a number I didn't recognise.

"Oh, hi," a woman's voice said. "This is Anna Fairweather. I understand you've been trying to get hold of me."

Chapter Twenty-Two

I told Anna what little I knew about Rob's arrest and how he'd been staying in Suzanne's flat above the gallery and she agreed to come straight away. Then I dressed, tried to cover the worst of my puffy eyes with makeup and went downstairs.

"Do you want some lunch, love?" Mum asked.

I shook my head. I wasn't sure I ever wanted to eat again. And certainly not whatever it was she was cooking which looked as unappetising as it smelled.

"Your grandmother's gone out," she said. "Meeting someone for lunch. She didn't say who or where. Only that they're then going on to a meeting of the Floral Arts Society where, she says, they're going to shake things up." She sighed. "I do hope she isn't going to make trouble. You know what she's like."

I did indeed. I nodded wearily.

"But I thought that would give us chance to sit down and have a chat. About the wedding."

I grabbed my coat and avoided looking at her.

"Sorry. I've still got the dogs to walk and I want to go via the pub. Norina's in a state. Her niece didn't come home last night. I'd like to go and see if she's turned up yet."

Mum put the lid on the saucepan and turned off the heat. "Poor Norina. What a worry. She came in here the other day, you know, asking about a job."

"Do you mean Rhianna? Black hair, tattoos and nose rings?"

"Actually, I quite liked her. Well spoken. Polite."

"Are you sure we're talking about the same girl?"

"Well, there aren't too many young girls with black hair, nose rings and a welsh accent around here, are there?"

"She was asking about a job? Here in the salon?"

Mum nodded. "I said I'd have a think about it and a talk with her aunt. But, if as it seems, Sandra won't be coming back…"

"But Rhianna's -" I stopped. I'd been going to say that even Norina admitted she was a pain in the neck most of the time.

But the girl was missing. Who knew what had happened to her? I was now pretty sure Dylan had been telling the truth when he said he'd dropped her off around the corner from the pub at her request. And Cordelia said she'd seen Dylan.

But had she also seen Rhianna? I wished I'd got to see inside the barn. But hadn't Mum just said Gran K was going to a Floral Arts meeting after lunch? Cordelia would surely be there. Maybe that would be the time to hop over the padlocked gate and check out the barn. Just to put my mind at rest.

"You said she didn't come home last night," Mum said. "She's probably had a sleepover with one of her friends. You and Jules used to do it all the time, remember?"

"Yes, but you always knew where we were," I said, although I couldn't help adding silently *At least, you thought you did.*

Was Dylan covering for Rhianna, the way I'd often covered for Jules? Never the other way around, more the pity. My teenage years were total dullsville, compared to hers.

"Are you in for dinner tonight or are you working?" Mum asked.

"I'm doing the lunchtime shift, but I've got tonight off. I'm going round to Suzanne's. She's cooking *kleftiko*."

"That's nice. Will's very fond of Greek food, isn't he?"

It was no good. I was going to have to tell her. And sooner rather than later. Goodness knows how far her wedding plans would go if I didn't. She'd have chosen her cartwheel hat and tracked down the 'perfect' mother of the bride dress complete with matching shoes and handbag by 5 o'clock otherwise.

"Will won't be there." I dragged the words out, figuring I might as well get used to saying them. "There's been a change of plan. We - we decided - the engagement's off. That we - that it wasn't going to work and we'd just got carried away. By - by everything."

152

Her eyes filled with tears. I thought she was going to go on about all her plans and how she and Sally had schemed and dreamed of this over our cradles.

Instead, she put her arms around me. "Oh, love," she whispered. "I'm so, so sorry, but it's best you find out now than after the wedding, isn't it?"

"You mean, you don't mind? The big wedding and everything?"

She shook her head. "Of course not. I only want what makes you happy. And if Will doesn't do that, then so be it. And I've been thinking about what my mother said - about how you should get out there and spread your wings. And, yes, she didn't put it quite the way I'd have done, but she had a point. It set me thinking. And maybe it's set you thinking as well? You worked so hard for your degree. You deserve the chance to do something with it."

"I had the chance, remember? I blew it."

"That was just bad luck. There are other jobs out there for you. But maybe not around here." She bit her lip. "Oh, poor Will. How did he take it?"

Poor Will? For now, I let her believe it was me who'd dumped him instead of the other way round. I promised myself I'd tell her the truth when I could do so without bursting into tears.

I called in the pub on my way to collect the dogs in the hope that Rhianna would have turned up.

But she hadn't. Norina was going to give it another couple of hours before going to the police.

As I rang Elsie's doorbell, Prescott set off a volley of shrill barking that made my ears ring. I asked Elsie how she put up with the noise, but she said she was used to it and hardly noticed it anymore.

"Lucky you." I reached for Prescott's harness and we began our usual 'game' where I try to put it on him while he dances out of reach. "Elsie, there's something I think you ought to know. It's about Cordelia."

Elsie snorted. "That woman!"

"You do know she was in the pub last night, cosying up to Gerald Crabshaw, don't you?"

Elsie's next snort was even louder. "That man!"

"It sounded like they were plotting something. About the village hall. Your name was mentioned. And I think they're trying to fix up a committee meeting without telling you."

"But they can't do that," Elsie said, with a smug smile. "I've got all the keys to the hall. They wouldn't be able to get in without me letting them in."

I decided this was maybe not the time to tell her that there was, indeed, another key to the hall, which was currently in Gerald Crabshaw's possession.

"It sounded like they're planning on holding it somewhere else. Cordelia's house was mentioned."

Elsie scowled. "I tell you, Katie, that woman is ruthless. She'll stop at nothing to get what she wants. Cosying up to Gerald Crabshaw, was she? So much for her being heartbroken over the poor vicar, wouldn't you say?"

"Different people show their grief in different ways, Elsie," I managed to say between breaths as I chased Prescott around the room and finally cornered him over by Elsie's enormous TV that took up one half of the wall.

Elsie sniffed. "What the vicar saw in her, I'll never know."

"You really think he was keen on her?" I said. "Because they seem a very unlikely couple."

"So do you and Will Manning," she said snippily. "There's no telling, is there, when it comes to matters of the heart."

I muttered something as I wrestled Prescott into his harness, glad that Elsie couldn't see my face as I bent over her little dog. Her sharp eyes missed nothing.

"And the way she leaves those posters around. Do this, do that. I tell you, she really gets my goat."

"Oh really? Which goat would that be?"

"You know well enough what I mean, young lady, so don't go getting clever with me. I meant she gets on my nerves. You should have seen her at the church fundraising committee meeting. Talking about that silly teddy bear absent. It was all her idea, you know."

The original idea had, in fact, come from my friend Jules but I knew better than to contradict Elsie. "Teddy bear absent? Do you mean abseil?"

"That's what I said, didn't I? When she first came up with the idea, I thought the vicar would never go for it, him being so sensible and serious." She frowned. "Well, he was usually. But not that day. It's stuck in my mind because he actually made a joke, which was very out of character. I'm not sure I can remember ever hearing him laugh before, least of all crack a joke. Not that it was a very funny one, mind you. At least I didn't think so. But everyone else laughed. And she wrote it down. For her writer's notebook, she said. I think he was quite embarrassed by that, making out he was some kind of comedian. Give me Des O'Connor any day. Now there was a funny man. No smut or swearing. And he could sing, too. They don't make comedians like him anymore."

"So, what was the joke? The vicar's, I mean. Not Des O'Connor's," I added quickly before she could get side-tracked again.

Elsie shook her head. "No idea. Like I said, it wasn't even funny. He was saying how he'd have to arrange a meeting with the health and safety man from the council before the absent could go ahead. And she asked if she could be there. He looked surprised and asked her why she'd want to do that. 'It's for my murder', she said. Well, that got everyone's attention, as you can imagine. Then she said she had this idea for a murder mystery play where someone ended up being pushed off the church tower."

"Have you told the police this, Elsie?" I asked.

"Why would I? Look, I can't stand the woman. But I can tell you now, there's no way she'd have done it. Not when there was a chance of her becoming the next Mrs Fairweather."

"And yet, last night in the pub she was really playing up to Gerald Crabshaw. Not exactly playing the grieving lover."

"And now we know why, don't we?" Elsie said. "She was using her feminine charm to get Gerald on her side. The pair of them are scheming to get me off the village hall committee.

They're plotting a coop, you'll see."

"So, who do you think did murder the vicar then?" I asked.

"Hah! Not as clever as you think you are, girlie, are you?"

I sighed. "No, I don't think I'm clever at all. But I think you are." A little bit of flattery went a long way with Elsie. "You see things. And hear things."

"For starters, I hear his wife was back in the area at just the right time," Elsie said. "And as Inspector Morse will tell you, it's usually the nearest and dearest who done it. There was no love lost between the two of them, that's for sure. He never smiled at Mrs Fairweather the way he smiled at Her Ladyship. And before you try and get funny on me, I don't mean Inspector Morse."

"I wouldn't dream of it, Elsie."

"And another thing, I hear her brother has also been seen hanging around the village. And that he was carrying Olive's mother's blanket which is now in police custardy. Olive's terrified her sister's going to find out about it. Those two have been arguing about which one should have that blanket for the past twenty years."

"I'm sure they'll get it back soon. What about your son? Is he still away at his conference? You were going to ask him about Cordelia's first husband."

"I had a quick chat. He was in a rush, as always. He said as far as he could remember there was some sort of scandal. To do with money. His company hushed it up though and nothing ever came of it. And then he was killed in a car crash and that was that. He left her a wealthy widow, though, didn't he? So, it all turned out quite nicely for Her Ladyship. Anyway, if you're going to walk that dog of mine, you'd best be going. He's getting impatient. And there's wrestling on the TV in ten minutes."

The more I learned about the Reverend Lionel Fairweather, the more confusing the picture was becoming. On the one hand was the man I knew, or, rather, thought I knew. Slightly vague, very serious, wrote deadly dull sermons and had a terrible singing voice.

Then was the side of his character that Olive witnessed that day in the church, the unfeeling bully who'd reduced his poor wife to tears. Mrs Denby's version was a man who was nothing but a living saint. While Rob's was of someone who falsely accused him and got him sent back to jail to get him out of the way.

And now this the most recent one was the picture of a man falling for Cordelia's charms and cracking jokes.

Would Anna Fairweather be able to paint a clearer picture of the man, I wondered? Somehow, I doubted it.

I walked the dogs around the lane past Cordelia's barn but was unable to investigate as there was no way Rosie the Labrador would get under the gate. Nor, I suspected, would Finbar. And Prescott would make enough noise to alert the entire village if I left the three of them tied to the gate post. But from what I could see by balancing on the top rung of the gate, it looked as if Cordelia was right and that a thick cloak of brambles encircled the barn, like Sleeping Beauty's castle.

"Where's Prince Charming when I need him?" I muttered, then wished I hadn't as my thoughts turned to Will. And how on earth was I going to carry on without him?

I pushed the thought away and went back to thinking about the barn. If Gran K was going to a meeting of the Floral Arts Society this afternoon, that would mean Cordelia would also be there. The meetings usually took all afternoon. Plenty of time, then, to check out the barn when she was out and I was dog-less.

The walk completed, I dropped Rosie and Prescott off and checked my watch. I'd left Finbar until last hoping I'd have time for a cup of Suzanne's coffee before going home to change out of my dog walking clothes and into my pub clothes.

"I haven't heard anything from Rob," Suzanne said. "But they can't keep him much longer, can they?"

"Not unless they charge him. Have you thought about what to do about that teddy bear and the note?"

She worried at the slender gold chain around her neck. "I don't know. I don't want to make things any worse for him. Or for his sister," she added as she handed me a mug of coffee.

"Thanks. I really need that this morning," I said. "It's been... one of those days."

One way of putting it, I suppose. It was certainly up there with one of the worst. Once again, I pushed the thought of Will firmly away. I'd think about that later, I told myself in true Scarlett O'Hara fashion.

In the meantime, there was the mystery of Rhianna's disappearance, the forthcoming re-appearance of Anna Fairweather - and, of course, the teddy bear. More than enough to keep my mind off Will. Hopefully.

"Anna's on her way here," I told Suzanne.

"You've spoken to her? Where was she?"

"Back at that homeless hostel in London, I think. Fiona Crabshaw gave me the number of the hostel, which, it turns out is run by Ben Chappell's sister."

"You mean, Mr Chappell, the physics teacher?"

"I mean, Mr Chappell, the *ex*-physics teacher. According to Elsie he left his job at St Philomena's, or St Philadelphia's as she insists on calling it not long after Anna left the village. Which is why everyone assumed they'd gone off together."

"Where is she staying? I've got a spare room, she's welcome to that. I always liked Mrs Fairweather. She was very kind to me when I was at school."

"She's planning on staying with Fiona Crabshaw," I said, taking a sip of coffee. "Wow, Suzanne, you do make a brilliant cup of coffee. Or rather, your machine does. You could -"

I broke off suddenly and rushed to the window. On the other side of the road, sauntering along with not a care in the world, was Rhianna.

Chapter Twenty-Three

I left my coffee and rushed outside.

"Rhianna?" I called after her.

She turned round. Her eyes looked heavy, the black lines around them had smudged into real panda eyes and her long hair was tangled. She looked like she'd just crawled out of bed.

"Where've you been? Your aunt's been going out of her mind with worry."

"What's it to you?"

"You didn't come home last night. Where were you?"

She stared at me as if debating whether or not to answer. Finally, she gave the slow satisfied smile of a cat who'd not only got the cream but the champagne and chocolates as well. "If you must know, I was with Dylan. You know, the tall, thin one who really fancies me. You jealous?"

"No you weren't. I spoke to Dylan this morning. I didn't tell your aunt this because I didn't want to worry her unnecessarily. Dylan said he dropped you off in the village, just around the corner from the pub, in the early hours of the morning."

"Then he's lying." Her dismissive toss of the head set her nose rings jingling. "Probably trying to protect my reputation, or more like it, trying to spare himself getting it hot and holy from Aunty Nora."

"He wasn't lying." I was happy to see a flush stain her unusually pale cheeks. "You were seen."

"Then whoever it was, was mistaken."

"I don't think so. She even described Dylan's car. And what you were wearing. What you're still wearing now in fact."

Of course Cordelia had done none of those things, apart from mentioning the car. But Rhianna didn't need to know that.

159

She looked startled. "But she said -" she broke off and nibbled at the flaking black varnish on her thumbnail. "Who was it?"

"I can't tell you that. So, come on. No more lies. Where were you last night?"

"I told you, I was with Dylan. His mum and dad were away so we…" She grinned and shrugged. "We made the most of it. You know how it is. Or perhaps you don't? Your love life isn't exactly going smoothly from what I hear."

I could see she was trying to deflect my questions, but I refused to rise to the bait. "I don't think you were with Dylan."

"I don't care what you think. But, for your information, we'd had a few words and I said he could drive me home. But after he dropped me off, I had second thoughts, realised I'd been a bit of a cow and phoned him to ask him to come back and get me. Which is what he did. And we had a very nice time of it making up, if you know what I mean. So you see, Dylan was telling you the truth, just not the whole truth. Satisfied? Now, if you'll excuse me, I need a shower and a change of clothes. You working this lunch time?"

"Yes."

"Good. I think I'm going to catch up on some much-needed sleep."

Only when I got to the pub ready for the lunchtime shift, Rhianna was not catching up on her sleep. She wasn't behind the bar either. Instead, Norina had her working in the kitchen.

"Where I can keep an eye on her," she told me as she came into the bar to get some beer for her batter. "She told me she stayed at a girlfriend's house, that they got watching something on Netflix and lost track of the time. And she thinks I was born yesterday and am going to swallow that one. Well, she can spend the lunch session prepping the veg and then washing up. The young lad who usually does it has hurt his hand and can't come in, so that's worked out pretty well, I'd say. Don't you think?"

It might have worked well for Norina, but Rhianna was not happy and made that very apparent by banging and crashing around. Gino and I exchanged smiles and kept out of her way as much as possible.

At the end of the shift, Norina went upstairs as she usually does as soon as she's finished cooking and that day, a Saturday, she was very quick to say that the kitchen was closed.

Wales was playing Italy in the Six Nations Rugby that afternoon and Norina was a mega rugby fan. Gino, not so much and, good Italian though he was, he was always relieved if Wales beat Italy. It was, he reckoned, 'less trouble all round.'

"Want a coke?" I asked Rhianna as she came into the now empty bar.

"No thanks," she said shortly. "Unless you've got a Bacardi to go in it. But then again, I've got a bomber of a headache. I'm actually feeling quite rough. I've had it in there."

"Have you cleared up in the kitchen?" I asked, surprised that she'd got through it so quickly.

She shook her head.

"Don't you think you should?"

She shook her head again. Then winced as if doing so caused her pain.

"Your aunt's not going to be very pleased," I said.

"I don't care," Rhianna snapped. "She can keep her rubbish job. I hate it. You wait. After tomorrow I'll have a proper job. I won't need this anymore."

"Doing what?" I asked.

A sly look crept over her pale face. "Wouldn't you like to know, Miss Marple," she sneered. "But someone out there thinks I'm good for something better than peeling carrots and washing greasy dishes. If it all goes to plan tomorrow, I'll be out of here faster than a rat out of a drainpipe."

I don't know why I did it. Well, yes, I did really. I didn't want to go home and be quizzed by my mother about me and Will. Or even worse, by my grandmother.

I wasn't clearing up in the kitchen as a favour to Rhianna. It just suited me to be on my own, doing something as mindless as unloading then reloading the dishwasher. From the groans and yells coming from upstairs, it sounded like Wales was not having the best of days at the office and I was really glad I wouldn't be working tonight as Norina was a very poor loser when it came to her national team.

At last, when every surface that could be wiped had been, there was no reason for me to delay any longer. The dogs had all been walked. And now that Rhianna was back there was no point going to check out Cordelia's barn. Nothing else to do but go home. And think. The last thing in the world I wanted to do.

Because every time I did so, my thoughts went back to Will.

But as I left the pub, I saw a taxi come down the road and stop outside Suzanne's. Rob got out and went towards the front door. I caught up with him on the doorstep.

"They let you go then?" I said.

"Well, put it this way, I didn't tie a load of sheets together and climb out the window or dig a tunnel to escape," he said snippily. But then he gave a quick apologetic smile. "Sorry, didn't mean it to sound as snarky as it did. It was a long night and I didn't get much sleep. Yes, they let me go but they did say they'd probably need to speak to me again. I honestly think they're going round in circles."

At that moment, the front door opened and Suzanne ushered us both in.

"Rob. You look terrible. Have you eaten?" she asked anxiously.

"Well, that's made me feel a whole lot better," he said. "And thanks, but I'm not hungry. Cup of coffee would hit the spot though."

While Suzanne bustled around setting the coffee machine off on a cycle that seemed to take longer than my mum's washing machine I crossed to the table and picked up the plastic bag containing the old teddy bear.

Rob stiffened as I held it up. "Where did you get that?"

"Archie found it," Suzanne said. "He came up with me when I went to change your bed and scrabbled underneath. Before I could stop him, he'd pulled out your rucksack and came out with this."

"So where did you get it?" I asked him. "Only I heard there was something similar to this near Lionel Fairweather's body. But when the police got there, it had disappeared. The police thought, as did I, that the original witness had been mistaken. But I think it was you. You took it, didn't you?"

His shoulders sagged. "Yes." His voice was scarcely above a whisper.

"But why? Did you recognise it? Was that it?"

"No. It was - I don't know why I did it. It was the shock, finding him like that. And - and I wasn't well." He looked across at Suzanne. "You saw the state I was in when I collapsed on your doorstep. I wasn't thinking straight."

"Did you tell the police what you'd found?" I asked.

"They didn't ask."

"But Rob," I said. "When the forensics come back, they'll find traces of you. If you touched the body."

"But I didn't. The bear was lying several feet away, I swear. I told you the truth when I said as soon as I saw that he was dead, I legged it. I'm not proud of myself for that."

At that moment, the doorbell rang, setting both dogs off. Finbar gave his usual deep throated woof, but Archie suddenly went mad and I knew before Suzanne opened the door who'd be standing there.

"Hello, Suzanne," Anna said. "I don't know if you remember me but - oh Archie." She bent down and hugged the excited dog who'd been winding himself around her legs in a bid to get her attention. "Archie, it's so good to see you again, little man."

After a short while, she stood up and brushed herself off. Archie continued to dance around her in a frenzy of excitement.

"Come along in," Suzanne said. "Come on, Archie. Let her in."

"I've missed him so much," Anna began then froze as, for the first time, she saw her brother who'd stood up as she came in, his face tense, shoulders rigid.

"Rob?" Her face creased with concern. "How are you? You

look ... awful."

"Well, thanks." His voice was icy. "That's what six months in prison does for you."

She flinched as if he'd struck her. "When did you get out?"

"Look," Suzanne said. "You two probably need some privacy. Here's your coffee, Rob. Why don't you both go into the sitting room and I'll bring you in a coffee, Anna. Or something stronger if you'd prefer?"

"No need," Rob said. "I've nothing to say to my sister that can't be said in front of you both."

"Anna?" Suzanne asked.

"I'm fine with that," she said, her hand never straying from Archie's head.

"I didn't steal that money, you know," Rob said. "I don't know who did, but it wasn't me. I wondered at one time if it was Lionel. To get rid of me. Certainly, he hated me enough to want me out of the way."

"He wouldn't have done that. But he was very protective of me. Overprotective," Anna said. "He believed the stress of having you around, worrying about you all the time, was making me ill. It wasn't that, of course. I loved having you nearby. It was - I was pregnant and nothing was going right. I felt ill from day one and eventually I miscarried. I hardly remember a thing from that time. Everything was such a haze. I couldn't eat. I couldn't sleep. I couldn't function. Goodness knows what I'd have done without Mrs Denby. She was so kind to me."

Rob stared down at his coffee cup without saying a word.

Anna swallowed and went on. "That was why I wasn't around for you. I was out of it most of the time. By the time I recovered, you'd gone. They told me at first that you'd left of your own accord. It wasn't until much later I found out what had really happened to you. I tried to contact you, but you refused to see me. I wrote to you though."

He scowled at her. "I didn't bother to read them. Chucked them in the bin. Just like you chucked away that picture I drew for you when we were kids."

She stared at him blankly. "What are you talking about?"

164

He turned to me. "Do you still have it?" he asked.

I nodded and handed it to him. As I did so, Anna gasped.

"Where did you find that?" she asked. "I've been looking for it everywhere."

"Archie found it in the bushes by the front door of the vicarage. The day you nearly ran us down."

She flushed. "I'm sorry about that. It must have fallen off the keyring when I got out of the car to speak to Mrs Denby. I was so upset when I realised I'd lost it." She turned to Rob. "I would never have thrown it away. It means the world to me. As do you." She took a step towards him. "I've come to take you home, Rob."

"Home?" His head snapped up and he moved away from her. "Do you mean Bay View? Have you seen the state of it? Yes, of course you have. I saw you there, didn't I? Only you didn't hang around long enough for me to have a go at you. To ask you what the hell you'd been doing to let it get into that state? The place our mother worked so hard for. Were you waiting for the place to be condemned so you could sell the land to a developer? How could you?"

"You were at Bay View? When?"

He shoved his hand through his hair. "I don't know now. A few days ago. I'm not even sure what day of the week it is anymore. But it was just before I came here. In fact, you were the reason I came, even though I vowed I'd never set foot in the place again."

"Was it you who broke the toilet window?" she asked.

"Why? Are you going to send me the bill?"

"Of course not." Her voice was so full of distress that Archie gave a little whimper and pushed himself closer into her legs. "The day you saw me, it was Thursday by the way, was the first time I'd seen the house in years. Lionel always said he'd look after it for me, that everything was fine and well maintained. I don't know why he let it go like that. Just to hurt me, I suppose. To destroy what was mine, like he did with everything else."

"Except Archie," I said softly.

"Except Archie. I imagine even he couldn't bring himself to

do something so awful to such a sweet natured dog."

"What made you go to Stargate that day, of all days?" Rob asked.

Anna looked across at Suzanne. "Could I change my mind and have that coffee now, please?" she asked. Then turned back to face her brother. "All the while I was in London, I'd managed to push Much Winchmoor and everything about it out of my mind. I worked in a homeless hostel and it was hard physical work, left me no time to think. But then, last week, we had a young man come in. He looked a bit like you. He was in a bad way. Been living on the streets and not looking after himself."

"What happened to him?" Suzanne asked as she handed Anna the coffee and put a plate of biscuits on the table in front of them.

"He died. And that was my wake-up moment. I didn't want that to happen to Rob and I decided then and there to go down to Stargate, give the tenants notice to quit and then start to make a home there." She looked steadily at her brother. "For you and me."

"But when I got there, Andrew Hunter, the agent who used to look after the property for us, told me that Lionel had sacked him ages ago, said he would see to the letting himself. But Andrew said he checked up on it from time to time as he'd been friends with Dad and was shocked when he saw the state of the place a couple of months ago. He'd informed Lionel who said it wasn't his problem anymore and that he was not going to spend any more money on the place. But even with Andrew's warning, I wasn't prepared for what I saw."

"Any more than I was," Rob muttered. But she carried on as if she hadn't heard him. She wrapped her hands around the coffee cup, as if she was cold.

"I was that angry with Lionel, I could have -" She stopped.

"Killed him?" I said quietly.

"No. But I wanted to hurt him. As he'd hurt me. That's why I came back to Much Winchmoor. To have a go at him. To ask him what the hell was going on. It's like he was deliberately setting out to destroy everything that had ever belonged to me."

I heard Rob's sharp intake of breath.

I picked up the plastic bag. "Anna, have you ever seen this before?"

She gasped and what little colour she had drained from her face. "Where did you find this?"

"It was found next to Lionel's body," I said. "By Rob."

She looked puzzled. "But I don't understand. What's it doing here, Rob? Why didn't you hand it in to the police?"

He shook his head and looked down at his hands, tightly clasped on the table in front of him.

"He was in the shed in the churchyard," I said when it looked as if he wasn't going to answer. "He slept there, hoping to see you when you turned up for your morning music practice. He didn't know that you no longer lived at the vicarage. Isn't that right, Rob?"

He still didn't answer.

"So, he heard Lionel fall. And then, as he was about to go and see what was going on, he heard footsteps. A man's footsteps. He assumed that whoever they belonged to had gone for help. That's what you told us, isn't it, Rob?"

Again he nodded.

"Only that wasn't quite true, was it? It wasn't a man's footsteps you heard but a woman's. And when you saw the old teddy bear lying there, you thought-"

I didn't need to say anymore. Anna had obviously realised the significance of it.

"You thought it was me," she whispered. "You thought I'd killed Lionel. How could you think I'd do such a dreadful thing?"

He continued to look down at his hands. "Good people do bad things. That's one thing prison taught me."

"But there was no way I could have killed him," Anna said. "Yes, I was in Much Winchmoor that morning but at the time he was killed, I was standing by the side of the road, waiting for someone to help me with my car. The police told me yesterday that the man who stopped to help had come forward to give me an alibi."

"But what made you so sure that the vicar was murdered

and not just the unfortunate victim of a horrible accident, Rob?" I asked. "Did you find anything else by the body?"

He hesitated. "Like what?"

"Like, maybe, a note?"

He raised his head at last and nodded slowly. "It was fixed to the bear. Only it's not there now. But I didn't take it."

"No. I did," Suzanne said. "I took it out of Archie's mouth. I'm afraid it's a bit crumpled and soggy."

She handed it to me. A bright pink post-it note. It was indeed crumpled and the purple ink had run in places but it was still readable. I straightened it out and looked at down the words.

"*Abseiling*," Anna read, "*is only the second fastest way down a church tower.* What does that mean?"

"It means someone wanted to make absolutely sure the police knew Mr Fairweather was murdered and not the victim of a horrible accident. Or indeed, suicide," I said.

Suzanne and Anna looked horrified. Rob looked confused.

"Why did you take the bear, Rob?" Anna asked softly. "Why didn't you leave it there for the police to find? It was evidence."

"Because I recognised it. It was your old bear that always used to be on your bed when we were growing up. I was trying to protect you. The note was stuck to the bear. It didn't make any sense to me. But I took it anyway."

"You took such a risk for me. Oh Rob." Anna gave a small cry, pushed her chair back, and the next moment she and Rob were wrapped in each other's arms.

Suzanne and I looked at each other, picked up our coffees and went into the other room to give them some space.

Chapter Twenty-Four

Suzanne was very keen for me to stay and eat with them that evening, as we'd originally planned, but I declined. I wasn't that hungry. I wasn't feeling terribly sociable either.

Besides, something was niggling away at the back of my mind about that note. I'd seen something similar recently. But where?

Rob and Anna, now completely reconciled, were full of plans for the future, of bringing Bay View back to the house they used to know and love. And Suzanne and Anna were having a fun time reminiscing about the old school days.

The feeling of gloom that had hung over the house had lifted, and Suzanne's comfortable kitchen was filled with laughter. It was also filled with the mouth-watering aroma of slow cooking lamb. And it was breaking my heart.

The subtle combination of lemon, garlic and oregano took me right back to my last birthday when Will had surprised me by taking me to this lovely Greek restaurant in Dintscombe where we'd both fallen in love with the delicious food and were making plans for a trip to one of the Greek islands as soon as our finances would permit.

I made my excuses and left. As I walked past the pub, the lights were on and I could hear bursts of laughter coming from inside.

Usually, on a Saturday night, even if I was working, Will would come down. He'd sit on the bar stool in the corner and chat to me. He'd even help out if we were busy. And he always walked me home.

But that evening I was alone as I walked on, past the pub, past the seat where we often used to stop, if it was a clear night, to look up at the stars. Past, too, the pond, where Will had once stood in the middle, in his boxer shorts, with a rose between his teeth and asked me to marry him.

I couldn't believe we'd never do that again. Not the standing in the middle of the pond bit, although he did look pretty hot in his boxer shorts. But the rest of it.

I couldn't imagine a life that didn't have Will in it.

I took out my phone. *Should I ring him*, I thought. *Should I ask him if he'd changed his mind? If he'd just said that to frighten me?*

But then I remembered the look in his eyes when I'd asked him if there was someone else. Saw that little sideways glance that he always did when he was trying to hide something.

I put my phone away. There was no point.

When I got home, I pleaded a headache, which was nothing but the truth and said that I thought I was coming down with a cold, which was not the truth. But it was enough to have Gran K shooing me away as if I'd just announced I had the plague.

"You know what I'm like with my chest," she said. "I can't afford to take chances."

But I had no intention of sitting in with her and Mum and Dad, watching old reruns of Family Fortunes, so I took myself up to my room and tried to read a book. Tried, too, not to think about what Will and I were doing at the same time last week.

I failed at both the reading and the not thinking about Will and in the end gave up before very quietly crying myself to sleep.

"Well, that's it. I've had it with that girl," Norina exclaimed as I walked into the pub next morning ready for my lunchtime shift. "She knows Sunday lunch is our busiest time and promised faithfully she'd be back in good time. But of course, she's not. I've had enough, Katie, and that's a fact. Loan or no loan, that girl's on the first train back to Pontypridd in the morning"

I didn't think now was the time to tell her that the last train to leave Much Winchmoor did so in 1962 and even then, it went to Evercreech Junction and not Pontypridd. But Norina didn't seem to be in the mood for my jokes that morning, if indeed she ever was. Not that I was in the mood for jokes either. But that's what I do when I'm stressed.

"Did she say where she was going?" I asked. "Or who she was meeting?"

"No. Just that it was very important, but she'd be back in good time to make up for letting us down yesterday. Said she felt bad about it and wanted to put things right. Little madam. And I believed her too. I'll bet she's with that boy again."

"Do you want me to ask him?"

"Would you? Only I've got to get back in the kitchen. My roast potatoes are at a critical stage. But let me know what he says, won't you? And if she is with him, you tell her to get back here right now or not bother coming back at all."

Still grumbling, she went back into the kitchen while I called up Dylan's number. "Dylan? It's Kat here," I said.

"Who?" Once again, he sounded like he'd just woken up.

"Kat. From Much Winchmoor. I phoned yesterday about Rhianna. Is she there please?"

"What? No. No, she's not."

"Are you sure?"

"Yeah. Course I am. Honest, she's not here. I haven't seen her since…"

"Since you dropped her off in Much Winchmoor in the early hours of yesterday morning. You didn't go back for her, did you?"

There was a long silence.

"Dylan, please. I need you to tell me the truth. Something's going on here that doesn't feel right to me. It could be really important."

He sighed. "Ok, you're right. She didn't call and ask me to come back for her."

"So why did you say she did?"

"Because she asked me to."

"Did she say why?"

"No."

"Did she say where she spent the night instead? Or with whom?"

"No. Only that it was someone her aunt wouldn't approve of. And when I started getting huffy and asking if she was with

171

another guy, she said it was nothing like that and she'd explain everything when she saw me. She can be very persuasive, can Rhianna," he added.

"I can imagine." My bad feeling began to get worse. The only person who admitted seeing Rhianna, who was out and about at the time she got back to the village after Dylan dropped her off, was Cordelia. And Cordelia had been acting very strangely when I went to see her yesterday. Why wouldn't she let me see the barn? What was she hiding?

Suddenly I remembered where I'd seen a bright pink post-it note similar to the one attached to the teddy bear. Or 'posters' as Elsie called them. Cordelia sprinkled them around like confetti. There was one in my notebook with her mobile number scrawled on it in her distinctive, purple-inked writing.

And there'd been another one stuck to the calendar in the vicarage kitchen. Why on earth hadn't picked up on it before?

I checked my watch. I had enough time before the pub was due to open. I told Norina that Dylan hadn't seen Rhianna but that I had an idea where she might be.

As I left the pub, Liam was walking across the pub car park. He scowled as he saw me. "Have you seen Rhianna?" he asked.

That seemed to be the question on everyone's lips. "No. Her aunt was asking the same question. Was it you she sloped off to meet this morning?"

"We were supposed to have met half an hour ago. In the churchyard. Said she had something to show me that would, as she put it, blow my mind. Only she wasn't there. I waited for a while but it's freezing cold, so I came round to see where the hell she's got to."

"Join the queue. According to Norina, she left ages ago. Said she'd be back in time to help with the lunchtime service. Only, of course, she isn't." I glanced at my watch. It was quarter to twelve. "What time did she arrange to meet you?"

"Quarter past eleven."

"But Norina said she left the pub just after ten thirty. So, if it wasn't you she was going to see..."

Then it was whoever she saw on Friday night/Saturday morning.

"I think I know where she might be," I said. "Are you coming?"

"Do we need my car?"

"No. Rhianna is in this village. I'm pretty sure of that." Without waiting for him, I hurried off.

"So where are we headed?" he asked as he caught up.

"To the home of our local celebrity. Mrs Cordelia Hilperton-Jones."

The sound of the heavy iron knocker on Cordelia's front door (the only bit of the original house to have survived her over enthusiastic updating) reverberated like distant thunder. But there was no yap from Princess Persephone. And if the dog wasn't at home, then it was one hundred per cent certain Cordelia wasn't either. Which suited me very well.

"Follow me," I said to Liam as I pushed open the gate that led into the back garden.

"Where are you going? You surely wouldn't be thinking of going in for a bit of breaking and entering, would you now?"

"Of course not. Although it wouldn't hurt to take a peek through the windows as we go past, would it?"

"And what would you be expecting to find?"

Good question. But I couldn't shake that uneasy feeling. "Not what. *Who*."

He gave a shout of laughter. "You don't surely mean Rhianna? What? You think Cordelia Hilperton-Jones has kidnapped her?"

"Why not? But I'm pretty sure she's not in the house." I peered through the kitchen window and then the study window but as expected the place was empty. Then I turned and picked my way across piles of builders' rubble towards the old barn. The trench had now been filled in, but it was still an obstacle course.

"For the love of Michael," Liam said, then cursed as he tripped over a pile of breeze blocks. "This place is a death trap."

A shiver crawled down my spine. "I hope not. I really, really hope not. But I think Cordelia's hiding something, or someone, in that barn. The first time I came here, she couldn't stop talking about it, wouldn't let me go until I'd pored over every page of the plans and was quite put out that she couldn't show me inside the barn because of the way the builders had left it. And yet, when I was here yesterday, she was very cagey. Wouldn't let me get anywhere near the place. So, while the cat's away, this Kat will play. You can come with me. Or you can stay there and keep a look out. It's up to you. I want to see what's in that barn that she didn't want me to see."

"I'll come," he muttered. "But I think all you're going to find in there's nothing but more of this damn rubbish. What sort of builders leave a place like this? It's a health and safety hazard, that's what it is. Now there's a good story you could follow up on. Make sure you take plenty of pictures. That will get Cordelia on side."

"I thought I was sacked?"

"Yes, well, I was maybe being a bit hasty. But you do try my patience some time, Kat Latcham, so you do. Anyway, it might be worth checking it out. Who are the builders, do you know?"

"A load of cowboys, according to Dylan's boss. The Dunning Brothers."

He lifted one eyebrow. "Is it now? Now that could well be very interesting. Come on then. What are we waiting for? Let's have a peek inside, shall we?"

We picked our way across the uneven deeply rutted wreckage that was once a well-tended and much loved garden. But before we reached the barn door, an angry voice boomed out behind us.

"What on earth do you think you are doing?"

At the same time, Princess Persephone flew towards us, teeth bared.

"Good morning, Cordelia," I said, keeping my eyes firmly on Princess Persephone who was still snarling but thankfully had stopped about two feet away from us. "You know Liam,

174

don't you? He's the editor of the Dintscombe Chronicle, and I was just telling him about the wonderful plans you and Suzanne have for the Winchmoor Festival of the Arts and how the barn will be the centrepiece of the entire festival. He said he'd love to see it, and that he thought your plan to turn the barn into a theatre would make a wonderful story. Maybe even a whole series, he says. With plenty of free advertising thrown in for good measure. Isn't that right, Liam?"

"Something like that," he muttered, giving me a glare.

"So, you thought you'd come and check it out for yourselves, did you?" Cordelia's voice was icy. "Throwing in a spot of trespassing for good measure."

"Well, I knocked on your door and when you didn't answer we thought we'd come and see if you were around the back somewhere." I beamed at her. "And here you are. We might as well see it now we're here, don't you think? Especially now it's a bit easier to access."

"No, you can't!" Her expression was so fierce I took a step back, glad that Liam was beside me.

"And why would that be?" I asked. "What is in that barn that you don't want us to see?"

"I haven't the faintest idea what you're talking about," she said. "Now, will you please both leave, or shall I call the police?"

"That's a good idea," I said. "I'm sure they'd be quite interested to have a look in your barn, as well."

"But you can't -" she began, then stopped and shrugged her shoulders. "Very well. But don't come to me if a lump of masonry falls on your head."

Liam reached the door first then turned back to Cordelia. "Do you have a key?"

"It's not locked," she said.

"Oh yes, it is," he said, pointing at a shiny new padlock that was attached to the door.

Cordelia looked bewildered. "But I didn't put that there. And I certainly don't have a key. The builders must have done it. I'll get in touch with them and you can come back another time, ok?"

175

Liam fingered the padlock. "I could pop that open in no time." He gave her his best smile. "With your permission, of course?"

Cordelia looked as if she was about to refuse but then she shrugged and muttered something about 'nothing to see'.

And she was right. The barn, when we finally accessed it, didn't look much different from when Arthur had used it. There were a few bits of machinery in one corner and not a lot else. Certainly there was no sign of Rhianna. I should have known by the fact that she gave in so easily. I put my hand in my pocket, took out a bright pink note with vivid purple handwriting and held it out to her. "This is yours, I take it."

She glanced at it. "Of course. It's my phone number."

"You gave it to me when you came into the salon, remember?"

"Did I? Probably. But what's the problem?"

"A note was found on the vicar's body, a sick, cruel note that made it very clear the poor man had been murdered. Same paper. Same purple handwriting."

She stared at me, her face white. Liam stared at me, too. But his face was as dark as thunder. He looked as if he was about to explode when Cordelia said: "You surely don't think I put it there, do you?"

"You walk your dog in the vicinity of the churchyard every morning."

"Not anymore," she said with a shudder.

"But you were seen there on the morning of the murder," I said.

Ok, Rob didn't actually say he'd seen Cordelia, but I was pretty sure that the barking that had woken him that morning had been her little dog.

"Yes, I was there. Although I didn't actually go in the churchyard. I told the police when they came to see me that I didn't see or hear anything or anyone. I was more concerned with getting poor little Princess home and dry. I told you how she'd gone missing, didn't I? And how when I did find her, tied up to the lychgate the poor little darling was soaking wet and shaking with the cold." As she spoke, she bent down,

176

picked up her little dog, and held her close. "I took her straight home and it wasn't until several hours later that I found out about the terrible tragedy. You surely don't think I - that I –" Her voice shook. "You can't think I had anything to do with Lionel's death."

"The note will be handed to the police later this morning. I'll also give them this one so that they can compare the handwriting."

"I have no idea what you're talking about," she said while Liam rounded on me, his face darker than ever.

"You have a note? Evidence in a murder enquiry?"

"No. But I know someone who does."

"And, of course, you were going to share that piece of information with me, weren't you?" he snapped. "I've had it with you, Kat Latcham. You've played me for a fool for the last time."

Before I could point out to him that, technically, I was still not working for the Chronicle, he strode off.

"But what about Rhianna?" I called after him.

He paused. "Looks like I'm not the only one being played for a fool," he said. "That young lady is pulling your strings, only you're too gullible to see it."

He strode off, leaving me alone with Cordelia. Suddenly I didn't feel so brave any more.

Chapter Twenty-Five

"If you'll hang on a moment, there's something I want to show you both," Cordelia said.

But Liam had already gone.

"Sorry, got to go," I said brightly. "I'd better see if I can catch up with him."

"No. Don't go." The look in her eyes made me curse Liam for running out on me. "I've decided to tell you the truth. Come along in and I'll explain over a cup of coffee."

She fished in her oversized bag for her back door key, opened the door and stood aside for me to go in. One minute she was threatening me with the police, the next she was inviting me into her home. What was she up to? Did she think I had the note on me? Or was she going to force me to tell her who did have it?

I'd once allowed myself, very naively, to be trapped in a room with a murderer. I had no intention of letting it happen again.

"Some other time, eh?" I said as I all but ran out of the garden, down the road and into the High Street. I got there in time to see Liam's car disappearing round the corner.

Nice one, Liam.

Now what? I'd really messed things up this time because I'd probably given Cordelia the nod that I had something that would prove she was the murderer and that the police would soon be on to her.

So why, I wondered, had Rhianna originally wanted Liam to meet her in the churchyard? What was she going to show him that would 'blow his mind? Had she found something about the murder?

I hurried towards the churchyard. After all, I reckoned, if

Rhianna could work it out then maybe I could as well. I pushed open the lychgate then stopped dead. I thought I'd heard -

It was a cry. Shrill. Frightened. Desperate. It was Rhianna. And it was coming from the top of the church tower. Was she being kept a prisoner there? Was that why Cordelia wasn't bothered about us seeing inside the barn?

I ran into the church, wrenched open the ancient oak door to the tower, and began climbing the narrow stone steps that rose in a spiral way above me. I hesitated for just a second. The steps were worn and uneven, with only a rope as a handrail. And I hated narrow, confined spaces.

Then I thought about that cry. It hadn't been the sound of someone messing about. Or playing me for a gullible fool, as Liam had put it.

I forced myself to go on and had almost reached the small landing that led to the bell ringing chamber when I heard footsteps coming up behind me.

I looked down and saw Cordelia making her way towards me.

I'd done it again. In spite of all my best intentions, I'd found myself trapped. With a murderer.

Chapter Twenty-Six

I had no choice. I had to keep going up. I've never been comfortable with heights and had only ever been up the church tower once before when I was seven years old and the church was having an open day. I got part way up and froze and my dad had to be sent for to come and fetch me down.

Will had teased me about it for years.

But there was no dad coming across the horizon like the cavalry that day. No Will either. This was all down to me.

So, I clenched my teeth and forced myself on. As I reached the door to the bell ringing chamber, I wondered about pulling on one of the bell ropes.

But that would have been madness. Just the sight of those massive bells, the size of a small car, scared me witless. I didn't fancy getting yanked up to the top of the tower by one.

I pushed on to the next flight of steps that became progressively narrower as they wound their way up, past the bell loft and on.

I forced myself to keep going. Every time I paused for breath, I could hear Cordelia's footsteps. But I was pulling away from her as I was a lot fitter - and younger - than she was. Maybe when I got to the top I could shout for help as Rhianna had done. It was obvious that for some reason Cordelia had been keeping Rhianna captive not in her house or the barn but in the church. Had Rhianna climbed the tower to call for help?

As I pushed open the tiny door that led out on to the top of the tower, I was almost knocked off my feet by the wind which then caught the door and slammed it so hard that it sounded like a gun going off.

The top of the tower was a slightly sloping square space with a flagpole to one side and a small spire in one corner. And there, I saw something that would have taken my breath away, if the wind hadn't already done so.

Rhianna was rolling around on the floor. But she wasn't the one being attacked. She was doing the attacking.

"Rhianna!" I yelled as I ran across, grabbed her arm and yanked her away. "What on earth do you think you're doing?"

I pulled her away and the woman on the floor sprang to her feet. The last person in the world I expected to see.

"Mrs Denby! Are you ok? What's going on?"

Mrs Denby scrabbled to her feet, her face flushed, her eyes frightened. "I'll tell you what's going on. That - that young woman there just tried to push me off the roof. She's mad. If you hadn't got here, Katie, I don't know what would have happened."

"I wasn't attacking her, it was the other way around," Rhianna said. "She tried to push me off the roof."

"Don't be ridiculous. Why would I do that?" Mrs Denby said. "Look, you stay here with her, Katie. I'll run down and call for the police. There's no point even trying to get a signal up here."

Mrs Denby hurried across to the door that led back into the tower and pulled on it. It had obviously stuck when it had slammed so hard behind me. As she reached to try again, the door suddenly flew open and hit her in the face with a sickening crunch. She dropped to the ground in a crumpled heap.

Cordelia, who was on the other side of the door, hurried across and knelt beside her. "She's out cold," she said. "I had no idea she was there. It wouldn't budge so I gave it a good hard shoulder barge and it suddenly flew open."

"Well, we'd better-" I'd been about to say we'd better wedge it open to stop it getting stuck again, but I was too late. Another gust of wind snatched it, just like before, and slammed it shut with a crack that sent the rooks in the nearby beech trees flying up into the air, in a panicked frenzy. The crack was followed by a dull metallic thud.

Cordelia knelt beside Mrs Denby. "She's out cold. But her eyelids are flickering, so I think she may be coming round."

I tried the door. At least, I *tried* to try the door. But the handle was on the floor at my feet, which explained the dull metallic thud. Goodness knows what had happened to the handle on the other side.

We were going nowhere. I was trapped on a church roof with three other people, one of whom was a murderer.

"We're trapped." As if she could read my mind, Rhianna's voice rose shrilly above the noise of the wind and the constant tap tap tapping of the cable on the flagpole. "First she tries to push me off the roof, and now we're trapped up here. I think I'm going to scream."

"Don't be silly. That isn't going to help anyone." I put my hand on her arm and drew her away from Mrs Denby and Cordelia. I didn't want Cordelia to hear. "But you've got Mrs Denby all wrong, Rhianna. She isn't the murderer."

"But she pushed…" There was a flicker of doubt in her dark rimmed eyes. "At least, I thought..."

"So, what exactly happened?" I asked.

"She was going to show me something that she said would prove how the vicar was murdered. We were leaning over that wall thing over there. Can't remember what she called it."

"The parapet?"

"Whatever. And then... well, I suppose I felt a bit weird. Dizzy-like. Coming up those stairs, particularly the narrow ones above the bells, really freaked me out and I was still feeling a bit shaky. Weird really because usually I'm ok with that sort of thing. But I'm feeling a bit off today."

"Too many late nights?" I suggested. As soon as the words were out, I could have bitten my tongue. What was I doing? I was turning into my mother. That was her stock answer for whatever was ailing me, from the common cold to ingrowing toenails. "Forget I said that, Rhianna. Go on."

"And then, it's a bit of a blur, but I remember - I thought... well, it was like this whooshing feeling, like someone had their hand on my back."

"But you can't be sure?"

"I suppose not. I panicked, turned and grabbed her. But I didn't try to throw her off the roof. I was just in a panic."

I looked across at where Cordelia was still kneeling in front of Mrs Denby. Poor Mrs Denby. Not having the best of days, was she? First off, she almost got rolled off the roof by someone who thought she was trying to kill them, and then she gets knocked out by a flying door.

"Is she going to be all right?" Rhianna asked. "I feel terrible now, especially as she was so kind to me." She lowered her voice. "And she knows who the murderer is, you know."

"So do I," I said, trying not to look in Cordelia's direction. I didn't want to set Rhianna panicking again as she realised she was trapped on the church roof with a murderer. "Did she say who?"

Rhianna shook her head. "She said she'd tell me later."

I took my phone out, even though I knew there was no point. And indeed, there was no signal.

"Do you think she's going to die?" Rhianna whispered. "I really like her. She's one of the few people in this village who were kind to me. Not like Aunty Nora. Do you know she locked me out the other night?"

"She runs a pub. She's hardly going to leave the front door unlocked, is she? And you did go off without telling her. So where were you that night? Because I've spoken to Dylan, and you weren't with him." I lowered my voice. "He says he saw Cordelia out and about at that time. Were you with her?"

"No. Why would I be? If you must know, I stayed at Mrs Denby's. She saw me huddled in the porch, hoping there'd be a key hidden somewhere. She was so kind. I was freezing cold, and she brought me in, gave me a hot drink, and let me sleep in her spare room."

"You stayed at Mrs Denby's Friday night? Why on earth didn't you say so?"

"Because she asked me not to," Rhianna said. "She told me that Aunty Nora didn't approve of her, although it sounded to me like it was Mrs Denby who didn't approve of Aunty Nora. Going on about how she was doing Satan's work, running the pub. But she was kind to me, or at least I thought she was." Her eyes widened. "You - you don't think she killed the vicar, do you?"

I didn't even have to think about that one. "No way," I said with a laugh.

At that moment, Cordelia looked up. "I think she's coming round," she said. "She's going to have one hell of a black eye. Have you got something to tie her up with?"

"What?" Rhianna and I both stared at her.

"Haven't you worked it out yet?" Cordelia glared at me. "I thought you were supposed to be the great detective around here."

"Yes. I *have* worked it out, actually. I think you had your sights set on marrying the vicar, only to find that he wasn't so keen on the idea as you were. Maybe he was planning to get back together with his wife, which was why you tried to implicate her in his murder by leaving her teddy bear by his body with that cruel note."

"You think I killed Lionel? Are you mad?"

"A teddy bear?" Rhianna said. "What is all this about bears? Mrs Denby was really put out with me this morning, about a bear. When I left her on Saturday, she asked me if I knew where the bear was, the one with the note about the abseil pinned to him. And I said yes because I thought she meant the bear that's in the bar, advertising the fundraising bash."

"And it has a note attached to him saying 'please sponsor me'. So it was you who took it," I said, remembering how annoyed Norina had been when the bear went missing.

Rhianna nodded. "But Mrs Denby wasn't best pleased when I turned up with it and muttered something about the wrong bear."

"She meant the bear that was found near the body," I said. "The one with the note in Cordelia's handwriting."

"What is this note you keep going on about?" Cordelia asked. "What exactly did it say?"

"It said that abseiling was only the second fastest way down a church tower," I told her and watched as the colour drained from her face.

"Oh, my goodness," she said slowly. "I remember now. It was at the fundraising meeting. Lionel was saying how he had to meet a Health and Safety man from the council before they'd allow the event to go ahead. And I said how I'd love to go up the tower with him because I was thinking of writing my next murder mystery when someone falls (or was she pushed?) off the church roof. And it was actually Lionel who jokingly said something about abseiling being only the second fastest way down. I thought it was a great line and so wrote it down on a post it note."

"Elsie's poster," I murmured as I remembered Elsie going on about the way Cordelia left 'posters' all over the place. She'd meant post-it notes, of course.

"Excuse me?" Cordelia said, while Rhianna looked more confused than ever.

"It doesn't matter. Carry on."

"Well, that's it really. I stuck the note in my book but I'm not sure what happened to it. I'm always losing the things."

She looked down at Mrs Denby, who was still out cold. "You know, I've a feeling she played me the morning of Lionel's murder. I was due to meet Lionel that morning here in the church, but I had a call from Mrs Denby to say she'd seen the Princess down by Long Ford."

"Princess who?" Rhianna asked.

"Princess Persephone, my dog. The postman must have left the gate open and she got out. I was out of my mind worrying about her and when Mrs Denby called, I rushed off to the ford. Only I couldn't find her and when I got back to the village, there she was, the poor little scrap. She was soaking wet and tied to the lychgate at the entrance to the churchyard."

"So, you admit to being at the churchyard that morning?" I said.

"I've already told you. But, like I said, just as far as the gate. And you know, now I think of it, I'm not sure the Princess would go as far as Long Ford. And what would Mrs Denby be doing down there that early in the morning? Hardly the type who goes in for long early morning walks, is she?"

"But why would you think she set you up?" I made an attempt to keep the disbelief out of my voice. "You're making her out to be some great mastermind. But she's not the brightest button in the box. In fact, according to Elsie

Flintlock, Mrs Denby is pretty useless and couldn't organise a drinks party in a brewery."

Those weren't Elsie's exact words, you understand. But I remembered in time where we were.

Rhianna snorted with laughter. "She's certainly got some weird ways."

I looked down at Mrs Denby and shook my head. "That's Elsie for you. She can be a bit outspoken about people she doesn't like."

"Tell me about it," Cordelia said.

"In fact," I went on, "this morning I was telling her that Anna and her brother Rob are both back in the village and that I wondered if Mrs Denby might have been behind the burglary that sent poor Rob back to prison. But Elsie said no way. If it wasn't Rob who took the money, then it had to be the vicar himself."

"Oh no. No." Cordelia jumped in. "You've got it all wrong. Lionel was a good man. He could never do such a terrible thing. He was -"

There was a sudden yell as Mrs Denby sprang to her feet. She launched herself at Cordelia, her hands outstretched as if she would scratch her face off. But I was ready for her.

I'd been hoping for such a reaction and pulled her back before she could connect with Cordelia's shocked face.

Chapter Twenty-Seven

I'd like to say that all the hours of judo training I'd done at college kicked in, and I had Mrs Denby safely down on the floor in one easy move.

But it didn't happen like that. Instead, we did an ungainly, shuffly sort of dance where I attempted to hold on to her while at the same time trying to keep out of range of those claw-like hands that were slashing out wildly, trying to find a soft surface, preferably my face, to sink into.

I'd never noticed her fingernails before, but it was like she'd suddenly turned into Edward Scissorhands on a bad day. And all the while, she was hissing, spitting and cursing like an angry cat.

Just when I thought I couldn't hold on to her any longer and was figuring out which bits of myself to protect, there was a bellow, a swirl of wild black hair as Rhianna launched herself at us with a flying tackle that should have earned her a place in the Welsh rugby team.

Mrs Denby made an 'oomph' sound, as if all the breath had been knocked out of her which, given the ferocity of the tackle, it probably had. The cursing stopped and she dropped to the floor, pulling me down with her. That seemed to jolt Cordelia out of her shocked trance. She caught me by the arm and dragged me clear.

"It was you, wasn't it?" Rhianna yelled, as she pinned Mrs Denby to the ground. "I didn't imagine it, did I? You really did try to push me off the roof."

"Please let me up and I'll explain," came the muffled voice. "And, of course, apologise. I owe you that."

"You're not kidding," Rhianna said as she tightened her grip on Mrs Denby's shoulder.

I put my hand on her arm. "Let her up, Rhianna. She's not

going anywhere."

And, indeed, she wasn't. All the fight, all the hissing and spitting and the Edward Scissorhands claws had gone. And although she was a bit red in the face, all the fire had gone from her eyes.

"Please, dear, let me sit up." Her voice was its normal, soft tone. "Like you said, Katie, I'm not going anywhere and I need to explain why I -" She swallowed, then took a deep steadying breath. "Why I did what I did."

"You mean, why you murdered the vicar?" I said as, closely watched by Rhianna, Mrs Denby pulled herself into a sitting position, her back against the wall. Rhianna, Cordelia and I stood in a semi-circle around her.

"It was all your fault," Mrs Denby said to Cordelia. "None of this would have happened if you hadn't come to Much Winchmoor."

"How do you make that out?" Cordelia asked.

But Mrs Denby ignored her and turned, instead, towards me. "I apologise for losing my temper just now. What the reverend would have said if he could have witnessed that, I don't know. He'd have been so disappointed in me. He worked so hard - indeed, we both did - on my anger management issues when I first arrived in the village. You see, my husband had just left me for a trollop -" She broke off as her voice began to rise. I began to worry that she was about to go off on one again. Instead, she took another deep breath, then lowered her voice back to its normal pitch. "He left me for a woman young enough to be his daughter. It upset me deeply at the time, but I'm over that now, thanks to the reverend. I owe him so much."

"And yet you killed him," Rhianna exclaimed. "Crazy way of settling a debt."

"But that wasn't my fault, dear." Mrs Denby spoke gently as if to a small child. "I told you, it was hers. Let me explain. You can record it if you like. I'm sure you've got something on your phone that will do that?"

I stared at her. This was starting to get really creepy. "You want Rhianna to record your confession? Why?"

188

"To set the record straight," she said. "I want the world to know what I had to do, and why."

"Ok. Fire away." Rhianna took her phone out and placed it on the ground in front of her. "It's sheltered down here so that should cut out most of the noise from the wind."

"Let's start with how and why you murdered the vicar, shall we?" I said. "Was it because you were jealous of the blossoming relationship between him and Cordelia? Were you in love with him?"

Rhianna snorted. "If so, she had a pretty weird way of showing it."

Mrs Denby held up a hand. "Please. Let me tell it in my own way. And no, I was not in love with him, although I must admit that when I first came to the village, after my divorce, I did have those sorts of feelings for him. But he explained to me, very gently and kindly, that he didn't believe in divorce and that people who made their marriage vows in the sight of God should keep them. He was deeply unhappy with the decision of the Church of England to allow divorced people to remarry in church and said that he, personally, would never allow that in his church. I respected and admired him for his principles."

Cordelia looked bewildered. "But Lionel and I were good friends, that's all. There was no mention of marriage."

"But you were working up to it, weren't you? I hear the gossip, you know, and it was all over the village, the way you were throwing yourself at him. And he, being weak, was falling for it." Her voice had begun to rise again and I could see that it took a huge effort on her part to keep it quiet and calm. "He'd started to redecorate the vicarage, you know. 'A fresh start, Mrs D'. Those were his exact words, the very same words he'd used before."

"How do you mean?" Rhianna asked.

"The year he went away for his usual holiday in Dorset, then came back and started changing everything around in the vicarage. He even wanted me to go and work in that ridiculous shed in the village hall, which I told him straight I had no intention of doing. Next thing he tells me he's getting married and talking about a fresh start."

"That was when he married Anna, I assume," I said. "How did you feel about that?"

She sighed. "She was all wrong for him. I saw that immediately. I knew I had to get rid of her. For his sake, you understand." She gave a fond smile. "Everything I did was for him. Always for him."

"How exactly did you get rid of her?" I prompted gently, not wanting her to stop now she'd started talking.

"She was making him so unhappy. I could see he realised he'd made a terrible mistake. And then she got pregnant. She probably did it quite deliberately to trap him further."

"Last I heard, it took two to make a baby," Rhianna murmured. I sent her a warning glance, but Mrs Denby showed no sign of having heard her.

"She had terrible morning sickness," she went on. "So I made her my special honey and herb concoctions that would, I told her, make her feel better." Her face softened as if she was recalling a pleasant memory. "Only, of course, they didn't. They made her feel worse. A lot worse."

I shivered. I think I preferred it when she was ranting and raving. This was beginning to freak me out, the way she was sitting there on the roof of the church tower, talking quietly and calmly as if she was telling a bedtime tale, rather than the very worst kind of Halloween horror story.

"Poor Anna." A horrible thought occurred to me. "She mentioned how kind you'd been to her at that time. Did you, or rather, your concoctions cause her to lose the baby?"

She shrugged. "I didn't set out to do that. But it proved to me I was doing the right thing. I took it as a sign. I persuaded the reverend that a lot of Anna's problems were in her mind, (which of course they were) and that the best way he could help her was to be cruel to be kind. Be firm with her. And, of course, he believed me. Called me his 'wise old bird', and said where would he be without me?"

"Are you talking about the crib service?" I prompted as I remembered what Elsie and Olive had told me.

She smiled. The fact that it was her normal, sweet smile

somehow made everything she was saying even worse. "I convinced him the best thing he could do for her was to insist she played the organ for the service. I said that once she got back into her music the healing would begin. But I knew perfectly well she'd never get through *Away in a Manger*. I planned it all, you see, down to the last detail." Her smile vanished as she glared up at me. "As for that fool Elsie Flintlock, daring to say such a thing about me."

Actually, Elsie had said nothing of the sort. I'd made the remark in the hope that Mrs Denby was, as I'd suspected, merely pretending to be unconscious. I'd goaded her, hoping to create a reaction, and it had worked.

"I knew, or rather I hoped, that playing *Away in a Manger* would tip her over the edge. Goodness knows, she'd been whining on about it enough, how she'd always imagined her child, their child, walking down the church to that particular carol. And how she was sure she'd never be able to play it again. She confided in me, you see."

I saw Cordelia open her mouth to say something. She was obviously as appalled as I was by the callous way she spoke, but I shook my head at her.

"And while she was so ill, you started on her brother," I said. "You took that money, didn't you? Not Rob."

"Believe it or not, that was a complete accident. I was counting out the money from the church fete when he banged on the kitchen window and frightened me to death. He'd cut himself, and so I told him to come in and I'd get the first aid box. I scooped the money up and shoved it into my bag. But after he'd gone, I went to go back to the money and couldn't find it. The reverend and I were both convinced he'd taken it, which he probably *would* have done if he'd had the chance.

"Only, as it happened, after the police had been called and he'd been taken away, I found the money. In my anxiety to get it out of his sight, I'd put it into another bag by mistake. Of course, it was too late to do anything about it by then. So, I put it down as a sign, as well, that I'd done the right thing. He'd probably already broken the terms of his probation and would have ended up back in prison anyway. His sort always does. I

191

was doing him a favour really."

"But he didn't do it," I protested.

She shrugged. "No. But he's probably done all sorts of other things and got away with it."

"So, you were quite happy when Anna upped and left?" I said.

"Happy?" She gave a short laugh. "I packed her bag for her."

"And Mr Fairweather was heartbroken, I suppose, and you were around to comfort him."

She gave that weird creepy smile again. "Not as heartbroken as all that. I told him she'd run off with that teacher, that they were living in sin and he believed me."

"But why? You've already said you didn't want to marry him yourself."

"I wanted things to go back to the way they were before she arrived. Which they did. Until she came along." Once again she glared at Cordelia. "She changed everything. I couldn't let him turn his back on his beliefs and principles, could I? He asked me if I knew how to get in touch with Anna as he was going to ask her for a divorce. When I reminded him that he didn't believe in divorce, he said he'd wrestled with his conscience. But in the end, he couldn't deny what was in his heart.

"That was when I knew I had to kill him. And so I came up with the perfect plan."

Chapter Twenty-Eight

"You didn't see Princess down by Long Ford that morning, did you?" Cordelia said. "That was just to get me out of the way."

"Of course. For the last week, I've been walking past your house every morning and giving that silly little creature a dog treat. All part of my carefully thought out plan." She emphasised the word plan as she glared at me before turning back to Cordelia. "You see, you always let her out at the same time into the front garden. The stupid animal started looking out for me. So that morning all I had to do was pick her up, pop her into a bag the way you do, and bring her back to the vicarage, then send you off on a wild goose chase while I met the reverend in the church in your place."

Cordelia gave a quiet groan. "How could you? In my panic at losing the Princess, I'd forgotten that Lionel and I had agreed to meet at the church that morning."

"I told him you'd just called me to say you couldn't make it, then I suggested we might as well go through what we needed to get in place for the safety check while I was there. Of course once we were up here, it was the easiest thing in the world to encourage him to peer over the parapet, come up behind, and give him the gentlest of shoves. And over he went." She turned to Rhianna. "Just like you should have done earlier."

Rhianna's heavy black eye make-up made a stark contrast to her deathly pale face. "Why would you do that?" she whispered. "What harm have I ever done you?"

"You took the bear and nearly ruined everything," Mrs Denby said. "I'd gone to a lot of trouble to make sure it was by his body, with the note attached. I didn't want anyone to think it was an accident, or even suicide. I wanted there to be no doubt that it was murder and to point the finger at her." She glowered at Cordelia. "And you were responsible for his death. If you hadn't come here, turning his head and making him forget the very principles he lived by, he'd still be alive now, God rest his poor soul. What's more, it was you who put the idea in my head in the first place."

Cordelia's eyes were brimming with tears as she stared at her, bewildered. "I haven't the faintest idea what you're talking about."

But *I* did. I could have kicked myself for not having seen it before. Had I done so, we wouldn't be in the mess we were in now.

"You're talking about the fundraising meeting, aren't you? About the note?"

She nodded. "First, all that silly talk about murder mysteries, then when the reverend made that joke about abseiling being only the second fastest way down and you made a big thing of writing it down, like he'd just said the wittiest thing ever. Well, it got me thinking." Her voice was beginning to rise again. "To hear the way you were planning to turn the churchyard into some sort of fairground really upset me. When I saw you write that silly note, it became clear what I had to do and how to go about it."

"You mean murder Lionel and set me up for it?" Cordelia said. "That's really, really wicked."

"But clever. You've got to admit that. Once he was dead, all I had to do was get you in the vicinity of the churchyard and hope that someone saw you. I was going to say I had if no one else came forward. Then I tied your silly little dog to the gate, knowing that you'd see the state of her and take her straight home without actually coming into the churchyard. But even if you had, my plan would still have worked. I had it all worked out. Down to the last detail."

"But how did she get so wet?" Cordelia asked.

Mrs Denby smiled. "A watering can. She wasn't too keen on it, I can tell you."

"That was so cruel. And, as it turned out, totally unnecessary. The police ruled me out quite quickly because while I was down at Long Ford looking for her, I bumped into

Fiona Crabshaw and Harvey and she helped me search for the Princess."

Mrs Denby's face darkened. "But Fiona Crabshaw always takes her walk around Short Ford. You can set your clock by her. Why would she change her habit?"

I figured I knew the answer to that one. It was to avoid me. But I kept quiet. I didn't want to say or do anything that would stop her talking.

"Poor little Princess," Cordelia murmured. "She was in a terrible state when I found her."

Mrs Denby sniffed. "Collateral damage." She pointed at Rhianna, "It would have worked, too if she hadn't taken the bear and the note."

"But I didn't take them," Rhianna protested. "How many times do I have to say that?"

"It could only have been you," Mrs Denby said. "When you took that dreadful photograph. You lied to me, Katie, when you said you didn't know her. But I found out anyway. Millie Compton told me."

"So that was what you were on about this morning," Rhianna said. "When I turned up with the bear from the pub."

"I had a good look through your bag on Friday night while you were sleeping. Also looked through your phone. Very careless of you not to use a passcode, you know."

Rhianna stared at her. "You went through my phone?"

"I did. And you should be ashamed of yourself, young lady." She shook her head. "I despair of young people nowadays. No morals whatsoever."

"No morals?" Rhianna shrieked. "How can you, of all people, say that? When you've confessed to murdering one person and setting up someone else for it, not to mention invading my privacy." She bit her lip, and her voice dropped to a frightened whisper. "Did you drug me?"

Mrs Denby looked scornful. "So melodramatic. It was only a bit of valerian and honey, mixed with one of my sleeping pills. Nothing more sinister. It gave you a good night's sleep, after your aunt locked you out of the pub, didn't it? Couldn't believe my luck when I saw you standing there in the pub porch. Another sign, you see."

Rhianna clapped her hand to her mouth. "You gave me some again, in that drink you made for me this morning, didn't you?" she said slowly. She was shaking as she turned to me. "That was why I felt woozy over by the parapet. If you hadn't come along when you did, Kat..."

I didn't like to point out to her that we were still trapped on the top of the church tower with no immediate prospect of rescue. And, just to add to the joy of the situation, the sky was getting darker and darker. It looked as if it was going to rain at any moment.

"But I swear I didn't touch your precious bear," Rhianna said.

"Then who did?"

"Anna's brother. Rob." I said. "He'd spent the night in the shed in the churchyard and heard Mr Fairweather fall. He also heard footsteps going up to the body then hurrying away. But he thought they were Anna's. When he saw the bear he recognised it as belonging to her so he took it, thinking he was protecting his sister."

Mrs Denby sneered. "I always knew that boy was stupid. Anna would never have the courage to do what I did."

"You crept up behind pushed Lionel off the roof," Cordelia said. "That's the most cowardly, despicable thing I've ever heard of. How can you think that takes courage?"

"But why did you try to implicate Anna?" I asked. "What was the point of that when she wasn't in the village?"

"Always have a backup plan, that's what my old dad used to say," Mrs Denby said. "I'd originally planned the murder for some time next week but when Anna phoned to say she was coming to 'have it out' with the reverend, well, I took that as yet another sign, didn't I? I knew the reverend wouldn't be back that afternoon which would annoy her. I wanted to keep things tricky between them, you see."

"And did the vicar burn all her things, like you told her?" I asked.

"Of course he didn't. He's much too soft to do something like that. She's so gullible, she'll believe anything. The dog

196

was a touch of genius which you nearly ruined." Another black look aimed at me. "I told you to keep him out for an hour, but you had to come back early, didn't you? But, as it happened, even that worked to my advantage because I then had a witness to Anna threatening the reverend. I told her to come back first thing next morning and I'd make sure she saw him." She paused and smiled. "And if things had worked out, she'd have done just that. She'd have seen him spread out on the church path. But her stupid car broke down which kind of scuppered that. But it didn't matter. It was only plan B. I wasn't even that bothered when you refused to hand over that tacky little keyring thing which I recognised as Anna's. She was always going on about how talented her waster of a brother was. So you see how ridiculous it is for Elsie Flintlock to say I can't plan anything. I'd like to see her do what I've just done..."

While she was speaking I heard something I'd been straining my ears for. Someone was talking way below us in the churchyard. Keeping my eyes firmly fixed on Mrs Denby, I edged over to the parapet and took a quick look down.

It was Ed Fuller and Gerald Crabshaw. I didn't want to shout and draw Mrs Denby's attention to them. Goodness knows how she'd react. True, there were three of us and only one of her. But she'd murdered a man and had nothing to lose.

And if I waved to attract their attention, she'd see that too. But, on the other hand, what choice did I have?

"Ed," I yelled. "We're stuck up here on the roof and the door's jammed. The handle's come off. Can you come up? Quick."

Rhianna came up beside me and leaned over. "Please hurry. We're trapped up here with -" She began, but her words ended in a scream of terror as Mrs Denby pushed Cordelia away and grabbed Rhianna before any of us could react.

"Now, don't any of you do anything stupid or she goes over the edge," she said. "And don't for one minute think I won't do it because I will."

"But you can't escape," I said. "Ed's on his way up now. It's all over, Mrs Denby. Let her go. You're frightening her."

"Who said anything about escape?" Mrs Denby's eyes burned fever bright as she tightened her grip on Rhianna. "How does it go now?" Her low laugh will stay in my mind for ever. "*Abseiling is only the second fastest way down a church tower*. Why do you think I had you record my story? I want people to know what I've done and why. But I have no intention of being taken by the police and now I'm going to go the same way as the reverend. I'm not going to spend the rest of my life locked up in a women's prison with drug addicts and prostitutes."

"It's what you deserve," Cordelia said. "You're an evil woman, and Lionel couldn't stand you. He was going to fire you."

Before Mrs Denby could respond the door flew open. Ed stood there looking bewildered.

"What the -" he began.

"Don't come any closer," she screamed at him. "Or I'll go over and take her with me. Get over there with the others where I can see you."

"But what's going on?" he managed to say.

"Ed. Move," I called out. "She means it."

"Wise words," Mrs Denby said as she tightened her grip on Rhianna's long hair, pulling her in closer, holding the terrified girl in front of her like a human shield. "Now, Katie, make sure that door doesn't slam again. And give me that phone. I've changed my mind about jumping. This young lady's going to be my ticket out of here and you're all going to stay where you are until I'm safely through that door. And in case you're thinking of rushing me ..." She put her free hand in her pocket and drew out a small knife. "It's my best pruning knife and it's very, very sharp. Isn't it, dear?" Rhianna screamed as the tip of the knife was pressed against her neck. "Believe me, I am not afraid to use it."

"We believe you," I said as Rhianna began to sob. "Let her go, Mrs Denby. She's just a kid."

"A very annoying kid," Mrs Denby said as she dragged the weeping girl towards the door. But as she reached it, she gave Rhianna a huge shove in the back and sent her, and the knife, sprawling across the uneven floor. Then she disappeared down the stairs.

Cordelia rushed to see if Rhianna was all right while Ed and I raced to the door. We reached it at the same time and bounced off each other in our hurry. Both desperate to catch up with Mrs Denby even though Ed was still asking what was going on.

But she hadn't got very far. Thanks to Gerald Crabshaw.

"Please, please, Mrs Denby. Don't leave me," he said as he held Mrs Denby's arm in a vicelike grip. His voice was shrill as he teetered on the edge of hysteria. "I can't move. I - it's vertigo. I should never have come up here. But if I could just hang on to you, we could go down together. Please, please don't go. I won't let you." His voice rose as Mrs Denby attempted to push past him and he flattened himself, and her, against the rough stone wall.

"I think this is what we could call a fair cop, don't you, folks?" Cordelia said in a creditable attempt at a slow, American drawl.

Chapter Twenty-Nine

Three weeks later

"It's disgusting, that's what it is," Morag Browne (with an E) sniffed while behind her there was a murmur of agreement from the crowd, mostly members of the Much Winchmoor Grumble and Gossip Group. They were clustered around the window of Suzanne's recently finished gallery. One single painting stood on an easel in the centre. It was the only thing in the window.

"She should take it down," Olive Shrewton said. "The children come this way to school. They shouldn't have to see things like that. It's not the sort of thing you expect to see in Much Winchmoor High Street on a Wednesday morning."

"Well, I think it's lovely," Millie Compton announced, raising her voice to make herself heard above the disapproving mutters. "It's art, that's what it is. And she has a beautiful smile."

"And she's as naked as the day she was born," Olive went on, like no one else had noticed that fact. "It's all very well for you, Millie. I dare say you and your Abe are liberal thinkers and all that. But I don't think it should be on display for all the world to see what's she's got."

Millie tutted and turned back to studying the painting.

"And I shall be having a word with the Parish Council to see about getting it taken down," Morag Browne announced. "What's wrong with a nice landscape? A picture of the River Winch, maybe, or the view from Pendle Knoll towards Glastonbury Tor. Now what's what I call art."

"Well, I don't know why we need a fancy pantsy art gallery at all," Elsie said. "What we need is a post office. Or a shop.

Like we used to have before they turned them all into holiday cottages."

"She'll be selling coffee and cakes as well as paintings," I pointed out. "And I can recommend the coffee."

Morag Browne huffed. "Give me a nice cup of tea any day," she said. "I don't know what she was thinking of, posing in the nude like that. How are we going to look her in the eye next time we're at choir? I won't know where to look and that's a fact."

It was the day of the grand opening of Suzanne's gallery which was taking place at noon and declared open by none other than our own celebrity (once-removed), Cordelia Hilperton-Jones. The builders had finally come good and had completed everything to Suzanne's high standards, which meant that she was able to open just a couple of weeks before Christmas.

I hid a smile as I elbowed my way through the small but vocal crowd to Suzanne's front door. Things had gone very quiet on the gossip front since Mrs Denby had been arrested and charged with the vicar's murder and the attempted murder of Rhianna. She was now on remand awaiting trial.

At least the nude portrait of Suzanne, which took pride of place in the window of the gallery (with a 'Not For Sale' sticker on it), would give the massed members of the Grumble and Gossip Group something new to talk about. And talking they certainly were.

"Well?" said Suzanne as she opened the door to me, her cheeks pink. "What do you think of it? No. Don't answer that yet. Come along into the kitchen. Do you want a coffee?"

"Do I ever say no?" I laughed as Suzanne switched on the coffee machine.

"So, what do you think?"

"I think you've shocked the ladies of Much Winchmoor," I said.

"Probably. But you? Have I shocked you?"

"Of course not. It's a beautiful painting. Rob's very talented."

Suzanne's eyes shone. "He is, isn't he? And wait until you

see the rest of his work. He's doing some brilliant stuff at the moment."

"You do realise he's in love with you, don't you?" I said quietly.

Suzanne busied herself with the coffee cups and didn't look at me. "Don't be silly. Of course he's not."

"Suzanne, I don't know much about art, but the love shines out of that painting. No wonder he doesn't want to sell it."

Her cheeks flaming, she turned away.

"Is he here?"

"He's on his way," she said. "He and Anna are getting quotes from some more builders today. They've already had a couple, and Anna thinks that they'll have Bay View up and running in time for Easter."

"Was the damage very bad?"

"Apparently not," she said. "Rob told me that the first couple of builders were pretty confident that much of the damage is superficial."

"Thank goodness for that. Well, let's hope the costs are reasonable."

"Indeed. And the best thing is, Anna discovered there was quite a lot of money in a separate account in her name. Mr Fairweather had been putting the income from the holiday lets, all neatly written down in a ledger. The money only stopped going into the account when Mrs Denby took over. Anna thinks she probably managed to persuade the vicar that it was all becoming too much for him and that she'd be happy to save him a job. Only of course as soon as she did, she sacked the agent, wasn't too careful about who she let the place to - with the inevitable results. I think she really was hoping for the place to fall down."

"But why?"

"Apparently she said that she was tired of hearing people always talking about Bay View. 'Going on about the place as if it was Narnia or something' were her actual words. And if he hadn't started going there all those years ago, he'd never have met Anna and he'd still be alive today. I think she really believes this is all Anna's fault. And, of course, Cordelia's.

Well, anyone really, except for her. Unbelievable, isn't it?"

I shuddered. "She really was – is a monster, isn't she?" I said as I recalled the screaming, foul-mouthed creature who had to be physically dragged by the police to the waiting car. Hard to believe she was the same person, with her apple cheeks and sweet smile.

"Anyway," Suzanne went on, "the good news is that the house, basically, is fine. It was built to withstand south-westerly gales and is tougher than it looks."

"That's great. I'll bet they can't wait to start on it." I glanced at my watch. "So, are you all set up for the grand opening? Anything I can do to help?"

"If you'll take the glasses through, that will be lovely. And Cordelia said she'd be along soon. You know, Kat, she's really nice when you get to know her. I can't think how you ever thought she was the murderer."

I picked up a tray of champagne flutes and followed her into the gallery. Finbar gave a huge sigh and padded behind us.

"Poor love," she smiled down at him. "You're missing Archie, aren't you, sweetheart?"

I placed the glasses on a side table and looked around the room. "This is stunning, Suzanne. You've made a great job of it. Are these all Rob's paintings?"

She nodded. "At the moment, yes. But I'm hoping, once I put the word around, that other artists will be keen to exhibit here. I've still got my contact list from when I worked in Bristol. I'm hoping some of them will still be around. Anyway, you didn't answer my question."

I'd been hoping she hadn't noticed. "What question?"

"I asked you what made you think that Cordelia was the murderer?"

"She admitted being around when Rhianna disappeared and I'm afraid I didn't believe her story about her dog going missing at the time of the murder and ending up tied to the churchyard gate. And then she was being so cagey about the barn." I said. "Acting like she had something to hide."

"But she did, poor woman. Those awful builders weren't proper builders at all but thieves. They had a nice little racket,

203

stealing farm machinery, builders' power tools, that sort of thing and selling them abroad. They were using the barn to store them. At first, they kept her out by digging a trench across her garden but when she started to insist that she saw inside the barn, they turned nasty and told her to stay away. Threatened to hurt her dog if she didn't. They also said she didn't have planning permission for the work on the barn. But she told me yesterday that Gerald had sorted all that out for her."

"Gerald?" I stared at her in astonishment. "As in Gerald Crabshaw?"

"The very same. Once again, he's the hero of the hour. He's coming to the opening as Cordelia's guest. Fiona, of course, is coming as a member of the Parish Council."

"The great and the good," I murmured. "I only hope we don't have to listen one more time to how he single handedly captured a dangerous murderer."

Suzanne laughed. "Poor guy. Cordelia told me how he was clinging to Mrs Denby like grim death. But only because he got part way up the stairs after Ed and had a panic attack. Couldn't go up or down."

"Yes, well, that'll be our little secret, won't it?" I said. "I'm just glad he was there - even if he didn't mean to be. But did you manage to find out what he and Ed were doing there in the first place that Sunday?"

"Checking out the village hall, while they knew Elsie wouldn't be around. Cordelia is very keen to get that shed taken off the stage, you know. And I for one support her in that."

I grinned. "Best not let Elsie Flintlock hear you saying that. And as for Gerald having a key to the village hall, best not tell her that either. She thinks she is the only person in the village to have a key."

At least that explained what Cordelia and Gerald were planning that evening in the Winchmoor Arms.

"Sounds like she and Gerald have become quite close. I wonder what Fiona makes of that."

"Cordelia says she invited him to thank him for 'sorting out' the planning stuff. Apparently, he still has (or so he says) contacts in the right places and said he'd put in a word with the planning department to persuade them to grant retrospective planning permission."

"So, she really didn't have planning permission for the conversion?"

"Apparently not. The builders told her they had it all in hand. It never occurred to her to check for herself."

Suzanne straightened a picture that didn't need straightening, moved a beautiful little bronze sculpture of a hare that didn't need moving and sighed.

"Come on," I said. "It all looks perfect. Let's go and get that coffee, shall we?"

She nodded and I followed her back into the house.

"How's Rhianna getting on with your mum?" she asked.

"Believe it or not, she's doing really well," I said. "She's only been working in the salon for four days but appears to have taken to it. And the clients all seem to like her. Well, almost everyone. Apart from Morag Browne. But then, she doesn't like anyone."

"Except her cat."

"True. And Rhianna managed to talk Minnie Compton into having a manicure and having her nails painted purple. Olive was shocked and muttered something about how she'd be getting a tattoo next. But Minnie just glared at her sister and asked her how did she know she didn't have one already? Olive spluttered a bit and then Minnie asked her if she'd heard any more about their mother's blanket and that shut her up completely."

Suzanne laughed. "They are a pair, aren't they?"

"Elsie reckons they were bickering from the day they were born. Not that she knew them then. But Elsie's never let the truth get in the way of a good line."

"Talking of Rhianna, you know those flyers she offered to do to publicise this festival that Cordelia is so keen on?"

"The Much Winchmoor Festival of Arts. Cordelia talks about nothing else."

"Well, this is what Rhianna came up with. She said it needed something short, punchy and memorable. And this is it."

MUCH WINCH F/ARTS
Coming Next Year
Watch this space

"Well, it's certainly eye catching," I said. "Not sure Cordelia will go for it though."

We both burst out laughing and Suzanne put the flyers in a drawer. As she did so, a small yellow car drew up outside.

"Looks like you've got a visitor," I murmured as Suzanne hurried out to let Rob in.

He certainly looked a lot better than the last time I'd seen him. In those three weeks, he's lost the hollowness in his cheeks and his eyes were clearer. It helped too that his beard was now trimmed to a trendy length and his hair neatly cut.

I put my empty cup down and stood up. "I'd best be going."

"Something I said?" Rob said with a grin.

"Of course not. But I've got dogs to walk and I want to be back in good time for the opening. Ready, Finbar? Shall we go and see Prescott?"

I was pleased for Suzanne and Rob. I really was. They were obviously very much in love. And the way he looked at her, the way his face softened and his eyes danced, it just reminded me that Will used to look at me like that.

But not anymore. I hadn't seen Will since that awful day he dumped me. And I missed him more than I would ever have thought it possible to miss anyone.

I collected the other two dogs and set off on our usual route around the fords. I hadn't got very far when my phone rang. My heart leapt as it did every time, wondering if it would be Will. And every time I was disappointed.

This time was no exception. "Oh, hi Liam." I still hadn't forgiven him for leaving me with Cordelia that Sunday. Ok, so she wasn't the murderer. But I didn't know that at the time. And neither did he.

But he'd explained that he'd recognised some of the stolen machinery that was in the barn as he'd been working on a piece following a recent spate of thefts in the area. He had to go back to the office to check it out and then contact the police.

"Well, you don't have to sound quite so pleased to hear from me," he said.

"Sorry, I've got a lot on my mind this morning."

"Funny you should say that, Kat Latcham. So have I." He sounded slightly out of breath and excited.

"Is everything ok? Where are you?"

"Everything's more than ok. And I'm walking along Dintscombe High Street."

Now that's not the kind of place to get many people excited, unless maybe you're a demolition contractor.

"So what is it?"

"I've come out of the office because I don't want to be overheard. I've been offered a job. In Manchester."

"Oh." I stopped walking and stared into the distance, while the dogs snuffled around in the ditch. I felt tears prickle my eyes and was glad there was no one around to see me. What was the matter with me? I always knew Liam would leave Dintscombe sooner or later. And indeed, there were several occasions when I would have happily settled for sooner rather than later.

"That's ... that's really good news." I swallowed hard and forced myself to sound like I meant it. "I'm happy for you, Liam. Really, I am. Congratulations."

"But that's not all." His voice was still bubbling with excitement. "There's a job for you there too, if you're interested."

It was like the world had stopped still. The dogs had stopped snuffling in the muddy ditch. The rooks had stopped doing whatever rooks do in the tall trees to my left. And I had stopped breathing.

This was it. My chance to leave Much Winchmoor. To leave all the gossiping, the claustrophobic goldfish bowl of a place. To leave Gran K who seemed to have taken up permanent residence. To be no longer being constantly broke, running around after three rubbish jobs, all of which paid peanuts. To live in a bustling vibrant city again.

"Are you there, Kat?"

"Yes. I'm - I'm just surprised, that's all."

"And your answer?"

I took a deep breath. "My answer is no, Liam. I can't leave at the moment. It's - the timing is all wrong."

"Oh." He sounded surprised. "Well, think about it. You've got until the weekend to do so. No pressure."

He ended the call and I finished the walk on autopilot. I'd turned the job down. Why had I just done that? Why had I turned my back on my dream?

When I got home, Mum and Gran were in the kitchen. Mum was getting lunch. Gran K was, as usual, sitting at the table, expecting to be waited upon. I went to head upstairs to get changed but Mum called me back.

"Katie." Her voice was very serious. "Your grandmother has something to say to you. Go on, Mother."

"Can it wait?" I said. "I'm sorry, but I've got to -"

"No, it can't wait." I don't know when I'd heard my mother sound so fierce. "She has something to tell you. And she will do it now. Come in and sit down please."

Chapter Thirty

I sat down at the kitchen table, opposite my grandmother, who was busy rearranging the knives and forks and moving the water glass an eighth of an inch to the left.

"What's it all about?" I asked.

Gran K shrugged her thin, elegant shoulders. "I just wanted to let you know that you can have your room back, Kathryn. I'm moving out."

"You're going home?" At least I'd had some good news today.

"No. I'm selling my place in Taunton. Or I might let it. I haven't decided yet. I'm moving into Crabshaw Crescent."

"Do you mean in Fred Wetherall's old bungalow? But that won't be possible. There's a waiting list for the bungalows in Crabshaw Crescent."

"Not if you know the right people," she said with a smirk. "And what better person to know than Councillor Crabshaw."

"*Ex*-Councillor Crabshaw," I reminded her.

"Whatever. He still has influence and friends where it matters. And he is such a charming gentleman."

Now I've heard Gerald Crabshaw called many things in the time I've known him. I've even called him a few myself. But 'charming gentleman'? Never.

"You do know Gerald's a lot of talk, don't you?" I warned her. "There's a world of difference between what he says he'll do and what he actually does."

She reached into her handbag and took out a key. "Well, as far as I'm concerned, the man was as good as his word. Your father's going to make a start on the place tomorrow for me."

It was good news - of a sort. "That's - um great," I said, although from the expression on my mother's face, I guessed she didn't exactly share my sentiment.

"Mother!" she said sharply. "Your move to Crabshaw Crescent wasn't what I meant, and you know it. Tell her about Will."

My heart started thudding against my ribcage. "What about Will?"

"Oh, that." Gran K moved the water glass an eighth of an inch to the right. "You mean, when I went to see him?"

"Of course that's what I meant," Mum said.

"When was this?" I asked.

"Two maybe three weeks ago. And the state of that lane outside the farm is a disgrace. I ruined a perfectly good pair of shoes that day. And I told him so too. I said it was people like him, leaving their muck all over public roads, that gave the countryside a bad name."

"Mother! You did not go to see Will to discuss the state of the roads with him," Mum said. "And if you don't tell Katie what you did, then I will."

"Tell me what?" I demanded. "Will one of you please tell me what's going on."

"Your grandmother took it upon herself to go and see Will. She even had the nerve to boast about what she'd done, as if it was something to be proud of."

"I did nothing wrong," Gran K said firmly. "I went to see the young man, Kathryn, and I told him how you were wasting your life here in Much Winchmoor and that, if he cared anything for you at all, he'd do the decent thing and let you go. Let you go after the sort of life you want - and deserve."

"How can you say such a thing, Mother! You really are an infuriating, interfering old woman."

My chair scraped on the floor as I stood up. In the background, I could hear Gran saying something to Mum. And soon, no doubt when I stopped to think about what she'd done, I'd be as mad with her as Mum undoubtedly was.

But, just at that moment, all I could think of was that Will had been told to 'do the decent thing' and let me go. And Will, being Will, would always do 'the decent thing', even when it was the wrong thing.

210

I hurried outside, took out my phone, and called him but, as always, his phone wasn't turned on. Will never did get the concept of a 'mobile' phone and his spent most of its time in a state of immobility on the dresser in the farmhouse kitchen.

The heaviness that had been my chest these last few weeks lifted as I ran out of the house and up the hill towards Pendle Knoll farm, hardly noticing the steepness.

When I reached the farm, I paused and for the first time noticed that I was out of breath.

I looked around, at the old farmhouse that I've known and loved all my life, saw the yard where I'd learned to ride a bike, the plum tree that grew up the front of the house and how Will and I would risk life and limb (and Sally's fury if we were caught) reaching out of the upstairs landing window to pick the ripened fruit.

This was the place where I was going to spend the rest of my life. And I loved it like I've never loved another place on earth. It was where I wanted to be.

How could I have ever doubted that?

I drew breath to call for Will but at that moment, Tam, his wild-eyed collie came out of the big barn and raced towards me, barking. I stood very still and hoped that he'd stop before he reached me.

"That's enough, Tam," Will called as he came out of the barn. "Katie? What are you doing here?"

"Trying to avoid getting nipped on the ankles by your crazy dog for a start."

Now that I was here, I didn't know where to start. "I -um, I was speaking to Gran Kingham just now and she said - she said she came to see you a while back."

"Oh, that." He pushed his hand through his hair and looked desperately uncomfortable. "Yes, well, I -"

Before either of us could say anymore, a voice called him from the barn. A female voice.

"Will, are you coming? Only I need you to -" She broke off as she saw me. "Oh, hello. It's Katie, isn't it? Sorry, but I'm going to have to drag him away."

It was the 'pretty young vet', which was how Elsie always described her. She was, also according to Elsie, single again. Not only that, but she was also the only person I knew who could look dainty and feminine in Hunters wellies and a set of green overalls with Dintscombe Vets embroidered on the pocket. I, on the other hand, looked like something the cat had dragged in.

As if in slow motion, I saw Will turn towards her, saw the smile on his face as he looked at her. Saw the way she smiled back at him.

"Got a bit of an emergency going on in there with one of the cows," he said. "What did you want?"

I shook my head. "Nothing that won't keep," I said as I turned back towards the lane. "I can see you're busy. I'll see you around, Will. Nice seeing you again," I said to the pretty young vet whose name I could never remember.

As I walked down the lane, the heaviness which had been temporarily lifted was back again, like an old unwelcome visitor.

I got out my phone, took a long steadying breath and waited for what seemed like ages for him to answer.

"Oh hi, Liam. It's Kat here. About that job...."

THE END

Read *Murder Served Cold, Rough and Deadly, and Burying Bad News, the first, second, and third in the series.*

Fantastic Books
Great Authors

darkstroke is
an imprint of
Crooked Cat Books

- Gripping Thrillers
- Cosy Mysteries
- Romantic Chick-Lit
- Fascinating Historicals
- Exciting Fantasy
- Young Adult and Children's
  Adventures
- Non-Fiction

Discover us online
www.darkstroke.com

Find us on instagram:
www.instagram.com/darkstrokebooks

Printed in Great Britain
by Amazon